I AM CHANGE

First published in Great Britain 2020 by Walker Books Ltd
87 Vauxhall Walk, London SE11 5HJ

2 4 6 8 10 9 7 5 3 1

Text © 2019 Suzy Zail

The right of Suzy Zail to be identified as author of this work has been asserted by her in accordance with the Copyright, Designs and Patents Act 1988

This book has been typeset in Chaparral Pro

Printed and bound by CPI Group (UK) Ltd, Croydon CR0 4YY

British Library Cataloguing in Publication Data:
a catalogue record for this book is
available from the British Library

ISBN 978-1-4063-9758-1

www.walker.co.uk

MIX
Paper from
responsible sources
FSC® C020471

I AM CHANGE

Suzy Zail

WALKER
BOOKS

For all the girls who are silenced.
And for those who shout.

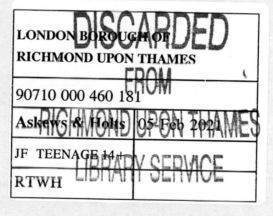

Foreword

My name is Namukasa Nusula Sarah. I met Suzy Zail in August 2015 in Kampala. Until then I had never told anyone my story, not all of it. I'm 24. I'm not old but my story is long and sad. Not sadder or longer than the stories of the other girls she met. I wasn't in the room when Suzy talked to them but I know they would have told her the same story about growing up without shoes or schoolbooks. There are thousands of girls like us, chased from school because our mothers can't afford to pay the fees.

Suzy was writing a book about girls like me who dreamed of wearing a school uniform. All the books I opened as a child had girls with light skin who had adventures or married princes. I wanted to read a book about a girl who was hungry to learn. A girl who sold porridge and washed other peoples' clothes so she could buy books. A girl scared to become a woman because everything changes once you bleed.

I wanted to read a book like that and I wanted other people to read it too – people in faraway places who'd never been to Uganda. I finished school because a kind lady doctor from America wanted to help. She set up an organisation called Concern for the Girl Child and paid for my school fees and bought me a uniform; a blue skirt, a short-sleeved cotton shirt, white socks and black shoes. My first pair of leather shoes.

I was lucky. Not everyone who wants to go to school has their prayers answered, so when Suzy asked if I was ready to tell my story I said yes. Because maybe if people read about the challenges we girls face they would help other girls go to school. I know what school can do; how it brings about change. I've seen it in my own family. Before I finished school, I was just another girl in the village. I didn't exist. Now when I go home to Wantete on break from university, even the men respect me. They give me a warm welcome. They split a goat and cook rice for me. I get a mattress and even sleep well. When I talk, my family listen. Now that I am studying conservation forestry they know I can help. I can take care of my brother in Primary Six when he's chased for school fees and show my grandmother the modern ways of farming.

Two years after I met Suzy in the offices of Concern for the Girl Child, I opened an email to find the chapters of a book. Suzy asked if I'd mind reading it. She wanted to be sure she got everything right – how we gripped the cassava when pulling it from the ground, the songs we sang around the fire, the things our aunties taught us so we would be good wives. The book was called *I Am Change* and the title made me smile. Just the week before I had convinced the girls in my hostel to advocate for better living conditions. We needed toilets that worked, a roof that didn't leak, a door that locked. We're in a new hostel now because I spoke up. *I am change*, I thought, starting to read.

I read every line watching for mistakes. I am good at English and love the language, ever since Primary Six when my English teacher, Madam Charity, made me stand on my desk and read my composition to the class. Afterwards, everyone clapped hands for me and the teacher bought me breakfast. I turned the pages of Suzy's book, adding a Luganda word here, typing the words of a song there. I added the names of the grasses we used for roofing and the name of the plant we use to clean ourselves after visiting the toilet but after a few pages I was lost in the story, in my story, and I cried, because I was Lilian. Me and my friends and the girls in my village. Everything that happened to Lilian and her friends has happened to one – or all – of us. Suzy had listened to our stories. It was all there. The lessons and the beatings, the laughter, the drums, the hunger and the fear.

It wasn't easy to move from trash to where I am now. Things are changing in Uganda. In some schools girls are made head prefect, but in the rural schools it's worse because girls don't have anybody to encourage them or tell them they are equal with boys. In the villages all sorts of bullying happens. If you go to the well and the well is crowded and here comes a boy who wants to fetch water he can pull you out of the line and take your place. If you go to school and the seats are limited, the girls who are sitting have to stand for the boys. And every year there are less girls in class as they start to bleed and can't afford sanitary towels or are married to a stranger for a goat or a cow.

Things can change. Me and my friends will make them change. We just need some help.

Namukasa Nusula Sarah
Wantete, Kayunga district, Uganda
April 2018

"Let us pick up our books and our pens.
They are our most powerful weapons."

–*Malala Yousafzai*

Chapter 1

The stars were bright by the time Lilian returned from the well. Sweat pearled down her back. It was more than an hour's walk through the bush and an even longer walk back, slowed by the weight of the slopping water.

"Where have you been?" Lilian's mother pulled the jerry can from Lilian's head. "Don't lie to me. I have better things to do than be lied to."

Lilian knew not to answer, knew that if she waited, her mother's fear would melt away and with it her anger.

"The dark is no place for a girl. Men lurk in the shadows–"

"Waiting to pluck children from the bush. I know, Maama. They bury our heads under their houses for good luck, but you told me yourself: they only want the heads of children with pure skin. You marked me, so I am safe. See?" Lilian twisted the thorn poking from the hole her mother had pierced in her ear with the tip of a safety pin. Her sisters, Nakato, Goodness and Sunrise, had all been marked by a piercing. Her brother Wekesa was protected by the scar on his left knee.

"Go bathe," her mother said, tipping the fresh water into a bucket. "And take your brother's uniform. It needs washing."

Lilian swung the bucket onto her head and walked to the bath hut to scrub the day's dirt from her skin. She tipped the bucket's contents into the plastic basin, dragged her dress over her head and stepped out of her knickers to crouch over the tub. The sponge had grown soft. Tomorrow, after school, she'd pluck a new one from the luffa trees that grew wild in the forest. She stood under the thumbnail moon and scooped water onto her body.

"You forgot your brother's socks." Lilian's mother stood in the slanting moonlight, her mouth hanging open, her eyes snaking from the patch of hair between Lilian's legs to her chest. Lilian grasped her dress to her dripping body but it was too late, her mother had seen her, seen how much she had grown.

"You haven't seen the moon yet?"

Lilian shook her head and her mother breathed out.
"Good. There is still time to visit Afia before you bleed." She circled Lilian like she circled the chickens before choosing the plumpest. "You should have come to me sooner. You are almost a woman and there is a lot for your aunt to teach you." She held out her hand and Lilian surrendered the dress. "Boys can't be trusted around a girl in a short dress. I will find you a long one."

She stepped from the bath hut and slung Lilian's dress over a tree branch.

"Try this on," her mother said when Lilian joined her in the sleeping hut. Lilian wanted to ask if the black bra had belonged to Goodness or Nakato, but she stopped herself. She wasn't supposed to use Nakato's name. *She's dead to us*, her mother had said, dragging Nakato's sleeping mat onto the fire the day she disappeared. *You will not speak of her again.*

Lilian fed her arms through the straps and stared down at her chest. Her family had gone for months without sugar so their mother could buy Nakato and Goodness bras. They were only bits of cloth but as soon as they slipped them on, Lilian's sisters had seemed more like their mother and less like Lilian. They stopped climbing trees and dancing in the rain. Their skirts grew longer and their tempers short. They weren't allowed to talk to boys, unless it was about schoolwork. They had to cross their legs and be careful of their manners. And then they were gone: Nakato slipping away without saying goodbye and Goodness bundled into the back seat of a car.

Her mother handed Lilian a dress. "It was Amara's," she said before Lilian could ask.

"Why doesn't Aunty come see us?" Lilian slipped the dress over her head.

"People in the city don't like leaving home." Her mother stared up at the flat black sky through the holes in the thatch. "They prefer their concrete boxes to the stars and the moon."

"What's she like?"

"Amara?"

Lilian nodded. All she knew of her mother's younger sister was that she was married to a rich man and lived in Kampala.

Lilian pictured a woman with hair grown past her shoulders. "They say she is beautiful."

"You can't eat beauty," her mother grumbled. "Learn to work." Her eyes narrowed to slits. "Pretty doesn't put porridge in the pot."

They walked the long way to Afia's hut, avoiding Sunrise's grave. Lilian didn't understand why her mother never sat by the small mound of dirt to keep her youngest child company, especially on dark nights like this one when lightning split the sky. Lilian didn't like the thought of her sister jolted awake by the crackling thunder, but she knew better than to ask her mother to stop and sit for a while.

Lilian hurried to catch up to her mother but she didn't take her hand. She could barely remember the warmth of her mother's touch; they hadn't held hands in so long. She remembered sleeping on her mother's lap when she was small and scared of the night. She remembered her mother's arms wrapped around her and her whispered words: *There's nothing to fear. I'm here.* But that was long ago, before Nakato disappeared, and their mother with her.

They walked silently through the dark bush, stepping over fallen tree limbs without stumbling. Lilian could have walked to Afia's hut blindfolded; she knew the track so well. She'd grown up chasing her cousins around the compound, dancing to the music on her aunt's battered radio, and had once visited her father's sister to learn how babies were made. Lilian had woken the night before and heard her father call out in a strangled voice and when she'd rushed to draw aside the curtain strung between their rooms, had found him lying on top of her mother, his back shiny with sweat. It was the first time her father had ever yelled at her, but not long after he'd come to her to explain. *I am fine, Tiny Mosquito. Your mother was resting and I was keeping her warm.* Her aunt had explained the noises on the other side of the curtain: her father's quickened breathing; a frantic, animal panting; someone's breath catching; then nothing. Afia's first lesson had been quick. Cover your ears when the moaning begins and keep your hands from the curtain. She would explain sex later, she had said. *It is my role as your Ssenga to teach you how to satisfy a man. You will become a woman soon. Your body will begin to change and, when it does, I will prepare you.*

And now her body *had* changed. She wouldn't have minded so much if everything else had stayed the same, but Wekesa had changed too and it wasn't just the deeper voice or the spots on his skin. He didn't tickle her or lie by her side counting stars through the thatch. He'd tied a sheet between their sleeping mats and stopped wrestling her in the dust.

She missed him. And she was jealous. Her body was growing but her world was still small. She was thirteen – a teenager – and as tall as her mother now, but she lived as she always had, rising before the sun to plant cassava and jackfruit, cooking for her brother and cleaning up after him. Apart from collecting firewood and feeding the animals, Wekesa had no chores. He exploded melons with his slingshot and was free to wander after dark. He ate when he was ready to eat and he didn't have to say thank you.

Lilian rounded a corner and saw, in the distance, the outline of her aunt's hut. Her stomach tightened. Her sisters had met with Afia when their bodies began to change. What had she told them about becoming Sabiny women? Lilian had wanted to know her aunt's secrets so badly, but now that she was on her doorstep, she wasn't so sure. Knowing was dangerous. It would make her one of *them*: a woman. And becoming a woman meant stopping school. Women didn't have time to read books. They had to weave mats and sell cassava and cook and dig. They had to have babies and hold onto husbands.

"Is there a problem at home?" Afia stood in the doorway, her face drained of colour. "Did something happen to my brother?"

"No, Kimanje is fine. He is still in Mukono." Lilian's mother nudged her forwards.

"*Yingila.* Come in." Afia bid them inside. A candle flickered in the corner of the room, casting dancing shadows on the faces of her cousins. Little Norris slept with his back to the door, a knotted ball at his feet. Ajani slept beside him, the shadowy beginnings of a black moustache above his lip. Mirembe slept on the other side of the room curled up like a question mark with gap-toothed MoreBlessing snuffling beside her.

"I am here about Lilian." Her mother shunted her into a chair. "It is time you talk. She hasn't seen the moon, but she is getting big. Soon the boys will notice." A firm look narrowed her eyes. "You will explain the ways of men?"

Afia nodded.

"*Weebale,*" her mother said, grabbing Afia's hands. "Teach her well, like you taught Goodness."

Afia grimaced. "I still don't understand why Nakato–"

"Sometimes they don't listen." Lilian's mother rushed to quiet her. "Sometimes they can't be taught."

Afia led Lilian to her bedroom, where baby Dembe slept in a cardboard box lined with leaves. She sat down and patted the space beside her. "Do you know why you are here?"

Lilian kneeled on the mat. "To learn how to behave like a woman?"

"That is part of it." Afia drew a pipe from her apron pocket and slid it between her lips. "But it is mostly about what is between your legs."

Lilian felt her face flush.

"You're becoming a woman." She waved her hands around, leaving a trail of pluming smoke. "You have to start thinking about how you package yourself."

Lilian groaned.

"You have a woman's curves." Afia sucked on her pipe. "If men see too much skin, they think you are not decent." She hooked a finger in Lilian's collar and peered down at her chest. "You wear a bra. Good. It will do the job."

"Job?"

"Controlling men." Afia snorted. "You will have to swat them away like mosquitos. You have inherited your taata's good looks."

Lilian liked having her father's high cheekbones and long,

long legs. She liked to think he'd gifted her his hunger to learn and hoped she had his strength. Afia took Lilian's hand and spun her in a slow circle.

"Shame," she said. "Men prefer a body like a guitar. Still, you might fill out."

"Fill out?" Lilian looked down at her chest. "I thought you didn't want men looking at my body?"

"Boda boda drivers and the boys from school, no. But men from good families with coins in their pockets ... men who can pay dowries ... they pay for the privilege." Her eyes landed in Lilian's lap. "As long as no one has been under your skirt before them. *That* has to wait until your wedding night."

"What if I don't want to marry?" Lilian held her breath. She'd never said the words out loud. She'd always wanted her own patch of dirt and a hut full of children, but not if it meant being yanked from school. Lilian hoped her aunt would say she could have both – a husband *and* a school certificate. A family *and* a job.

"Not want to *marry*?" Afia frowned. "What else would you do?"

"I could teach?"

Afia rolled her eyes.

"I could write stories," Lilian said, warming to the idea. "I could write down all the stories Taata has ever told me so they'd never be forgotten. I could write my own."

"Look at this fool!" Afia cut her off. "You are just frightened. Too much talk about boys." She plucked a hand mirror from a cardboard box and passed it to Lilian. "I told your mother I would warn you about boys; and I have. Now it is time to talk about your body."

Afia lowered herself onto her mat and beckoned Lilian to sit beside her. "Your mother is Sabiny. Daughter of the *Kapchemweny* clan. She was birthed on Mount Elgon and came here, already grown. Your taata and I are Sabiny too, from the *Kapchebasa*, but we grew up here, a long way from our people. Here, among the Baganda, when a girl approaches womanhood her *Ssenga* takes her to visit the bush. My aunt taught me about my body in the forest." Afia's eyes shone with the memory. "She took off her clothes and told me to do the same, and then she sat down and spread her legs." Afia hugged her belly and rocked back in her chair, laughing. "You look like a panicky chicken. Don't worry. I will let you discover your secret places by yourself. Use this." She passed Lilian a small jar of oil. "The best way to learn is to touch yourself. You will soon find your fingers will disappear."

Lilian's eyes grew wide.

"What?" Afia's smile fell away. "Have you never touched yourself?"

Lilian could hear her heart pounding. "Only once," she whispered, her cheeks hot. "Maama saw me and flew into a fury. She told me my first touch should be from my husband."

"You need to understand your own body before you can please a man." Afia rose from the mat to turn down the lantern. "Get to know yourself. When you have done that, I will teach you how to prepare your body for marriage. If you know how to keep your man happy, you will never be cast out. *This*," she said, putting her hands between her legs, "is a powerful thing. You just need to know how to use it."

Lilian emerged from Afia's bedroom, her body still tingling. She didn't have a name for what her fingers had found but it felt like a kind of freedom, a rippling that had almost stopped her breathing and made her want to cry. She tried to concentrate on what her aunt was telling her – something about putting leaves inside her to dry herself out – but everything in her that had been screaming an hour ago was now relaxed and all she wanted to do was rest her head on her aunt's lap and close her eyes.

"There are things husbands like you to do in bed." Afia lifted Lilian's chin in her cupped hand. "I will teach you. I know *all* the secrets. I'm not your uncle's favourite wife for nothing." She winked. "The Baganda also like their wives to look a certain way." She dropped her voice to a whisper. "I will show you how to lengthen your *enfuli*. Start pulling now and by the time your parents find you a husband," she held up her middle finger, "it will be *this* long."

"You want me to stretch it?" Lilian's mouth fell open when she realised her aunt meant the soft skin between her legs. "Doesn't that hurt?"

"You will get used to it." Afia bent to blow out the candle.

Chapter 2

Lilian woke before the sun to make her way home. The garden had been emptied of most of the jackfruit but there was still cassava to be pulled. When they could afford paraffin, her mother would set a lantern on the ground and they would dig in the circle of its glow. Lilian was glad there was no lantern this morning. She preferred the soft moonlight fading at the sun's approach. She crouched next to her mother, the still-cool morning breeze blowing about her knees. Somewhere in the distance a hyena howled.

They dug in silence, Lilian wishing – as she always did when her father was away – that he was kneeling beside her, filling the quiet hours with stories of Mount Elgon. Her mother liked the quiet.

"It is late," her mother said, shaking the dust from her dress and turning for home.

Lilian tugged a passionfruit from a low-hanging vine, bit it in two and sucked out the pulp. Behind her the sun climbed the distant blue hills, colouring the clouds orange. There was a belief among the Sabiny that mornings brought good news. It was true. It had brought her little sister Sunrise into the world, squealing and wet. Her mother had returned from the bush, her face puckered by disappointment. *Another mouth to feed*, her mother had said, setting a slug-shiny baby down in the dirt. Wekesa had said their mother was in a dark mood because they'd wanted another boy, but Lilian had seen her father's smile, wide as the sky. *Girls bring cows*, he'd said, scooping Sunrise from the ground.

That was true too. When Lilian's older sister Goodness was married, Lilian's parents got a cow. A man with wet armpits and eyebrows like caterpillars had delivered the animal at dawn, passing the halter to Lilian's father and a bag of coins to her mother. Lilian remembered her mother beaming as she closed her fist around the bag. It wasn't often that Lilian's mother smiled and never after dark. She was suspicious of the moon and wary of the shadows that swallowed the light. But occasionally, in the morning, if there was sugar for the porridge or a neighbour at their thorn fence waiting for milk, the corners of her mouth would lift into a smile.

Lilian closed the gate and hurried to the hut after her mother.

"Wake your brother. The porridge is almost ready," Lilian's mother said, poking at the embers of the cook fire. She snapped their old broomstick in two and tossed the broken sticks into the flames. "I am going to the garden to find a stronger branch. If anyone comes to the fence, tell them the bananas are ripe. If they want to trade, we need beans and papaya."

"Porridge, porridge, porridge!" Lilian called, blowing on the cook fire to keep it alight. "The porridge is ready!"

She poured milk into the pot to flavour the maize and scooped some into a bowl for her brother. Wekesa emerged from the hut, shirtless, his hair standing in uncombed spikes.

"No sugar?" he asked, opening the trunk where the food was kept safe from the animals.

"None left." Lilian snatched her brother's school shirt from the ground. It was dung day and she had to stack the papyrus mats and mop the hut before collecting the cow dung her mother would smear on the floor to keep the jiggers away. She tossed him the shirt and bent to examine her calloused feet, brushing the dirt off to scout for jiggers. Dung smelled bad, but having her mother pierce her skin with the point of a thorn to dig out a tick, big as a piece of rice, was worse.

"Come," Lilian's mother said when Lilian returned from the cowshed, lugging a bucket of dung. She held a dripping razor over a pot of water. "Your hair is too long." She dragged the razor over Lilian's scalp, drawing blood only once, above Lilian's left ear.

"Sorry, have to run!" Wekesa dodged the razor and made for the gate. Lilian shovelled some leftover cassava into a banana leaf and ran after him, her mother's voice following her down the rutted path. "Don't talk to boys!"

"Dimple?" Lilian glanced at the sagging couch in the front yard where Dimple's father slept surrounded by empty bottles and the bananas he used to make gin. Dimple's father brewed *Waraji*. Lilian had tried the drink once, on a dare. The *Waraji* was bitter as a cola nut and had made her head spin but Dimple's father liked it so much he sampled every bottle. *He prefers it to company*, Dimple had told her. *That's why Maama left*. Dimple remembered everything about her mother; all Lilian could recall of Madam Lakico was a huge bottom squeezed into a skirt and toes pink from nail polish.

Dimple had missed a week of school and Lilian worried that if her friend missed another week she'd fail Primary Five. *Write small; the pages last longer*, Lilian had whispered when Dimple had neared the end of her book. Dimple had tried, abandoning punctuation and making her capital letters dwarves, but still the letters filled the pages, until there was no white space left in which to squeeze Mr Lwere's words. *Get out if you are not writing!* Their teacher had pointed at the gate and Lilian had watched Dimple run, the pink soles of her feet kicking up dust, a black ant against the red earth.

"Can you come to school?" Lilian asked.

Dimple grinned and held out a soiled exercise book with half its pages missing. "I bought it yesterday. The trick is to ask for money when he is halfway through a bottle." Dimple threw a blanket over her father. "Once the bottle is empty, it's too late, because his mood turns black, and before he takes his first sip, he is mean as a mongoose, but if you get him at just the right time ..." Dimple pulled a handful of coins from her pocket, her face lit by a smile. Dimple was as poor as Lilian, maybe poorer. She stole her father's bananas for breakfast and went without dinner. "He gave me enough for the rest of the term. As long as I stay home on market days, I can go to school. It's my lucky day, Lala. First the money, and then I find *this*." She showed off a shoe dangling from her left foot.

When they left the path to walk through the overgrown bush, past deserted huts and darkened homes, Lilian was especially glad for Dimple's company. Lilian's mother had raised her to stomp on spiders and chase away hyenas. Scorpions didn't frighten her, but men did. Men could snatch you from the forest or lure you to an abandoned hut. *Men*, her mother warned, *would spoil her.*

The girls stopped to let a boda boda pass when they reached the main road.

"Take you to school cheap," the driver called, slowing his motorbike, but neither of them had money to spare. Lilian stopped to watch Trinah Mutete take a chapatti wrapped in grease paper from a man standing over a hotplate. She watched her peck at the soft bread, the smell of oil and fried beans making Lilian's mouth water. *Do they taste as good as they look*? Lilian had asked her friend the first time she saw her holding an oily wrapper. *Better*, Trinah had whispered. Trinah had ragged fingernails and dirty feet, but she was pretty, with shiny teeth and big dark eyes. Pretty, but poor. *How much did it cost*? Lilian had asked. *I don't know*, Trinah had answered. *The man at the stall gave it to me. He said I looked hungry. I'm going to try to look hungry again tomorrow.*

Lilian hurried through the school gate just in time for assembly. The head teacher, Mr Okurut, stood before the students holding a loudspeaker, well fed in his dark blue suit. Madam Charity stood next to him. She wore a striped blue dress and the same pink cardigan she had worn the first time Lilian met her.

The first time they met … Lilian's heart lifted. She returned to that day, that conversation, often. It was the day everything became possible: words and books, a desk and a pen. *Why aren't you in school?* Madam Charity had asked her and Lilian had shrugged. She knew from her parents' whispered discussions that school cost money and that they'd wasted too much of it on her sisters' schooling, and besides, who would help with the cooking and cleaning? *How old are you?* Madam Charity had asked, and Lilian had told her, *ten or eleven*. Lilian would never forget what the woman said next. *Would you like to go to school?* Lilian had thought about her mother alone in the garden, the beans left unwashed and the jerry cans empty. She thought about wandering through the market with Dimple, and the girls from her village waiting to play *sonko* and she'd started to shake her head. But then she saw a schoolbag like her brother's, hanging from a hook above her sleeping mat and a uniform folded on her bed and all twenty-six letters of the alphabet strung together to form words. She'd pictured herself reading a book to her father – and she'd nodded.

Uganda's flag climbed the school's wooden pole. *That'll be me, one day, standing next to Madam Charity wearing a prefect's badge*, Lilian told herself. She stared at the boys on the podium standing straight as a spear, the timekeeper, the flag-bearer, the sports prefect and the head boy. *How do I get to be timekeeper?* Lilian had asked Nasreen at her first assembly. Nasreen knew everything about Walumira Primary. She had started school two years before Lilian and was in Primary Three with Amal and Wekesa. *You don't have a watch, Lala. Timekeepers need watches*, Nasreen had told her, eyes dipping to Lilian's bare feet. *And sports prefects need shoes.*

A gong sounded and Lilian hurried to class. It clanged a second time and Ephraim Kakooza pushed past Dimple to get to the door. "Hey, One Shoe." He pointed at Dimple's plastic sandal, his face hard and sneering. "Forget something?"

The boy next to him laughed. "One Shoe!" he shrieked, nudging the boy behind him.

"One Shoe. One Shoe." The taunt became a chant and Lilian watched her friend's heart splinter into a thousand small pieces.

"Jobs." Mr Lwere snatched a piece of chalk from his desk. "Last lesson Peter Bukirwa told us he wants to be a lawyer when he finishes his A levels. Ephraim Kakooza hopes to be a chef." *Lawyer. Chef.* He wrote the words on the blackboard then swung around to face the class.

"Dimple, please tell us what you hope to be."

"Smart," Dimple said, and the teacher's mouth tightened.

"And you?" His gaze fell on Lilian. "What do you want to be?"

"I want to be a teacher." Lilian forced her eyes from her lap. "A teacher or a writer."

"A writer?" Mr Lwere threw his head back and laughed. "A writer! Why not an astronaut or an engineer?" Lilian heard a scuffle of laughter from the back row. "Let me try to explain this to you in a way you'll understand." The teacher's smile fell away. "Do you grow cassava?"

Lilian nodded.

"And bananas?" He didn't wait for her reply. "And what about apples? Do you have apple trees?"

"No," Lilian bleated, confused by the question. No one in Walumira planted apple trees.

"Exactly." He smiled but his face was hard. "You could try planting an apple tree, but nothing would sprout because the conditions aren't right. The soil can't support them." He lowered his eyes to gaze at her bare feet. "Your parents can't afford shoes, Lilian. Don't cultivate dreams that are beyond your reach."

Chapter 3

Dream big. That's what her father had said and there was no taking it back. He'd planted the thought in her head and it had taken root. Lilian lifted her eyes from the floor and regarded Mr Lwere's leather shoes and linen pants. She tucked the fraying hem of her dress under her legs and stared down at her lap. Her father had said there was no shame in being poor. *That may be true*, she thought, flicking a spider from her skirt, *but there was no joy in it either.*

She opened her book and tried to forget what Mr Lwere had said and concentrate only on the rhythm of his words, and the words themselves. *Cultivate. Beyond. Reach.* They were good words, useful words.

"Lawyer." Mr Lwere grabbed his wooden stick and jabbed the board as if to skewer the word. "Write it down."

Lilian wrote a comforting capital *L* in her exercise book:

an *L* like the one her father had scratched into the ground so many moons ago. *L for Lilian*, he'd explained, introducing her to the alphabet.

Dream big. Lilian repeated her father's words under her breath. She wished she could talk to him now. He always knew exactly what to say to make her feel better. Even when the boys at school had called her a beggar. *It is not what they call you that matters*, he'd said. *It is what you answer to.* And when she failed her first English test because she couldn't spell *Wednesday*, he'd sat her down and fed her smaller words. *If you want to move mountains*, he'd said, *you have to start by lifting rocks.*

Her father was still lifting rocks, heavy bags of charcoal that bent his back and bowed his legs. He hadn't finished primary school. *If I'd finished*, he'd told her before sending her off to her first day of school, *I could have been a doctor. Close your eyes*, he'd whispered, *and imagine you're grown.* Lilian had squeezed her eyes shut. *Dream big, Tiny Mosquito. What do you see?*

I see a classroom and a blackboard crammed with letters, and I'm writing on the board. A teacher, she'd said. *I want to be a teacher.* Teachers wore nice clothes and shiny shoes. They ate lunch in a cafeteria. They didn't collect dung or sell cassava chips. They sat in classrooms and read stories all day. Her father had given her a lopsided smile. *If you study hard, Tiny Mosquito, you can make those dreams real. You can do better than this.*

This. Lilian remembered the disappointment that sat like a stone in her belly. They had everything they needed in Walumira: umbrella trees for shelter and wild sugar cane. Baobab trees for building and acacia to feed the fire. They had milk from the cow and *nalongo* for fever. Lilian had looked at the washing line strung between the mvule trees and their small round house that her father had built from a skeleton of sticks. She had always thought her father was proud of their home and it had hurt to think that his smile might mask sadness.

She glanced up at the empty space on the blackboard next to her name. Mr Lwere hadn't written *teacher* or *author*; he'd left it blank. "I'll make you proud, Taata," she whispered. "I'll do something big."

Lunchtime was almost over by the time Lilian reached the front of the food line. She'd waited and watched as the Primary Sixes and Sevens claimed their plates of porridge before her, waited and quieted her stomach as the wealthier children poured from the canteen, shovelling cassava chips into their mouths. Lilian ate her porridge standing in the hot sun. The swings were taken, the yellow patch of grass by the front gate too. She scooped the claggy maize into her mouth, washed her plate and lowered it back into the sisal sack which hung by the open door of the canteen. Inside the dark building, the prefects and teachers sat at wooden tables, their knives shredding beef.

A flat-faced boy with a jungle of acne pushed past her on his way out.

"Smells good, doesn't it?" he said, waving an egg roll under her nose. He took a bite and brought his face close to hers, so close she could feel his oily breath on her neck. "Want a bite?" he whispered, his mouth at her ear. Lilian felt his hand on her back.

"*Nedda*," she spat, regretting the word as soon as she'd spoken it.

"Mr Namagembe!" the boy called to the teacher on duty. "I caught another one!" He pointed to Lilian and turned to his friend. "You heard her. She was speaking Luganda."

"She was, sir," the boy said. "Samuel asked if she was hungry and she said *nedda*." He whispered the last word.

Wekesa pinched his nose between his fingers. "Eeeh! I forgot how bad that thing stinks!"

Lilian lowered her gaze to the rotting dog's bone that hung from her neck by a piece of twine.

"I *know* it stinks. I'm *wearing* it!" She knew students weren't allowed to speak Luganda at school. Knew also that the quickest way to rid herself of the bone was to catch someone else speaking their native tongue.

"The gong has rung. Time for class." Madam Charity circled the yard, her smile emptying as her eyes dipped to the bone at Lilian's neck. "I'm sorry." She rested a hand on Lilian's shoulder. "It is a harsh lesson but it is good you learn English. Mr Okurut is only thinking about your future."

Future. Lilian tripped over the word. "Mr Lwere thinks I don't have one."

Madam Charity raised an eyebrow.

"He said I shouldn't dream about things that are beyond my reach."

"I've *always* had dreams." Madam Charity bristled. "I got my first pair of shoes at thirteen and, soon as I slipped them on, I started dreaming of a coat. It is okay to be ambitious, Lilian. Ambition is good."

She pulled a cellophane-wrapped sweet from her bag and dropped it into Lillian's palm. Lilian had never eaten candy before. She unfurled the orange sweet from its wrapper.

"Tastes like sunshine," she said, trapping it with her tongue.

"There are lots of sweet things in life, Lilian."

"Like books?" Lilian offered.

Madam Charity nodded.

"And shoes," Lilian said, staring down at her feet.

Lilian walked home with Dimple and Nasreen, Wekesa bounding ahead of them, snatching up scraps of bark to build the fire.

"See you at the well, later?" Lilian asked when they reached Dimple's yard. Dimple stopped to scoop an empty bottle from the dirt. The girls could hear her father crashing around inside.

"Useless," he yelled, his voice thick with drink. Something was hurled against a wall and clattered to the floor. Dimple rushed inside and closed the door behind her.

"You want to come over?" Nasreen looped her arm through Lilian's. "I have a new book we can read."

Lilian smelled the pancakes and fried onions as soon as she stepped into the yard.

"Is that ...?"

"*Ugati naamaggi*." Nasreen swung the door to the kitchen hut open and smoke billowed out. "My maama makes the best in all Walumira."

The girls weaved their way around bunches of drying sorghum and earthenware pots to stop beside Nasreen's mother. Madam Yawe's black veil lay puddled on the ground. Lilian had never seen Madam Yawe's face before. She'd seen long black lashes and almond eyes but the thick black veil Nasreen's mother wore whenever she left the house covered most of her face.

She was beautiful. Lilian looked from Madam Yawe to Nasreen. They shared the same oval face and small, slender nose. Lilian wished she had something in common with her mother, something to bind them together.

Madam Yawe was kneading an egg into a knob of minced chicken. She folded the meat into a neat parcel and handed it to Nasreen's aunt who sat over a sizzling skillet.

"Stay for supper?" Nasreen took Lilian's hand.

"I wish I could but Maama needs me at home," Lilian said, watching the pancake's edges brown and curl. A pan of milk was warming on the fire and Nasreen made tea, sweet and milky. They carried their cups to the sleeping hut where Nasreen shared a room with her sisters. Lilian sipped her tea silently, her eyes drifting from the tin roof to the mess of quilts covering the beds. "What should we read? How about *Cinderella*?"

Nasreen read the book out loud, while Lilian lingered over

the pictures of the girl with the pale skin and yellow hair transformed from a servant girl to the prince's bride.

"If I had a Fairy Godmother," Nasreen lowered her voice, "I'd ask her to pick a husband for me who was as handsome as that." She planted her finger on the prince.

"I wouldn't ask for a prince; I'd ask for money," Lilian said. "Enough for chapattis and donuts and a whole hut of books."

Lilian walked home, hugging Nasreen's book to her chest, grateful for her friend's generosity. She knew it was only a thing made of paper, glue and ink but it held more magic than a bewitching powder. Things happened in books, in the spaces between words and the gaps between paragraphs. Lilian wished her father were home to fan through the pages and listen to her read. He'd been gone only a few weeks, but his leaving felt like a door slamming shut. The hut seemed darker, the days gloomier.

Lilian tilted her face to the sun and assembled the day's events into a story she could tell her father on his return. She'd start the story with the dog's bone and end with the orange candy. Her father liked to hear about school. He liked Madam Charity best of all the teachers because her English sounded like the voices on Afia's radio, her sentences like songs.

She wore her hair loose, she'd tell him. She wouldn't need to describe Madam Charity's face or tell him she wore shoes. Her father knew that when Madam Charity smiled, her teeth were the same bright white as her eyes because he'd seen her at Walumira Primary, the day he enrolled Wekesa, and again, years later, when she came to their home to convince Lilian's mother to let her start school.

The first time she met Madam Charity, Lilian was bent over a plastic basin with an *akeyeyo* stick in her hand. She'd spat a mouthful of ash into the tub and put the toothbrush down. She didn't have time to go inside and change out of her ragged work dress; the woman was striding towards her.

Wasuze otya nno, Madam Charity had asked, stopping to peer at the pecking chickens and the drowsy cow, thinned by the dry season.

Lilian kneeled before the older woman. *Bulungi.* She switched to English. *I am fine, Madam. How are you?* Lilian's father preferred English to Luganda. *Luganda is home*, he'd said, *but the English language is the future*.

I'm well, the woman answered.

Should I find Maama for you? Lilian began. The woman shook her head, her long hair like a mane.

Don't disturb her. I can wait. She motioned for Lilian to rise. *Have you lived in Walumira long?* Her eyes drifted to Lilian's bare feet. Lilian wished she'd bathed. She didn't like being pitied.

I was born in the bush behind the banana garden. Lilian picked up a stick and drew a line in the dirt. *Maama planted the garden and Taata built the sleeping hut. Taata says if you own a home, you are never really poor.* She scrutinised the woman's shoes, black leather with a small heel. *He says that as long as we have a place to call home and land to grow food, we're as rich as the King of Buganda.*

Wise words. The woman smiled. *I'm Madam Charity. I teach Primary Six and help Mr Okurut run the school.* She extended a hand and Lilian shook it, feeling taller, smarter, older somehow.

I'm Lilian Chelangat, but my friends call me Lala. Her father called her *Tiny Mosquito* because she was skinny as a sesame pod and had big eyes, but Lilian wasn't going to tell the teacher that, she'd talked too much already.

What have you drawn? The woman gazed down at the dirt.

Oh, Lilian's cheeks reddened, *it's an L. L for Lilian.*

Do you know how to read? the teacher asked.

No, Lilian said, her eyes drawn to the crumbling mud hut in the distance where her grandfather had lived. *I tell stories like my grandfather.* It had been three years since Jjaja Wange Olufeni had died but if Lilian closed her eyes she could still conjure up the old man's face, black as midnight. She remembered his leathery hands and the holes in his ears plugged with wood and the stories he told, pounding at the ground with his thunder stick. *Jjaja is dead*, her father had whispered, lowering the gnarled stick into his grave the day he was buried, *but his stories will always live inside you.*

If you're here about Wekesa's school fees, Lilian's mother said, when she caught sight of Wekesa's teacher, *I paid them last week.* Lilian's mother spoke slowly, frowning as she always did when she switched from Luganda to English.

Oh, I haven't come about that. Madam Charity's cheeks flushed. *I wanted to discuss your son's homework.*

He hasn't finished it?

No, he finished it. His homework is excellent.

Excellent. Lilian repeated the word under her breath.

There's been a huge improvement in his writing, so much, in fact that Mr Okurut was considering recommending he skip the rest of Primary Three and start Primary Four with Mr Namagembe.

The teacher rummaged in her bag. *Here.* She brandished a piece of paper. *It is the last story he handed in. Do you want to read it?* Lilian's mother shook her head.

Madam Charity smoothed the paper out on her skirt and began to read. *Once upon a time there was a girl with long golden hair and skin like milk.*

Lilian bit her lip.

It is quite a shift from his previous stories about catching snakes and trapping lizards. Madam Charity waited for Lilian's mother to speak but she remained silent.

We just wanted to make sure he'd cope with Primary Four because there was quite a discrepancy – Madam Charity looked from Lilian's blank expression to her mother's baffled one. *There's a big difference,* she slowed her speech, *between the work he does at school and his homework. There's a depth and sensitivity in the homework that isn't evidenced* – she searched for a better way to explain – *his schoolwork is more typical of a boy his age.* She stopped to gaze at Lilian and when she finally spoke it wasn't to Lilian's mother. *Did you write it, Lilian?* she asked kindly. *It is okay if you did.*

Lilian's mother laughed, revealing a space where a front tooth had once been. *Lilian spends her days in the garden. She has no time ...* She stared at her daughter. *She doesn't know how ...* Her smile vanished.

Wekesa wrote the story, Lilian began, searching for the right words to placate her mother. *He wrote the words. I just made them up.* They'd struck a deal. Lilian would feed her brother stories for school and he'd teach her to read, one word at a time.

You don't need to know how to read to pluck feathers off a chicken, he'd said the first time she asked.

I want to learn to read so I can help you, Lilian had replied, thinking quickly. *It's not fair that I play kakebe while you do homework.*

Once upon a time, Lilian had begun, watching her brother trap her words on paper, *there was a girl with long golden hair and skin like milk*. Lilian had tried to remember the words her father had used when he'd told the story. English words she'd never heard before. *She grew strong and big and the people loved her and called her Joy but her name was Sorrow.*

Lilian snuck a look at her mother. Her face looked like thunder.

I just wanted to read the books Wekesa brought home from school, Lilian tried to explain. *Taata is always away and when I asked you about the strange letters, you said not to waste my time on words, that numbers were more useful, and that you'd teach me to count and add, so I could sell cassava chips on the street.*

And I also said your brother needs to read because it will help him get a job. You won't need one; you'll get married. Lilian's mother glanced at the teacher. *School would be wasted on her.*

Wasted? Madam Charity raised an eyebrow. *She needs to prepare for her future.*

Her future as a wife, Lilian's mother interrupted, *and I'm doing that.* She handed Lilian a broom and pointed to the hut.

You have a clever daughter, Lilian heard Madam Charity say. *She'll learn fast ... if you let her.*

Chapter 4

"It's late," Lilian's mother grumbled. She didn't ask about school. What would Lilian have said? That school was hard? Her mother had survived worse. Much worse.

"The clothes need washing," she said, lifting Nasreen's book from Lilian's lap. "I said you could go to school; I didn't say you could waste time."

Lilian washed her brother's socks and scrubbed the dirt from her school dress. She untied the bundle of banana stalks her mother had left by the door and planted them in rows. She washed the cook pot and fed Moses. The heat was stifling but Lilian felt refreshed by the work. Feeding the goat made sense. There was a purpose to keeping the cook pot clean and the work made her strong.

She picked a half-finished doll from the classroom of dolls propped against the back of the hut. She'd made them all: girl dolls, boy dolls, white-skinned *mzungu* dolls and dolls black as tar. Nakato had taught her how to strip the fibre from the banana trees, tie the dolls' limbs and ball their heads. That was moons ago. Lilian didn't play with the dolls anymore. Now that she was older, she made them for her cousins and for Sunrise too, who was trapped under the ground and would forever be three.

Lilian laid the half-made doll on her knee and pressed two black stones into place for her eyes, wondering whether her mother would spare a piece of fabric so she could make her a dress.

"Faith," she whispered the doll's name, taking the razor blade from its hiding spot to cut her a mouth. She wove the loose banana fibres into plaits and added Faith to the ragged collection of disintegrating dolls that lay splayed on the ground, mouths wide, waiting to be fed.

"Have you fetched water?" Lilian's mother found her at the back of the hut. "It will be dark soon and I won't have another child stolen at night." Lilian lifted the jerry can to her head and walked towards the well. When her mother was no longer watching, she slipped from the path and ran toward the acacia tree that measured her growth but she didn't stop to see if she was taller than the notch her father had carved at the last full moon; she headed straight to the graveyard, past her grandfather's grave and then her grandmother's, stopping to kneel at the smallest of the three unmarked graves. She wasn't worried that her mother might have followed her; her mother never came to the place where her youngest daughter was buried.

The sad mound of dirt under which Sunrise was sleeping seemed small next to their grandmother's plot. Jjaja Nia had been a tiny woman, but Sunrise's grave was smaller still. Lilian kneeled beside her sister's grave and brushed the leaves from the dirt. She'd long ago stopped trying to picture her little sister grown healthy and strong, but she couldn't help imagining how things might have turned out if her sister's cough had gone away. Their mother might still know how to smile. Lilian stared at the swept earth. There may have been one body lowered into the ground, but two hearts had been buried beneath the soil the day of her sister's funeral: Sunrise's just-stopped heart and her mother's.

Lilian scraped at the earth. When the hole she'd dug was deep enough to hold a doll, she lowered Faith into the ground to keep Sunrise company. Lilian had peered into the coffin the day of her sister's burial, before the lid had been closed, and seen her sister's small body wrapped in bark cloth, a picture Goodness had drawn of her lying flat on her stilled chest. She remembered everything about Sunrise, from her new teeth, which were too big for her mouth to her biscuit-brown bottom, but she recalled little of her death, only that she'd been taken at night. Lilian remembered the indifferent stars and her mother holding Sunrise in her arms and gulping for air like a wounded animal. She remembered her father's thin scream as the first clod of earth hit the coffin and her sisters holding hands by the graveside, their faces wet from crying.

Lilian had cried too.

Come, Tiny Mosquito, her father had said, lifting Lilian into his arms and carrying her to bed. Lilian hadn't wanted to sleep. She had so many questions. Mostly, why her sister – who was only three – had to die.

Lilian wiped the tears from her face and stood to leave. Her mother didn't like it when she cried. Lilian supposed it was because her mother had no tears left. Death had visited her too many times. Or maybe her mother was too angry to cry. Angry at the witchdoctor for taking her money, angry at the herbalist for giving her medicine that didn't work and angry at Death for choosing to take her lastborn child.

"You'd like my new classroom." Lilian talked to her sister of happier things. In Primary Four she'd sat on a dusty dirt floor in a room that smelled like wet armpits. In her new classroom they sat on bench seats and when she swung her legs, her feet skimmed a cement floor. Best of all there was a big round clock suspended on the wall with a face white as the moon and slender black hands trapped behind glass. "You can hear it tick," she told her sister.

"Tiny Mosquito!" Lilian's father called as he hurried towards her, his woolly hair damp with sweat. "I guessed you might be here." He bent to wrap his arms around her, his smile a crescent moon. "How are you?" He kissed her forehead. "How is school?" Lilian laid her head on his shoulder and breathed in his woody smell. "The boys are always disturbing me. They say I am poor." She had never been able to lie to her father.

"As long as you have a place—"

"To call home. I know." Lilian sat up. "They *all* have a place to call home, Taata, but they have shoes, too, and when I make mistakes they laugh at me." She watched her father smooth the dirt on Sunrise's grave as though he were tucking her in for the night.

"Let them laugh," he said, laying a wilted rock flower on the rectangle of earth that cradled his child. "And while they are laughing, *you* will be learning."

"And fetching water," Lilian griped, lifting the jerry can onto her head.

She could hear Wekesa's laughter floating over the long grass before she glimpsed the plastic buckets balanced on the heads of the waiting children. The line for the water was long and the sun still mean, but Lilian took her place at the end of the queue so her family could wash the dirt from their feet and eat supper.

"*Mpulira ebbugumu,*" Dimple complained, hauling her jerry can to the ground to stand behind Lilian. A stream of sweat trickled down her neck.

"I'm hot too," Lilian answered in English. No one would punish her for speaking Luganda at the well. As soon as you were outside the school gates, you were free to speak Sapiny, Swahili or any other of the dozens of languages Lilian heard every day. Still it was better to break the habit, she thought, wiping the sweat from her face with the hem of her work dress.

Wekesa and Amal stood under the cloudless sky, dousing each other with water. Amal wore a pair of shorts, Wekesa faded underwear. Lilian brushed a mosquito away and watched Amal empty his bucket over Wekesa's head, his spiky hair glistening in the sun. When the last boy in line had filled his jerry can, Lilian filled hers, lifting it onto the base of banana leaves balanced on her head.

"Don't go yet. Let's join the water fight!" Dimple began to undo her buttons, slowing when she caught Lilian staring at the purpling skin on her chest. "I am fine, Lala. I was late with dinner. My dad was hungry. Looks worse than it feels."

"*Owange!*" A girl with sticking-out teeth scooped Dimple's dress from the ground. "Hasn't your maama told you about the *kongolambere*?" She glanced at Dimple's flat chest. "If a praying mantis sees you naked, you'll never grow boobs." She shoved the dress at Dimple. "It happened to my Ssenga and she's flat as chapatti bread."

"You look like a mosquito trying to hold up a hut." Lilian's father laughed when he saw her walk into the yard. He grabbed the bundle of sticks from under her arm and lifted the jerry can from her head. "Help me light the fire?"

They broke the sticks into short lengths and set them alight so Lilian could put the fish on to steam. They only ate *Luwombo* when Lilian's father was home and she always served him first. *Taata first*, her mother always said, *then Wekesa, and don't stand while you cook. Kneel or sit cross-legged.* Lilian dropped to her knees. There were so many things to remember when you were a girl, so many rules. *No wonder boys do better at school*, Lilian thought, *they walk into class with empty heads. Ours are already full.*

The moon was bright by the time Wekesa came home.

"May we thank the Lord for this meal." Lilian's father sat by the fire, his children on one side, his wife on the other. Lilian didn't speak until her father addressed her, eating the *Luwombo* with her fingers, the food hot from the fire. She thanked her mother when the meal was finished and waited for her to scold Wekesa for standing without permission.

"Take the lantern for your homework," her mother said instead.

Lilian stood to collect the plates. "Sit for a while." Her father patted the mat beside him. "Let's listen for the owls."

Her mother left with the dirty dishes and Lilian sat beside her father in the dark, the soft moonlight shining silver above them. Bats swept through the yard and Lilian listened to her father talk, wondering whether the lines on his face numbered the mountains he'd crossed to settle in Walumira.

"What is Mr Lwere teaching you these days?" her father asked and Lilian told him about Lake Victoria and the Great River Nile.

"Maama never asks about school," she added, "except to warn me about talking to boys."

"Your mother was born wary." Her father stared into the fire. "Her mother taught her to be afraid of anything that moved. It was wise advice for a Sabiny child who lived among thieves and animals with sharp teeth."

"But you are Sabiny."

"My father was Sabiny. I grew up in Kampala, not far from here. Your mother grew up in a small village. She was already a woman when she landed among the Baganda."

"Come," her father said when Lilian asked if he could spare

money for a sharpener. They walked to her grandfather's hut with the help of the moon. "I might be able to find one in here," her father said, disappearing through the door. Lilian stepped into the cool darkness of the empty hut, her eyes adjusting to the bluish light. A tin trunk sat in the corner of the room and Lilian's father crouched over it, his hands shaking as he lifted the lid. "I thought Nakato would come back so I saved her things." He pulled a plastic bag from the trunk, spilling its contents – a pencil, a plastic sharpener, a spool of thread and a pair of scissors – onto the floor.

Lilian took a deep breath. "Why did she go, Taata?" Lilian had wanted to ask the question so many times but something in her father's expression always stopped her.

"I don't know. I was in Mukono for a month and when I came back she was gone." He picked through Nakato's things and handed Lilian the sharpener.

"Gone where?"

Her father shrugged. "No one knows."

They walked home together, her father's stories blunting her sadness. "That's all the stories for today," her father said, kissing her on the forehead when they reached the hut. "Do your homework then go to bed."

Lilian sat on a rock and settled her exercise book on her lap.

"Lawyer." She stared at the moonlit word, covered it with her left hand and wrote with her right. *Lawyer*. "Chef." She whispered the word, then trapped it on the page, trying to shut out the sound of her mother's voice.

"What's the point of wasting money on somebody else's

wife?" Her mother's words leaked through the thatched walls.

Lilian gripped the pencil hard. *I'm thirteen and she already thinks of me as somebody else's wife.*

"Wekesa is the one who needs—" Lilian jammed her fingers in her ears to mute her mother's anger.

"Chef," she said, reciting the words she'd copied off the board. "Author," she said, the word ringing in her ears.

Dreams.

Beyond.

Reach.

Chapter 5

"Lilian, wake up." Lilian opened her eyes. Her mother was standing over her. "We need to go to the market."

"Again?" Lilian groaned. "I missed a day of school last week. I am going to fall behind and Mr Lwere–"

"Mr Lwere will eat *lwombo* tonight. If we don't sell the jackfruit, we don't eat." Her mother's voice was low. "Don't wake your brother."

Lilian tugged her dress over her head and crept to her father's room.

"Taata," she whispered, nudging him awake. "I have to go to the market. Will you be home when I get back?"

Her father dragged himself onto an elbow and yawned. His black bushy hair, usually parted at the side, stuck up like a crown. "I am afraid not, Tiny Mosquito, but we still have time to pray." He folded up his sleeping mat and dropped to his knees.

Lilian preferred to pray on Sundays in the pink-walled church at the edge of the village, her father dressed in his suit, and Lilian wearing the good dress she saved for church. She could sit for hours staring at the purple-red sky through the stained-glass windows. She didn't feel as close to God kneeling in a room without a cross, but it was still time with her father, so she kneeled beside him and bowed her head.

By the time the sun was touching the acacias, Lilian and her mother were already on their way, their arms loaded with baskets of jackfruit. They walked without speaking, past sleeping huts and blinking cows, skirting sugarcane plantations and coffee fields.

Her mother swiped the tall grass with a stick as she walked five steps ahead of Lilian. Lilian didn't need her mother by her side to protect her. She knew that if a forest cobra surprised her she should reach for a stick to beat its head, and if she was bitten, the yellow pods of the sausage fruit would draw out the poison, but still, she couldn't shake the feeling that it might be nice to rub shoulders with her mother as they walked.

They stopped only once to buy a packet of blue soap. Lilian poked her head through the shop door. She'd bought soap and oil for her mother from Madam Kiyonga dozens of times but she still liked to run her fingers along the shelves and touch the packets of paracetamol, the bottles of soda, the spoons, toothpaste and candles. She pressed her back to the fridge packed with ice, the metal cold on her skin.

They reached the market mid-morning and laid their fruit out on a tattered rug under the shade of an oak. The smell of fire-charred corn made Lilian's empty stomach twist. Lilian's mother traded a jackfruit for two sticks of corn and handed Lilian one with instructions to manage their stall while she bought the dried fish and tomatoes they would need for the week.

Lilian waved at Dimple and her sister who sat with their knees tucked under them, surrounded by bottles of *Waraji* plugged with cork. When Lilian's mother returned and set her free to wander the aisles, she grabbed Dimple's clammy hand and pulled her from her rug.

"So, what are we buying today?" Lilian asked, picking a silver ring from a table.

"Maybe this?" Dimple looped a scarf around her neck. Neither of them had money and the woman standing behind the clothing stall lifted the scarf from Dimple's shoulders and sent the girls on their way. They walked arm in arm through the line of traders, fingering bolts of cloth and trying on shoes. They lifted pumpkins to guess their weight and sniffed at the tangled roots at the herbalist's stall. They strolled past watermelons sliced open and tubs of grasshoppers, buckets of goat's milk and parcels of salt. The girls inhaled the smell of the meat hanging from the butcher's hooks, and although they envied the boys buying tubs of peanut butter and the girls seated on blankets having their toenails painted, they were happy just to be there, in the maze of stalls, trying on masks and bangles, amid the buzzing chatter of preachers and hawkers.

The day slunk away.

"We must hurry before the sun disappears." Her mother grabbed their empty basket and made for home as the sun slipped from the sky. When she stopped to squat in the high grass Lilian turned away to give her privacy and saw a girl of two or three standing in her front garden clutching a doll. The doll was white-skinned – a *mzungu* – made from the palest banana fibres. The girl was paler, her white skin luminous, her light eyes the colour of sky. Lilian had never seen a *mzungu* in the flesh. She had seen them in English books, all white skin, blue eyes and straight, straw-colour hair, but this girl had white hair knotted into tight little spikes and a nose that lay down flat.

"I don't want you talking to that girl." Her mother grabbed her by the skirt.

"The *mzungu*?" Lilian asked.

"The *mzungu*?" Lilian's mother frowned. "White people are *good* luck. That one brings bad fortune. Touch an albino and bad luck will follow you the rest of your days."

"She's filthy." A boy's voice echoed in the hushed yard.

"It's disgusting." A different voice, then scouring laughter. "I can smell her from here."

A crumpled ball of paper landed beside Lilian's feet. She didn't stoop to pick it up. It wasn't her fault her dress was dirty. Mr Lwere had made her come to school early to clean the yard. Lilian kept her arms by her side and her eyes on the school flag. Nasreen reached down for the crinkled note.

"No," Lilian whispered, batting Nasreen's hand away. "Don't let them disturb us."

"No talking at assembly." Mr Lwere followed Nasreen's gaze to the ground at Lilian's feet. "The two of you passing notes?"

Nasreen lowered her head.

Mr Lwere scooped the paper from the dirt and held it above his head.

"Whose is this?"

Mr Okurut lowered his loudspeaker and the yard fell silent.

"Denis wrote it, Mr Lwere."

Lilian turned at the sound of a familiar voice. It was Samuel, the boy who'd tricked her into speaking Luganda. "Denis was just trying to do her a favour." Samuel wore a mean smile. "Go on, tell him, Denis," he said, nudging the boy beside him.

"She got her ..." The boy stammered, raising his hand to point at Nasreen, at the dark patch at her bottom where her uniform was streaked with blood. Nasreen wheeled around, craning her neck to see what the boys were laughing at, why the girls in her row had bullfrog eyes.

"No. No. No." She swiped at the stain on her dress, her face purpling with shame. She looked up at Lilian, her eyes filling with tears. "What do I?" She held out a hand speckled with blood.

Mr Lwere stood over her.

"I'm sorry, sir," she said, balling her skirt in her hands. The yard was silent, the blood bright and loud.

"Go home," Mr Lwere said, his mouth curling in disgust.

Lilian watched Nasreen's panicked escape, saw her friend flee the yard with her hands behind her back, her fingers splayed to cover the dark blot on her skirt. If Lilian had a handkerchief, she could have passed it to her. If she owned a coat, she could've tied it around Nasreen's waist. *I should have done something, said something*, Lilian chided herself. She'd seen blood like that before. A lake of crimson blood. And Goodness lying in it, her thin legs tied together at the ankles. It was the day after Nakato had disappeared. Lilian had gone searching for her sister and found Goodness curled on the floor of their grandfather's abandoned hut, her thighs streaked with blood, her dress too. It was the first time she'd seen proof that her sisters had become women. They were normally careful to hide their rags. She'd opened her mouth to ask if she could untie her sister's legs – *why were they tied?* – but her mother had come in with a cup of steaming tea and shooed her away.

Lilian sat in class after assembly copying English words from the blackboard, joining them tentatively, one by one, into sentences. *Kamukamu-gwemuganda*, she whispered under her breath, *one by one makes a bundle*. She stared down at the list of words she'd copied into her book. Know, knot, knife. *What was the point of letters being in a word and remaining silent? What was the point of being in class* – she slumped in her seat – *if she was too afraid to speak?*

At lunchtime Lilian ate her porridge by the school gate. If Nasreen had washed and hung her dress in the sun, it would be dry enough to wear. All she needed was an old shirt she could tear into strips to soak up her shame. Lilian settled herself under a tree and took Nasreen's book from the plastic shopping bag her father had given her. The bag had a hole in it so she'd tucked Nakato's sharpener into the elastic of her knickers and buried the rest of Nakato's things under the acacia tree.

Lilian opened Nasreen's book to the first page. *Once upon a time* ... Lilian knew the words by heart. Storybooks about *mzungu* always started with *Once upon a time* and ended with *Happily ever after*. Lilian flipped to the last page. *And they lived happily ever after.* There was life; that was true. And there was happy: a full stomach, a room with a light bulb, a sister picking you up and carrying you on her hip. But happily *ever* after? Lilian wasn't so sure. There were good days, happy days, but she knew good days were always shadowed by bad days: days when your baby sister died or your uniform was stained black with blood.

"Hey, you mind if I share the shade?" Amal sunk to the ground beside her, his face shiny with sweat. "I'm out. Anyway, it's too hot for *Kwepena*. What are you reading?" Lilian blushed. She had known Wekesa's best friend all her life but this was the first time he had sat beside her. He plucked the book from her lap.

"It's Nasreen's," she said.

"You want me to read? The English might be tricky." A smile brightened his face and Lilian noticed for the first time that he had dimples.

He didn't wait for her to answer. He opened the book to the first page. "Once upon a time there lived an unhappy young girl." He grabbed a carrot from his bag and took a bite. "Her mother was dead and her stepmother didn't like her. Cinderella wore her stepsister's hand-me-downs." Lilian tucked her unravelling hem under her. "She ate nothing but scraps and had to work hard. Only when evening came was she allowed to sit for a while by the fire, near the cinders." Amal lifted his eyes from the page. "That is why they called her Cinderella." Lilian knew this, of course, but she nodded just the same. "Her stepsisters had everything they desired," he went on, "but Cinderella had something neither of them had, and that was beauty." Amal's cheeks darkened. He closed the book and handed it back to Lilian. "I should go. Class is about to start."

Lilian waited until he'd left before standing to examine her dress. It was fraying at the hem and bleached almost white by years of washing but there was no embarrassing leak so she dusted herself off and walked to class. *It could have been me,* she thought, *me with a circle of blood on my dress.* She wasn't ready to bleed. It was hard enough keeping the yard tidy and conjugating verbs. She didn't have time to scrub bloody rags or visit her aunt.

The gong rang and Lilian returned to class, then it rang again, it seemed much too quickly, and she was forced out of the dark classroom and into the sun. Madam Charity stopped Lilian at the school gate on her way home. "I have something for you," she said, setting a pair of sports shoes on the ground at Lilian's feet. "I hope they fit."

"I can't," Lilian said, nudging a shoe with her toe to feel the soft leather. "It's too much." She peered into their dark mouths.

"They were my son's. They are too small for him. Please."

"I'm not supposed to accept gifts." Lilian eased her foot into a shoe. "I could work for them? I could empty your bins or dust the shelves in the library?" She slipped the other shoe on, guilt niggling at her heels. She wasn't sure helping in the library *was* a job. She would've cleaned the latrines, spread dung on the walls, anything to keep the shoes on her feet.

"Dusting shelves sounds like a fair deal." Madam Charity held out a hand and Lilian shook it. "You can start tomorrow."

Lilian ran to Nasreen's house, her laces dragging in the dust. "Your laces are undone," Madam Yawe called out. Lilian didn't stop to tie them.

She found Nasreen in bed, a pot of spiced tea at her feet. "I'm not going back, Lala."

"What? Ever?" Lilian slumped on the bed.

"Not until I stop bleeding."

"But if you miss a week now and again in a month, you'll fall behind. They won't let you run for class monitor."

Nasreen shrugged. "There's nowhere to change my rags. Anyway, my mother has started looking. She'll find me a husband whether or not I'm class monitor. Don't make that face! Be happy for me. He'll be rich and well read. It won't be like Salwa."

Nasreen had told Lilian about Salwa, her aunt's firstborn. Salwa who was forced to marry her uncle's eldest boy – her cousin – when she was eleven. Salwa who had clawed her way out of the wedding dress her mother had sewn for her and been married in a sheet, kicking and screaming.

"My father is kind. He will find me a kind man."

Kind men break promises, Lilian wanted to say. The man with the caterpillar eyebrows had brought Goodness a pair of slippers and a scarf as a wedding gift. He'd put her schoolbooks into the back seat of his car, but she never went to school. She had a baby instead.

Chapter 6

The dry season made way for the dripping rain. Huts filled with water and the air grew thick with mosquitos. The days were short and the afternoons dark, but the months of the long rains were Lilian's favourite. The rain filled the air with the scent of wildflowers and everything smelled new. When it rained, Lilian would hold her head up to the sky and swallow mouthfuls of fresh water, letting the huge drops spatter her arms and legs. When it pelted, she'd collect hailstones and suck on the ice. She didn't have to visit the well on those wet, dark days, just put the buckets and pots outside and wait till they filled. There were only two seasons in Africa, rain-wet and bone-dry. The rainbows melted away in the dry seasons, but in the wetter months, they coloured the sky.

The wet season was for growing, so as soon as the sky grew gloomy, Lilian and her mother started to plant. They built embankments into which they sunk their seeds so when the slanting rain came, the water ran off the little hills instead of carrying the seeds away. They dug in the morning, dropping their jackfruit seeds and cassava stems into the holes, and waited for them to sprout. Lilian's body, which had begun to bud during the last wet season, flowered. The stray hairs trapped under her knickers grew thick and curling. Her hips widened and her breasts continued to swell. She couldn't hide them under loose clothes any more. With each passing moon she grew taller. A ladder of gashes climbed the acacia's trunk and the soles of her runners came unstuck, her toenails forcing holes at the ends of her shoes. She didn't throw them away; she bound the flapping soles with twine and cut the fabric away with her father's knife, leaving just a strip at the front so she could wear them as thongs.

She fell ill once during the wet season, with malaria, and missed three days of school. On the second sweaty night when sleep wasn't enough to stop her head from pounding, her mother fed her *Nalongo* and let her crawl in to her lap. The herbs made her head spin, made the walls of the mud hut close in on her and then melt away, leaving her in the wild green beside Sunrise's grave. Goodness lay next to Sunrise, her legs bloodied, her ankles tied. "It's okay," Nakato whispered, pitching a shovel into the earth, and then they all disappeared, scattering at the sound of their mother's voice.

"It's okay," her mother whispered, "I am here. I won't leave."

When the pain had fled and the delirium passed, Lilian lay in her mother's arms a little longer, hoping her sisters might reappear. "Nakato?" she called out, pretending it was the fever.

She closed her eyes and waited but her mother never spoke, just laid a cool hand on her head and sang her to sleep.

By the end of April, when the wind and rain were at their worst, Lilian had learned to multiply fractions and change past to future tense and singular to plural. She had also learned that if you were pretty or rich, you were less likely to feel the sting of Mr Lwere's stick or spend time sitting cross-legged under the Shame Tree, a sad-looking mvule with gnarled boughs. Lilian still wasn't assigned homework – only the rich children could afford the teacher's quizzes – but she could pick any of the English books from the box on her teacher's desk and read them aloud from cover to cover. She collected words, running her finger along the pages of Mr Lwere's books, joining them one after another until a story sprang up.

She couldn't beat her brother to the top of a tree, but in school she'd found something she was good at, something she liked. When the rain pelted down on the school's tin roof, like a band of drummers and the wind turned fierce, ripping leaves from trees, the school closed down and Lilian was forced to run home in the sheeting rain, water at her shins. There were five very bad days that wet season: five days school was closed and Lilian forced to spend her days in the garden, trying to save the cassava from drowning. On those days Lilian couldn't help thinking that maybe her mother was right; she would learn to read and write but she wouldn't finish school. She would go back to tending the farm until her mother found her a man to marry.

On good days, when Mr Lwere begrudgingly gave her full marks on a spelling test or called on her to answer a question none of the boys got right, she'd imagine herself as his number one student. When she finally earned the title, at the beginning of term three, Mr Lwere, who was anxious to be rid of her, shipped her off to Primary Six and Lilian found herself in Madam Charity's class.

Lilian was accustomed to moving classes. She had started Primary One late in the year, and spent only half a year in Primary Two before jumping to Primary Three, but this was different; this was her brother's class, and he didn't hide his displeasure. He rolled his eyes whenever Lilian raised her hand to speak and ignored her at break time, but he couldn't ignore the fact that she was smarter than him: better at writing and better at maths.

I can help you, she'd offered, after he'd complained to their mother.

You help me? Your head is jammed. You are a year younger than me. And a girl. He'd raised his voice so their mother could hear him. *It is bad enough sharing a room with you. Now I have to share my friends too.*

Lilian didn't let his stony silence dampen her mood. It felt good to be called on when you had your hand up and see the teacher smile, not sneer, when you answered a question correctly. It felt good to be seen.

Madam Charity handed back the students' maths tests. "Let's put the tests to one side and focus on English," she said, distributing a page of typewritten text. "Nasreen, how about you read to the class today?" Nasreen's reading had fallen behind. She had returned to school after her first period but her mother kept her home every month when she bled. *At least she's here,*

Lilian reminded herself. There were only a handful of girls left in Primary Six, even fewer in Primary Seven. Most had married. Nasreen often talked about Zaina's handsome husband or Mariam's good luck marrying a man with a car. Lilian couldn't imagine how keeping house for a man could ever come close to following a line of words into a new world.

Nasreen finished reading and sat down.

"Anyone know who wrote that story?" Madam Charity addressed the class.

"Is it Enid Blyton?"

"Well done, Amal. Enid Blyton wrote dozens of books, mostly about children who solve mysteries and get tangled up with criminals."

Lilian's eyes grew wide. She'd read stories about wars and wizards but never about children who were adventurous and congratulated for it.

"Novels aren't like encyclopaedias or newspapers." Madam Charity walked between the desks to quieten the noisemakers. "They don't present facts so why do we read them?"

"Because she tells us to," Wekesa whispered under his breath.

"We read to escape so we don't have to think about where we are," Lilian blurted.

The boys in the back row sniggered.

"We read for different reasons." Amal's voice shut down the laughter. "That's the best thing about books. You can take what you want from them."

"Exactly," Madam Charity said. "And now it's time for you to write a story as engrossing as Mrs Blyton's Famous Five."

Mrs Blyton. Lilian hadn't thought for a second, that the author of the Famous Five might be a woman.

Madam Charity instructed the class to open their books to an empty page and free their imaginations. Lilian's stomach grumbled. She ignored her hunger and picked up a pen. "Enid Blyton once said," Madam Charity continued, "'I make my mind a blank and wait, and then, clear as day, my characters stand before me.' Now it is your turn. Make your mind a blank and find your story."

Lilian touched her pen to the page and wrote the first tentative words, her own *Once upon a time*, the words that followed making so much noise in her head she had to scribble them down quickly before the next rush of words came. The girl with the grass-coloured eyes who appeared in the second paragraph arrived without a name but Lilian felt as though she knew her, and knew that if she wrote a lake for her, the girl would dive in and swim to her sisters who would be waiting for her in the deep cool blue. Lilian wrote the last word and put down her pen, something loosening inside her.

"Madam." Lilian stopped at Madam Charity's desk as the class filed from the room at break time. "I just wanted to ask about the maths test."

"You are confused?" Madam Charity rested a hand on Lilian's shoulder. "I gave you 13/18 and—"

"A gold star," Lilian looked puzzled.

"You're new to this class. Primary Six is tough. I gave you the gold star because if I focussed on what you got wrong, you'd feel hopeless but if I tell you what you did correctly, you might be inspired to work harder. Keep studying." Madam Charity held Lilian's gaze. "I know you can do better."

Lilian found Dimple at break time sitting under the Shame Tree.

"I failed maths." Dimple shook the rain from her hair. "Mr Lwere said not to come back until I wrote down all the times tables. I'll use up my book. My dad wasn't happy when I needed a ruler." Her fingers found the ghost of a faded bruise on her cheek. "And books cost *more*." She frowned. "Do you think they are smarter than us?"

"Who?"

"The boys. They do better on tests. Maybe they *are* more clever."

"You missed most of last week." Lilian said, wishing her mother could spare a few rags for Dimple. "If your teacher won't catch you up when you have your P's, how are you supposed to pass? Hey," Lilian said, looking over Dimple's shoulder. "Isn't that Masani, the girl from the well who told you that you wouldn't grow boobs?" She pointed to a girl at the far end of the yard talking to a boy in long pants from Walumira Secondary. "We should stop him," Lilian said when he slid a hand up Masani's shirt.

But then she saw Masani smile and let him press his mouth to her lips. Masani took a step backwards and held out her hand.

"What is she doing?" Dimple's eyebrows arched in surprise

as the boy pulled something from his pocket and dropped it into Masani's palm.

"Is that a *pencil*?" Dimple swung around to face Lilian, her eyes enormous. "Did she really just do that for a pencil?"

Chapter 7

Lilian sat in the dripping rain. She pulled up the collar of her dress and held it closed around her neck. When the showers finally passed and the clouds drifted away, the slanting moon lit the page on Lilian's lap and she picked up her pen. *On a dark and windless night*, she wrote, every word taking her further from the tossing trees and soaked bush, from a mother who disapproved of her and a brother who wished she'd disappear.

Lilian glanced up from her page to see her mother standing over her.

"Men don't marry smart women," her mother said, snuffing out the fire. "Especially women who are smarter than them." She stared at the damp page on Lilian's lap. "Just because you can draw those lines and dots, doesn't mean your dreams will come true. Your father can read and where is he now? Fighting boys half his age for a job loading trucks. And all those extra hours just so you can go to school. You don't know what it's costing him." She turned away, mumbling. "What it is costing all of us."

Lilian didn't want to think about the long hours her father worked or how little he slept or whether her brother would like her better, if she wasn't so smart. She'd learned things this past year – about the world and herself – that she couldn't unlearn. Didn't *want* to unlearn. Things that would help her find a job as a teacher.

She tore her story from her exercise book. She'd write another tomorrow night and the night after that, until she had a mountain of stories for her father. Lilian folded the page in two and slipped it under her mat, tilting her head to gaze up through the gaps in the thatch. There were no stars in the sky, just grey clouds and the promise of more rain, and her brother snoring on the other side of the curtain and her mother worn down by worry.

She didn't need her mother to be proud of her. She didn't need her brother's understanding. That would come, when she was a teacher at Walumira Primary and came bearing gifts. They'd forgive her everything, then.

Lilian walked the narrow path to school alone, her feet making sucking sounds as she pulled them from the mud. She pressed her hand to her stomach to quiet the rumbling. She hadn't had breakfast, just a cup of boiling water flavoured with *mujaaja*. Anything they managed to grow, they saved for supper or sold.

Lilian couldn't complain. The school fed her porridge for lunch; her mother stayed hungry.

"Have you seen Dimple?" Lilian asked Nasreen as they lined up for assembly.

"No," Nasreen said, shucking off her raincoat. "And she just had her period, so it can't be that."

Lilian's stomach lurched. Dimple's father wouldn't have been happy about paying for her new book, but that didn't explain her absence from school. She'd come to class with bruises before.

"I haven't seen her either," Masani said, though no one had asked her. "Do you think she's been stolen? There's a new factory going up on the edge of town. The last time a building went up around here, a girl in Primary Two went missing." She paused as the flag bearer hoisted the school flag up the pole. "You know what the witchdoctors say," she continued as the school anthem drew to a close. "If you want a strong building you have to bury something – or someone – under the foundations."

"And now Dimple's gone missing," Nasreen whimpered.

"Probably that time of the month." Thomas Kobego turned around and flashed Lilian a smile, his gaze drifting from her face to her soaked cotton dress where it clung to her chest. Lilian hated her classmate's sticky gaze and the way he let his eyes linger on her body. Lilian tugged the clinging fabric from her body wondering, for a moment, what he might give to slip his hand around her waist.

"Or maybe she ran out of money?" Masani whispered. "Did you see where she lives? I told her if her father can't afford fees, there are other ways to–"

"We saw you yesterday." Lilian cut Masani off. "You were with that senior boy. Do you even like him?"

"*Like* him?" Masani glanced at the boys milling at the gate to Walumira Secondary. "He buys me things. If Dimple was smart, she'd do the same."

Lilian emptied the library's picture book shelf and ran her rag across the splintered wood. She had paid off the shoes Madam Charity had given her but had asked to stay on. She'd lived a hundred lives since discovering the library's fiction section. She'd walked paved roads, hiked ice-capped mountains and slept in a four-poster bed, reading the books over and over till their pages were tattered and the words became her own. And then one day she caught herself thinking in English and realised it had become the language of her dreams too.

She returned the books to the shelf and found an empty desk. A Division 2. Lilian pulled her homework from her bag. Madam Charity had given her a *D2* for her last story. She traced the line of the *D* with her finger and pictured a *1* next to it. Amal had gotten a *D1*.

"Want a bite?" Trinah Mutete slid into the desk beside Lilian's. She peeled the wrapping from her chapatti and held the bread out. "It's okay. Abraham will give me another one. We're friends."

Lilian took a bite of the chapatti and licked her lips clean of sauce, wishing for the first time that she was pretty, as pretty as

Trinah whose feet were bare but pockets full. Being pretty didn't make you smart or funny, but it had a power and magic all its own.

The magic seemed to be working on Amal too, Lilian noticed, as she watched him stop beside Trinah to whisper in her ear. Lilian liked the two of them. She should have been happy they were friends, but something twisted inside her as she watched Amal hand the girl a note, and then her stomach lurched again with – what was it, pride? – as Trinah reached towards Lilian to pass the note to her.

Congratulations on your first D2, Amal's note read. *Finally, some competition!*

Dimple's father lay snoring on the couch, his mouth ringed with spit. One bloated hand was flung across his belly. An empty bottle dangled from the other.

"Dimple!" Lilian's voice caught when she saw her friend. A bruise dirtied Dimple's left cheek and her eye was swollen shut.

"It's my fault." Dimple shrugged. "Prosper dropped a bottle and he chased her into our room. I told him to leave her alone."

"Did he?"

"My face sort of got in the way." Dimple attempted a smile. "And then the neighbours came and said if I didn't stop carrying on they'd call the police. That sobered him up." She spat on a finger and worked the dried blood from her forehead. "Is it gone?" she asked, tipping her head towards Lilian.

Lilian wiped a bead of dried blood from her friend's brow. "See you at school tomorrow?"

Dimple's face crumpled. "I can't Lala, not with Prosper at home ..."

"She can come to us while you're at school. She can help Maama in the garden. You can both sleep over until you work things out."

"I don't know." Dimple's father was beginning to stir. "He needs us."

Mr Lakico opened one eye, then the other. "Wotstha time?" He wiped a grubby sleeve across his mouth.

"Dinnertime, I'm making beans." Dimple ushered Lilian to the gate, stopping at the couch to hold her hands out so her father could grab hold of her and pull himself up.

"I got a Division 2 for my story," Lilian said, before her mother could chide her for being late. She pressed the page into her mother's hands. "It's about Sunrise and Goodness and–" Lilian stopped. She didn't want to anger her mother by mentioning Nakato's name.

"What? Can't you see?" Her mother lifted her dripping hands from the basin and shook them at Lilian. "Put it there." She pointed to the flat stone Wekesa used as a desk. "You can read it to me when I am done."

The page was still there after Lilian raked the leaves and

when she returned from herding Moses her mother was sitting on the stone weaving papyrus leaves into a mat, the page blown against the sleeping hut and spattered with rain. Lilian peeled the page from the mud wall and held it near the fire to dry.

"I'm hungry," Wekesa complained, stalking into the yard. He dropped his bag on the ground and picked up his ball.

"Your brother is hungry." Lilian's mother set the cook pot on the firestones and handed Lilian a knife. It made no sense – Lilian opened her mouth, but thought better of it and closed it again – letting Wekesa go into the world, unable to feed himself. What was the point of teaching him to spear a hog if he couldn't cook it? It was the cooking of it that led to the eating.

"Maama," she said, slicing a cassava in two. "I saw Dimple today. She looked bad." Lilian didn't say more. She didn't have to. Her mother had known Dimple since she was the size of a cola nut. She had seen her eye swollen big as a man's angry fist. She'd seen her face bruised and her arms caked with blood.

Lilian waited for her mother's outrage, but she said nothing. Her face was blank, her mouth a slit. She scooped the cassava into the pot, threw some salt into the water and continued to stir.

"I told Dimple she could sleep with us," Lilian continued. "Prosper too."

"So, I'm expected to make room here, for another two children?"

"Just until Dimple works out what to do. She was really bad, Maama, and she won't go back to school unless Prosper is safe."

"It is not our place to interfere. He's feeding them?"

Lilian nodded.

"And they have a roof over their heads?"

Lilian put down the knife and looked at her mother. "He hits her, Maama."

"Fathers hit children. Husbands hit wives. My father hit me." Lilian's mother struck a match and flung it at the firewood.

"Please, Maama. Just for a day or two."

"It is not that simple." Her mother lifted the pot from the fire to add another log. "I take them in and I'm responsible for them, responsible for their behaviour. They have reputations."

"Reputations? For what?"

"For being out late, for being unruly."

"They're out buying food, doing things their father should be doing."

"Decent girls don't roam the street after dark. If they move here, people will say I don't keep a good home." Her mother heaved the pot back over the embers. "One should never rub bottoms with a porcupine."

Chapter 8

School closed for the long dry season and Lilian returned to the garden to harvest the jackfruit. With each passing moon she grew taller and more tempting to the men her mother worried would steal her honour. These men lurked in bushes and hid in abandoned huts. They sold trinkets at the market and drove buses. They were everywhere. Lilian was not to stop when they greeted her in the street or engage in conversation. She wasn't to talk to the boys in her class either, unless it was about schoolwork. *And you are not to see Dimple*, her mother had told her. *People judge you by the company you move with and who is to say she is not already spoiled, without a mother to look out for her.*

Lilian's mother didn't need to know that they met at the well every afternoon. It would only anger her. Though Lilian was now a head taller than her mother, she still felt like a child when her mother's anger took hold, so, she kept things from her, like the secret spot in the dark wild green where she hid to do as Afia had instructed. Lilian had tried to pull at the soft skin between her legs, but the stretching hurt, so she'd stopped, preferring to make her body tingle, as it had the night in Afia's hut. And, as she grew more adept at reading her body, she discovered a power both magical and frightening. *If she could make herself quiver, imagine what she could do to a man*, she flushed, *and what he might do to her.*

Lilian tried to stop the thoughts before they took hold of her. It was bad to let boys touch you; wrong even to think about those touches. *Bad thoughts make you ugly*, her mother liked to say. Lilian knew that if a boy touched her, she would end up pregnant. Afia had told her that friendship led to feelings and feelings led to sex and sex led to babies. She was better off not talking to boys at all; she'd worked too hard to be thrown out of school. *Dream big*, she reminded herself whenever her thoughts drifted to Amal.

The days were hot and long and lonely. In their father's absence, Wekesa was the man of the house and he took the role seriously, ordering Lilian to cook when he was hungry and clean up after him. Their mother encouraged his authority. He didn't have to say sorry when his words stung and he could come to supper without washing his hands, but he also had to be fearless, strong and hard and Lilian wondered if he ever felt cramped in his cage.

Lilian would have chosen his confinement over hers, but still, it was a type of prison.

Her father came home only once during the dry season. They'd cooked for days in anticipation of his arrival. Wekesa had shot a pigeon with his catapult and Lilian had basted it in groundnut sauce before cooking it over the fire with the maize cobs.

He arrived the day before Christmas, looking thinner and older. Deep crags marked his face but his smile was still as wide as the sky and Lilian ran to him like she always did, arms outstretched.

"Where's my Tiny Mosquito?" He laughed. "What have you done with her?"

Lilian's smile fell away. She knew her father was just teasing but she'd wanted a hug, the same crushing embrace she got every time he returned. She was older but she'd hoped her father wouldn't care. She needed it not to matter, at least, to *him*.

Goodness arrived, later that day, with a baby in a sling and another tugging on her skirt. Her husband had continued on to Mukono, where she would join him the next day. Lilian had so much to ask her sister but there was always someone crawling onto her lap wanting attention. Lilian's questions about the wedding night and the bloodied sheet she'd found soaking in the tub had been answered by her aunt the second time Lilian visited her.

Did he hurt her? Lilian had asked Afia.

No ... Her aunt had hesitated. *Well, maybe a little, but that's expected; they had sex.*

Lilian knew about sex. She knew it meant letting a man

inside you. It was the blood that had made her panic and the thought of the man with the caterpillar eyebrows tearing at her sister's insides.

But he was happy she bled, Lilian had told Afia. *I saw him smiling.* Lilian had hated him for that smile.

Goodness was a virgin, a mbelela, Afia had said proudly. *She was properly brought up so her husband was pleased.*

That's why he gave Maama the coins?

Afia had nodded. *When you take something valuable, you have to pay for it.*

Lilian sat shelling groundnuts by her sister's side. Their mother was in the sleeping hut with baby Rose and Kaikara was playing ball with Wekesa.

"Have you seen Nakato?" Lilian whispered, feeling lighter for having spoken her sister's name. "I miss her."

"I don't." Goodness said, stoking the fire. "She was a coward. *I* did it. She should have too."

"Did what?" Lilian asked, catching sight of her mother walking towards them.

Goodness batted the question away.

When the humming of the cicadas slowed with the heat, they made their way to church in their best clothes. Lilian sat in the cool shade of the church's thatched roof, her face washed of dust. Around her the congregation rose to their feet to sing about Jesus and ask forgiveness. Lilian listened to the moaning and clapping with her eyes half-closed, the music swirling and escaping through the open windows. She opened a hymnbook and pretended to read. "Please let me finish school." She lifted her eyes to the big wooden cross. "Do this, one thing, God, and I'll do whatever you ask."

They ate Christmas supper with their cousins and when the children were shooed from the fire to let the adults drink, Lilian kept them busy, handing out groundnuts to see who could cram the most into their mouths. MoreBlessing won the competition with twenty-three nuts forced through the gap between her front teeth, but then Ajani swallowed a boiled egg that hadn't been peeled and claimed first prize: a banana fibre doll.

"I wanted a ball."

"You mean this?" Wekesa asked, scooping his soccer ball from the ground. "If you can hold a hot coal longer than me, it's yours." He dragged two glowing coals from the fire with his stick and batted one to his cousin.

"Ready?"

Ajani scooped the smaller one into his hand. "Woo-wee!" he yelled, lobbing it into his other hand, before dropping it and running to the bucket at the other end of the yard. Wekesa laughed, juggling his coal back and forth between his hands until its orange glow paled.

The drums started up and Lilian rushed to sit on the warm earth by her father's side. If she stayed there long enough, he sometimes let her play and she'd strike the skin with her clenched fists, nervous to keep the beat, her heart thumping under her dress until the beat was inside her.

"You'll sit with us." Her mother reached to grab her skirt. "Leave the men to make the music."

There were no stories that night; her father was too tired, so Afia kept the children spellbound with a story she'd heard on the radio. Lilian slipped from the knot of wide-eyed children to follow her father to their hut.

"Feel like a story?" She held up a book.

"If you are reading it." He sat on his bed and shifted over for her.

She read the first chapter of *Robinson Crusoe* without stumbling, hoping her father might step into the story with her. Her father had returned home with money for another term of school and Lilian had taken the coins he'd offered. *You don't know what it is costing him*, her mother had said, but Lilian knew. She'd seen his sticking-out ribs and pocketed the coins. Reading was the only way she knew to pay him back.

"You really make those words talk, Tiny Mosquito!" Her father's eyes shone in the half-light.

"It's like slipping inside someone's skin," Lilian whispered, cradling the ragged paperback in her hand. "You can be anyone. Do anything ..." Lilian so badly wanted him to understand, to know his money wasn't wasted on her. But how to explain that being in the middle of a story was like being everywhere and nowhere at the same time? Her father had been pulled out of school in Primary Four. How could he hope to understand that she read to escape but also to find herself?

"It's like dancing, Taata. The same magic spreads through me when I open a book. I've started writing too." She slipped from his side and ran to the bundle of papers she kept hidden under her mat. There were at least twenty stories, some of them written on paper she'd torn from her brother's exercise books, some scrawled on bits of bark, all flattened by the weight of her sleeping body. She didn't want her father to see how hard it was to come by paper so she left the bark under her mat and returned to his side clutching the papers.

"I wrote this for you." She handed her favourite to her father. "It's about a wise man who won the king's favour by taming a snake with seven heads. All the warriors in the land had tried and failed. Their arrows and spears couldn't pierce its skin."

"So how did the wise man overpower the snake?"

"With a story," Lilian whispered. "He hypnotised the snake with words."

"Words make powerful weapons," her father said. His eyes were wet but he grinned as though she'd given him a present.

Goodness left the next morning as Lilian and her father were setting off to dig a latrine. Lilian's grandfather had dug the last *toyii* when Lilian was small but it was now full so they had to sink their shovels into the earth to dig another deep hole, and build a mud hut around it. Her father carried the buckets of mud and papyrus reeds. Lilian carried the sisal sack they would hang over the doorway for privacy. She'd known the walls wouldn't be made of bricks like Nasreen's *toyii* but she'd hoped for a hard wood door so the lizards couldn't get in. She didn't mind them watching as she squatted over the hole – they were just there to catch flies – but the lizards attracted wild rats and the rats drew snakes.

"*Nnina okugenda,*" Goodness called from the yard. "I have to go, Taata. Tiginda is expecting me at his uncle's house in Mukono and the boda boda driver is here." Lilian ran at her sister and flung her arms around her thick waist. She'd been without sisters for so long. There was so much she wanted to ask but her mother was always hovering.

"Do you love him?" Lilian whispered into her sister's ear.

"Love who?"

"Tiginda." Lilian stared at her sister.

"Oh!" Goodness said as if she were surprised by the question. She thought for a moment. "He was a hard worker and reliable, so I married him. I was fifteen. It was time."

Lilian was about to ask Goodness if she'd wanted to finish school when their father joined them.

"Say goodbye to your sister. The driver is waiting," he said gently. Lilian fetched a banana fibre doll for baby Rose and kissed Kaikara's pillowy cheek. When they were just black dots against the red earth, her father took her hand and the two of them set off. "Why does Maama never come see Sunrise?" Lilian asked when they neared her grave. Lilian's father lowered his head. She was used to her mother's silences. She wasn't accustomed to his.

He stuffed his hands in his pockets and looked up at the sky.

"She doesn't come ..." He kneeled beside Sunrise's plot and Lilian dropped down next to him. "She doesn't visit because ..." He crouched close to the earth as though he were speaking to Sunrise, apologising to her. "She doesn't come because she's scared."

"Scared?"

He smoothed the dirt on his daughter's grave. "That pouch she wears–"

"The one around her waist?"

"Yes. You're too young to remember. She got it when Sunrise–"

"Was sick. I remember. I wasn't allowed to touch it. Was there magic in it?" Lilian held her breath.

"She thought so. It contained a powder. The witchdoctor promised it would stop Sunrise's cough."

"But it didn't?"

Her father shook his head

"So *omusawo* lied."

Her father stood. "Your mother visited him again, after the funeral. She wanted answers. He asked if she'd taken off the pouch before Sunrise died."

"And had she?"

The light went out in her father's eyes.

"Once. She took it off once to bathe." His voice faltered "Imagine," he said, his face crumpling, "believing you killed your own child."

Chapter 9

Lilian pulled her schoolbag from under her mat, looped it over her shoulder and slipped into her mother's room to admire it in the mirror. The last time she'd visited her aunt, Afia had sat her down with a pair of scissors and a pile of old clothes and shown her how to cut them into rectangles to catch her blood when it came. But Lilian hadn't gotten her period that week, or the following one, so she'd sewn the scraps into a schoolbag instead.

She ran her fingers along the seams. Her stitches weren't straight and the scraps of old cloth had faded with washing, but still, it was an improvement on the plastic bag her father had given her. She fastened the buttons on her dress, fingering the pale blue button she'd discovered hanging from a thread on the inside seam of one of Uncle Lwanga's old shirts. Lilian had used a thorn, and the thread, to fix it to her school dress where it gaped at the neck, but the dress still wasn't right. It was too tight. Lilian held the cracked mirror at arm's length, and hunched her shoulders in an attempt to hide her breasts, but there was no hiding them. Not even in the new bra Afia had given her. *No parent wants to see her girl with big boobs*, Afia had said, pulling the elastic straps so tight they cut into Lilian's skin.

Lilian hid her schoolbag under her mat and joined her mother for breakfast. They drank their tea in silence.

"Go find Wekesa and make sure he reaches school on time," her mother finally said when Lilian stood to leave. "If he is not at Amal's," she eyed Lilian suspiciously, "I want you to leave. I don't want you alone with that boy."

Lilian repeated under her breath what her father had told her at Sunrise's grave. *She's hard on you because she wants to keep you safe.* She tamped down her anger and steadied her voice.

"We won't be alone. His parents will be home."

"From now on, Wekesa waits for you and you walk to school together. Together," her mother repeated.

Lilian slunk to her room and picked up her bag. How was it that the taller she grew, the smaller she felt?

She walked past Amal's empty yard, disappointed he wasn't there, and wondered if he'd notice her changing shape. Part of her wanted him to. Part of her liked this new body of hers. Her mind didn't seem to matter and her opinions didn't count but her curves did. They signalled she was an adult, and the boda boda drivers who offered her lifts and the chapatti sellers who called her to their stalls wanted her business. She always refused them but she liked the sound of her voice, rising to meet theirs, and their disappointment. At home she was always agreeable, always doing what she was told.

"I'll talk to Amal if I want to," she grumbled, wondering when talking to her friend had become an act of rebellion. Or wearing a short skirt. Lilian wore her uniform long but she wouldn't be ashamed of what was under her dress. She had a woman's shape but she was still Lala. She hoisted her skirt above her knees and admired her strong, long legs, wondering why anyone would want them hidden, those clever legs that could run and climb and dance.

"Chapatti for you?" A small man with bushy eyebrows stepped out from behind his stand. "Trinah likes them." His smile was kind. "I've seen you walk to school together."

Lilian wasn't supposed to talk to strangers but Trinah had talked of Mr Musoke's chapattis so often that Lilian felt she knew him.

"She was just here." He pointed to a girl further up the road. "I try to help out when I can." His voice dropped to a whisper. "Her mother is not well and her father left so she has to fend for herself. You hungry?" He scooped some cabbage onto a flatbread and hid it under a pile of onion. "A girl that's doing so much growing needs to eat!"

Lilian eyed the flames, which leaped through the grill to lick the meat. "I don't have money."

"Any friend of Trinah is a friend of mine." He wrapped the chapatti in a sheet of newspaper and held it out. "First one's on the house."

Lilian grabbed the steaming parcel, shoved it into her bag and ran towards school, her feet as fast as fire sparks. She knew she should've thanked Mr Musoke instead of waving as she flew off but she was shot through with doubt and didn't want to change her mind and hand it back, not with the smell of meat in her nostrils and her fingers wet with oil. She stopped at the gate to Walumira Primary, unwrapped the chapatti and brought the soft bread to her mouth.

"You didn't pay for that, did you?" Wekesa's bike skidded to a stop, his lightning fingers pulling the chapatti from her grasp before the bread grazed her lips.

"Wekesa!" Lilian's hands balled into fists. "You can't–"

"Do what?" He took a bite and wiped the oil from his chin. "Who are you going to tell? Maama? I'm sure she'd be interested to hear how you got your hands on a free meal." He demolished the chapatti in two bites, tossed the greasy newspaper at Lilian's feet and wheeled his bike through the gate.

Amal slowed his bike to stop beside her. "Hi," he said, scooping up the litter.

"Hi," Lilian said, losing grasp of her anger. "How was your break?" She forced the words out.

"Fine. Yours?" He climbed off his bike. He was taller than Lilian remembered, tall as a stem of maize.

"Long." Lilian reached into her bag to return his books. He had asked her to mind them while he spent the Christmas break working on his uncle's farm and she blushed as she thought of the lazy afternoons she'd spent flipping through the pages and thinking of him. She had dreamed of him too, and when she'd sat down to write stories, had found him hovering in the margins and filling the spaces between words. She'd given her explorers the small scar on his chin, her hunters his long fingers and her princes his confidence.

"I got something for you," he said, taking her hand and dropping a stone into it, blue as the river Nile.

Lilian lowered the stone into her bag and pulled out her English book, opening it to the first page. She was in Primary Seven. Just thirteen loops of the moon around the earth and she would be in Senior One. When she'd started in primary school, all she had known of the moon was that it hung in the sky. She remembered her first day, standing in front of the head teacher, so proud in her uniform. Mr Okurut had pulled a pen and a square of writing paper from his pocket. *Just a few formalities*, he'd said. *Date of birth?* Lilian remembered shrugging. She knew she was born in Walumira early in the year during the dry season, but had guessed that wouldn't do.

Mr Okurut had cleared his throat and asked for her telephone number. *If you have one*, he'd said, his face round and gentle. *Never mind.* He'd looked exhausted. *We'll start you in Primary One and see how you go.* Lilian remembered a door being swung open on a dusty room and a gaggle of children cross-legged on the floor with books on their laps. Lilian had dreamed of desks.

Mr Igbe's Primary Seven room was hot and airless. It didn't matter. Lilian was in her final year at Walumira Primary and would finally wear the class monitor's gold pin and eat with the prefects. She hadn't been made a prefect. The boys voted for boys and half the girls did too. *They're smarter*, Masani had said, casting her vote for Amal at the end of Primary Six.

"I will repeat the rules," Mr Igbe said, leaning back in his chair. He clasped his hands behind his head and swung his feet onto the desk. "You have fifty minutes. The person who writes the story that has me on the edge of my seat will be named class monitor tomorrow. Your time starts now."

Lilian chewed on her pencil, racking her brain for a story that would have Mr Igbe frantic to turn the page. *Once upon a time.* She put her pencil down and stared at the page. *Once upon a time.* She picked up her rubber. *Once upon a dark time,* she started again, *in a place where you can't sing or dance ...*

Lilian didn't stop at Mr Musoke's stand the next day. She ran all the way to school and was at her desk before the gong struck. Mr Igbe walked between the aisles, dropping papers onto desks. Lilian could feel the drumbeat of her heart.

"What did you get?" Amal swivelled around.

"A Division 1," she whispered, clutching the page. "You?"

Amal turned back at the sound of Igbe's voice.

"So, without further ado," their teacher paused, waiting for the class to settle. "Your class monitor for this year ..." he drummed on his desk, "is Amal Nakasule."

The boys clapped Amal on the back and hooted their approval.

Lilian's mouth drooped; he'd beat her again.

"Primary Seven is a busy year," their teacher continued. "Amal will have a lot to do, so I'll be appointing an assistant." He rose to his feet. "For always trying her hardest, my assistant this year will be Trinah Mutete." He rested a hand on her shoulder. "Stay back after class and I'll explain what I expect."

"*I* know what he expects," Masani leaned over and whispered. "My cousin was his assistant last year."

Lilian congratulated Amal. *An Adventure for a King.* She peered over his shoulder and found the title of his paper, then scanned the margins until she found his mark: a Division 2.

Lilian's smile fell away. "You got a Division 2?"

The gong sounded and Mr Igbe dismissed the class.

"Mr Igbe?" Lilian raised her hand.

"Yes."

"Sorry sir, but I think there's been a mistake," Lilian said, knowing, as soon as the words were out, that there'd been no mistake.

"A mistake?"

Lilian glanced at the D1 scrawled across the top of her page. "Amal got a Division 2. You said the student with the highest marks–"

"No. If you had been paying attention, you would have heard what I said." Mr Igbe spoke slowly as if Lilian were stupid. "I said the *boy* with the highest mark will be appointed class monitor. The job was never meant for a girl."

"*You* should have been class monitor." Nasreen stalked into the yard.

"Or at least his assistant," Lilian said, trying not to sound bitter.

"Trust me, you don't want to be his assistant." Masani waited for Mr Igbe to leave Trinah's side. "Congratulations on the big promotion. I guess you will be eating with the prefects from now on." She pointed to the cafeteria.

"Guess so," Trinah said, looking from Masani to Lilian. "I'm sorry, Lala," she said. "I thought *you* would get it. You are so much smarter than me."

"He must like *something* about you," Masani smirked. "So what did he say?"

"Nothing," Trinah blushed.

"Nothing?"

"Well, just that I was pretty, and that as long as I work hard I don't have to worry about buying pens or books. We can share." Trinah took Lilian's hand. "He doesn't have to know."

"So what's the job?" Lilian asked, forgiving her friend for being pretty. It was Mr Igbe she was angry with, not Trinah or Amal.

Trinah shrugged. "He never said."

"It's for you." Masani held out a stick of *ekiikajjo*. "From Thomas. He wants you to wait at the gate."

"I'm not interested," Lilian said, pushing the stick of sugar cane away.

"Who said you have to be interested? Just take what he's offering and I'll get a few shillings for passing on the message. We both win." She pressed the stick into Lilian's hand.

Lilian had eaten sugar cane before, chewed the soft, wet stalks till her jaw ached and they were just a mess of dried fibres. She could smell the sweet juice – taste it on her tongue – but the thought of Thomas Kobego's fingers crawling up her dress made her want to retch. She waited until he walked into class, and when she was sure he was looking, grabbed the stick of sugar cane and dumped it in the bin.

Chapter 10

"You haven't eaten, have you?" Mr Musoke wound a piece of old newspaper around a chapatti and offered it to Lilian.

"No thank you." Lilian waved the food away, though she hadn't eaten breakfast and her dinners had dwindled to a small scoop of Posho and a cup of tea. It took all her strength not to snatch the chapatti from his hands. Mr Musoke held the wrapper out to her. "We're friends. Friends help each other."

He is not your friend. Her mother's words buzzed in her head. Lilian had tried to convince her mother that Mr Musoke wasn't a bad man, but she wouldn't be convinced. *Men are slipperier than snakes. You think that chapatti was free? Nothing is free,* her mother had said with a ferocity Lilian hadn't witnessed before. *You're a smart girl.* Lilian had waited to hear those words for so long, hoping her mother might say them in a quiet moment after reading one of her stories or seeing her report card. *Too smart to be tricked into an old man's bed.*

If I was smart, Lilian thought, stopping at the cart, *Wekesa wouldn't have caught me eating a chapatti and told on me.* She peered around. At least her brother wasn't following her. Their mother had told him to keep her safe, but he was too lazy to keep an eye on her. She was almost at school and he was probably still deep in the forest, his legs wrapped around a tree trunk, shaking the branches for fruit.

"Let's worry about how you'll pay me later. You're hungry *now*." Mr Musoke's face was round and bright. "I don't like seeing children go hungry."

"I can't," Lilian said, feeling ungrateful.

"Tomorrow, then," he said and Lilian nodded, though there'd be no chapatti tomorrow, or the next day.

Not if she wanted to avoid a thrashing. *Mark my words*, her mother had said, *if he gives you something, he'll want something in return*. And maybe that was true back in Kapchowra, where Lilian's mother had grown up having things taken from her. First her maama, then her brother, then her little sister too. *The first time the Karamajong attacked, Maama saw their crops set alight and their cows lying down dead*, Nakato had explained when they woke one morning to find their mother asleep outside, curled around a tin drum. *The second time they came Maama told her little sister Baako to run and hide.* Nakato had steered Lilian inside before continuing the story. *Baako climbed into a tin drum but there wasn't room for two of them so Maama dragged the lid closed and hid high in a tree. The raiders burned down their home but they didn't take Baako. Maama climbed to the ground when they left. It was hours later, the sun still beating down. It was a hot, hot day, so hot that when she grabbed the lid to drag it from the drum, it burned her fingers.* Nakato never said what Maama found when she lifted the lid, and Lilian never asked.

Amal handed Lilian her algebra test. She found the Division 1 and waited for his smile. He'd been helping her with maths but the last time he'd visited her with a practice test, her mother had told him that Lilian had work in the garden, and that if he wanted to stay he could study with Wekesa, so this mark was all hers.

Masani tapped Trinah on the shoulder. "How did you go?"

"Don't," Lilian whispered, glaring at Masani. Trinah had just scraped into Primary Seven and hadn't yet mastered long division.

"I got a Division 1!" Trinah said, her eyes wide with surprise.

"Told you." Masani slumped back in her seat. "She could hand in a blank page and still get a Division 1."

At least Trinah had worked for it.

The assistant's job is hard, Trinah had told Lilian. *I have to stay back late, sometimes after dark and then Mr Igbe has to walk me home.*

On Tuesday Trinah got a Division 1 on her spelling test and on Thursday a Division 1 on a social studies assignment. On Friday she left an exercise book on Lilian's chair and a sharpener for Masani.

"Igbe thinks she's pretty," Masani said, dropping the sharpener into her bag, "but Thomas likes *you* and he has better shoes than Igbe and a fatter wallet. He wasn't happy about the sugar cane, but he'll forgive you if you meet him after school."

Lilian had gotten into the habit of walking home with Amal and sharing his snacks: a chicken wing, a comb of dripping honey, a fistful of fried white ants. She had no intention of walking home with Thomas.

"He gave me a pen just to pass on the message. Imagine what he could buy you."

"I can't be bought with a pen."

Masani laughed. "So, ask for a pencil case."

The final bell rang and the class spilled from the room. Masani had followed one of the older boys to the back of the sports shed. Lilian snuck after them to watch. She wanted to look away, wanted to feel angry with Masani, but she couldn't muster disgust, or even disappointment, just guilt that the watching warmed her body.

She imagined, as she stopped to rest under the shade of a mvule, what it might be like to have *her* back pressed against the shed and Amal's hands in her hair. She grabbed a library book from her bag and dived in, glad to free herself of Amal. She touched her hand to her chest and felt, beneath her bony ribs, the thudding of her heart slow.

"Hi." Amal stood over her, holding a ball. "Mind if I sit here? It's too hot for soccer."

"Sure," Lilian said, staring at the bench where the boys sat, watching the game, the bench he could have sat on if he hadn't chosen to sit right next to her. She stared at her book and tried to read but nothing sunk in, just the smell of him and his even breath and his knees so close to hers.

Lilian felt his eyes on her.

"You should have been Igbe's assistant." Amal shifted closer.

"You mean I should have been class monitor. You knew I got a Division 1 for my story. Why didn't you say anything?"

Amal seemed confused. "About what?" He pulled a fist of dried grasshoppers from his schoolbag and tossed them into his mouth.

"About Mr Igbe choosing you." Lilian tried not to sound angry. "About the class monitor always being a boy."

"Oh." Amal shrugged. "I thought you knew."

Lilian wanted to be mad at him but then he smiled an apology and she couldn't be mad, not when he was grinning at her like that. And he hadn't said what Igbe did was *right*. Just that it was what Igbe always did. He chose boys.

Lilian waved to Nasreen's brothers and stepped into the dark house, hoping to find her friend in bed with a hot water bottle and a cup of *Nnalongo*. Nasreen hadn't been in class for six days and Lilian prayed it was a stomach bug or malaria – something that could be treated. Lilian found her in the sitting room with her mother and aunts, plunging needles into fabric, their black robes puddled around them, their faces unmasked. Nasreen's lips were painted red and her eyes lined with kohl.

"Lala!" Nasreen leaped to her feet, sending a bolt of orange fabric rolling onto the floor. Her black eyes shone. "I'm getting married!" She flung her arms around Lilian then scooped the cloth from the earth floor and wrapped it around her waist. "Isn't it beautiful?"

"When?" Lilian whispered, a dark ache spreading through her.

"Soon. And he's handsome and tall. Well," she hesitated, "I haven't met him ..." She dipped her head so her mother could slip a rectangle of orange silk over her head. The fabric had been cut away at the front to reveal her eyes. The rest of her face was hidden.

"Your father has made a good match." Madam Yawe tucked a strand of Nasreen's hair under the elastic at her face. "We'll make a dozen in black," she turned to the aunts, "lighter fabrics for the dry season and heavier for the wet."

Nasreen scooped a fistful of *obuutiiti* from a basket and held one of the glass beads up to the light. Her black-rimmed eyes shone but her words were muffled.

Lilian tried to imagine Nasreen walking into a mosque, but instead she pictured Goodness, her pillow wet with tears and her legs smeared with blood. Lilian had seen her sister's stained wedding sheet. Afia had thrown the bloodied sheet over the washing line so everyone could see it. There had been cheering and drums.

"Touch it." Nasreen held the half-sewn wedding dress out for Lilian to admire. Lilian swept her fingers over the orange fabric and hoped the blood would wash out.

"Can you say no, if you don't like him?" she whispered when Nasreen's aunts and mother had left for the kitchen hut.

"I'll like him," Nasreen said, lifting her veil. "My parents will choose someone who will take care of me."

"And love you?"

"Love marriages are stupid," Nasreen said in a voice Lilian didn't recognise.

"What about *not* getting married?" Lilian ventured. "I don't mean not ever, just not until we finish school."

Nasreen shook her head as if to dislodge the thought. "My father has already spent the bride price on a second-hand car for my brother."

Lilian lifted Nasreen's niqab from the floor and wondered if her friend would like wearing a veil. Would she feel safe cloaked in black, or tethered?

"I hope he likes books." Nasreen picked up a comb and dragged the spikes through her hair. "Now that I won't be going to school I'll have more time to read." She pulled a book from under her mattress. "Do you want to read *Rapunzel*?"

Lilian sighed. She didn't want to read a fairytale about a girl trapped in a tower waiting for her prince.

"Are you scared?" Lilian asked.

"Why would I be scared?" Nasreen looked offended. "I've never been with another man. I'll bleed on my wedding night and my father will get more cows."

Lilian agreed that Nasreen would make a beautiful bride and her husband would be handsome and rich and kind, though she'd never met a man who fit that description. Lilian's father was handsome and kind but his pockets had holes in them and, even then her mother liked to say he was one of a kind. *Men are snakes*, she said whenever the Waraji loosened her lips. *Snakes and scorpions.*

Chapter 11

The cassava was infected, disease shrivelling the stems and turning the brilliant green leaves yellow.

"It all has to go," Lilian's mother said, flattening herself against a tree so she wouldn't collapse. Her face was slack, her eyes shadowed by dark gullies. "No one will buy it."

Lilian stared at the sad plants, their green-grey tendrils limp and stinking of decay.

"I'll help dig them out tomorrow. It will be okay," Lilian promised, though she didn't know how they'd pay for new stems.

Lilian walked her mother back to the hut and fetched her a cup of water.

"Maama," she said, fishing a story from her bag. "I got a Division 1 today." She didn't pass the page to her mother. *She can't read*, her father had told her the first time Lilian's mother swept her words away with a broom. Lilian had pointed to the letters etched into the dirt, but her mother hadn't stopped to admire the crooked line of words. She'd attacked the mess with a broom, sending the sentence billowing upward in a cloud of red dust. "I can read it to you?" Lilian offered, determined to prove to her mother that she was smart enough to finish school.

Her mother took the page and laid it on her lap. "Read, read, talk, talk." She pulled a fistful of groundnuts from the tin at her feet, cracked the shells open and dropped the husks onto the page. "I have work to do."

Once upon a dark time, the story unfurled in Lilian's head, *in a place where you can't sing or dance or dream.* Her mother poured another handful of nuts onto her lap burying the story's middle and end. *A girl was born*, Lilian continued, willing her mother to lift the page from her lap. *Her father cried when he saw the child was a girl, for he knew that, in this land that made girls invisible, his daughter would suffer.*

Lilian kneeled beside her mother. If she could just read her a paragraph, even a sentence …

"Maama, I can do that for you." Lilian reached for a groundnut.

"Did I call you to help?" Her mother didn't wait for an answer. "Go wash before dinner."

"I'll just read the first paragraph." Lilian didn't care if her mother angered. She just needed her to hear the first line.

A gripping story, Mr Igbe had written across the top of the page.

Her mother pulled the sheet from her lap, her eyes travelling over the jumble of letters that spelled the story's title: *The Land of Forgotten Girls.*

"A Division 1." Her mother looked up from the page. "The cassava are rotten. Can we eat your sentences?"

Lilian felt as though she'd been kicked in the stomach.

She stared into her mother's hard, empty face but saw nothing. Not a yearning for all she had lost or pride for her daughter's achievements. Lilian lifted the sheet from her mother's lap and staggered back to the hut.

She could have taught her mother to read. They could have learned together. Lilian tried to rein in her anger. Why hadn't Lilian's father taught her after they married? Lilian buried her face in her hands. There was no hope for her. Her mother would never know the power of her stories, would never understand the effect of her words or her hunger to learn.

Lilian pulled her stack of stories from under her mat: stories she'd hoped reflected the wonders and sadness of life, stories that told the truth. But the truth was darker and sadder than she'd ever guessed, and too hard to unravel. Lilian thought about Nasreen hurtling towards marriage, convinced that love was stupid. She thought about Goodness's fading smile and the last time she heard her mother laugh out loud. Were all grown people unhappy, or just the married ones? She swatted the tears from her cheeks, picked up the sheath of papers and slipped *The Land of Forgotten Girls* between the flattened pages.

"No!" Lilian said, rising from her bed, her mouth round with shock. "No!" She stared down at the wet mat and her sticky, blood-streaked thighs. "No, No, No!" She tore off her nightdress and mopped the blood from her legs. *Maama can't find out. Not yet. Not now.* Lilian dragged the clammy dress across the mat to collect the blood, then turned it inside out and crammed it into her underpants. *I can't miss school.* She crept from the hut. She had a maths test after break time.

I won't tell her. Lilian snuck into the bathroom and peeled off her underwear. She filled the plastic basin and plunged the soiled clothes into the water, then flung in the soap. *I'm not ready to be married. I don't want to stop school.* The soap turned red and the water too. Lilian scrubbed at the stains till her knuckles were raw, then hunched over the basin to sponge herself down. She rested a hand on her stomach and waited for the pain, the searing pain that had caused Goodness to shriek. Lilian had heard her all the way from their grandfather's hut, even with her hands clasped over her ears. Nakato hadn't covered her ears. When the shrieks became howls, she'd fled to her twin sister's side.

What had Nakato seen that day? Lilian hugged her knees to her chest. If her mother found her now, crouched over the pink water, would she drag Lilian from the tub and carry her to her grandfather's hut? Would she bind her ankles with rope and leave her shivering on the floor? How long had Goodness lain there with blood leaking out of her? At least seven days, Lilian guessed. Seven days away from school. And six months later the man with the caterpillar eyebrows had come for her.

Six months. If her mother found out, Lilian would have

six months at best. With the cassava crop ruined, her mother would be hunting for a husband with coins in his pockets. Lilian flung her wet nightdress over a branch and snatched a handful of leaves to line her knickers. If she kept her body's betrayal a secret, she could buy some time.

They pulled fifty-two plants from the red soil, Lilian's mother grieving the loss of each one. When the garden had been turned into a graveyard, they put down their hoes and returned to the hut. Lilian disappeared behind the curtain to drop her knickers. The leaves that had soaked up her blood had torn the thin skin between her legs and it was angry and red. She balled the leaves in her fist. There was nowhere to hide them, except maybe under her mat. If she spread them out side by side no one would know. She bent to lift the sleeping mat.

"What is *this*?"

Lilian looked up to find her mother standing over her, holding a wet dress.

"It's my nightdress."

"And?" Lilian's mother waited.

"It needed a wash," Lilian stammered, stepping into her school dress, "so I washed it."

"I'm sure it did," her mother said, turning the dress over to show Lilian the pink stain. "What were you thinking?" Her brow creased. "Your brother could have seen it."

Lilian stayed mute.

"How long have you bled?"

"It just started," Lilian surrendered. "I woke up and the mat was covered in blood, and I was going to tell you, but we had work to do."

"You should have told me sooner." Her mother found a dark corner and laid the dress out to dry. "If we hurry, we can get to Afia before the sun starts to bite. What's that?" She pried Lilian's fist open. "You're using leaves? Where are the rags Afia gave you?" She searched the room.

"I used them."

"To make *this*?" Her mother scooped her bag from the floor.

"I didn't have anything else to use. Everyone has bags. Even Wekesa ..."

"And *you* have your period." She brought the patchwork shoulder strap to her mouth to gnaw the thread.

Lilian had sewn the squares of cloth together with just a small spool of thread. They came apart easily, Uncle Lwanga's shirt scraps fluttering to the ground.

"Maama I have to get to school," Lilian said, willing herself not to cry. She turned away from her mother to slip a scrap of cotton into her pants. "I have a test." She scooped the rags from the floor and stuffed two into her bra. "I'll use them, I promise and I'll go to Afia." She collected her books. "As soon as school's done."

Her mother shook her head. "You will go to Afia now."

"You know, my cousin threw herself off a cliff after a boy made her pregnant."

Lilian kept her eyes on the path. She waited for her mother to continue, but her mother said nothing, not until they passed a couple slouched behind a hut. The man's hands were on the woman's bottom, his mouth at her neck, their faces in shadow.

"*Totuunula!*" her mother scolded, shielding Lilian's eyes, as if it were Lilian with her skirt hitched up around her thighs. "Don't be coming to me with a stomach."

"I won't." Lilian frowned. "I don't want babies until I finish–"

"School? School is no good. Too many boys, too much danger. You start talking to them, you start liking them and next thing you have a belly and you're bringing me a boy. Don't bring me a boy," she said, glaring at Lilian. "I want a man who can shop for us."

They walked on, the silence between them a warning. When they reached Afia's house Lilian's mother lifted her fist to the door and rapped on the wood.

"No school until the bleeding stops. You don't want to bleed on the seat."

"I'll be fine," Lilian whispered, as the door swung open, though she didn't know how she'd change her rags with no locks on the *toyii* doors.

"How long do you want to bleed?" Afia led Lilian to the back of the hut. "Two days? Three?"

"I thought you had to bleed for seven?" Lilian stared at her aunt. "Goodness bled for seven."

"Goodness bled for three." Afia looked at her oddly. "She asked for three days and that's how long she bled, regular as a clock."

"Maybe I remember it wrong." Lilian tried to cast her mind back. It had seemed like forever before Goodness was allowed out of their grandfather's hut. Lilian remembered the night Goodness crept back to their room. Nakato's mat was gone but Goodness didn't ask after her twin. She called her a coward and their mother didn't punish her.

"You're probably right," Lilian agreed, remembering the *mujaaja* leaves she used to pick to ease Goodness's stomach cramps. The pains never lasted more than three days.

"Is the first bleed always the worst?"

"Sometimes." Afia stopped and surveyed the hut's mud wall. "Everyone is different. You might be lucky. Now, how many days? Two? Three?"

Lilian wished she could ask her aunt to stop the bleeding, if not forever, for at least a few years.

"Two," she finally said.

"Two." Afia pointed at the hut's crumbling wall, a mix of grass, mud and manure, smoothed onto a wooden frame.

"All huts have a skeleton. See those sticks where the mud's been worn away?"

Lillian nodded.

"Put your left foot on the bottom rung and count ... one ...

two ..." She waited for Lilian to lift her bare foot to the second rung of the ladder of sticks that climbed the wall.

"Stop!" Afia held her palm out. "Don't step on the third rung. Leave it on the second and every month your bleeding will stop after two days."

Lilian wiped her feet on the grass and followed Afia to the front yard. They sat side by side, their faces turned up to the sun.

"I've never seen you so quiet. There is no need to worry." Afia patted her knee. "Blood means you are a woman and can have babies."

"I don't want babies. Not yet."

Her aunt threw her head back and laughed. "Well, that's good, because you don't have a husband and if you came home with a stomach, your mother would have your head and then come for mine." She brushed a thread of silver hair behind her ear. "Do you still have the rags I gave you?" Lilian reached into her top and pulled out the rectangles of cloth.

"Good. Wash them at night. When you are married, if you can afford one, buy an iron. The heat kills the germs."

"Germs?" Lilian frowned.

"The blood is dirty." Afia waved the question away. "Dry them in your room under your mat so–"

"Wekesa won't see them?"

"Wekesa ... your father ... Also if they are hidden, no one can use them to blow their nose." She winked at Lilian. "If you run out of rags, you can use anything as a *kitenge*." Afia scooped a few leaves from the ground. "Leaves if you need to, straw, a kitchen sponge. In two days, when the blood stops have a hot bath. It will get rid of the smell and the last of the blood. Do it when Wekesa is out, and when you're done, scrub the floor."

Lilian felt a heavy sadness sweep through her.

"It is a lot, I know, everything is changing, including your body." Afia reached over and fastened Lilian's top button. "Keep it done up. Sometimes men can't help themselves. A girl walks by with a short skirt and a low-cut top ..."

It was so confusing. Lilian smelled and the blood was dirty, yet now she was more irresistible than ever.

"Just stay away from boys." Afia stood to fetch some water from the bucket at the other end of the yard.

"I sit next to them in class," Lilian called after her. What she meant to say *was I don't want to keep my distance, not from Amal*. Her aunt could tell her how to behave around boys; she couldn't tell her how to feel. "There's one boy. We're friends. He's nice."

"I am sure he is," Afia said kindly. "He's probably tall? And handsome too?" Lilian nodded. "And he told you he loves you?" Lilian shook her head. "If he hasn't, he will. He'll tell you he wants to marry you and buy you things." Afia looked at Lilian as if she were simple. "He will ask to come visit when your father is away and your mother is at the market."

Lilian opened her mouth but Afia held up a hand to silence her. "You will get pregnant and he will deny it and there'll be nothing left but to marry you off to old Mr Wakabi. There are ways to end a pregnancy," she lowered her voice to a whisper, "but Wakabi will know, because your wedding sheets won't be stained and he'll march back to your parents and take back his cows. Your mother will be blamed for not raising you right and your father will be broken." Afia leaned closer and took Lilian's hand. "Wait for your husband."

Chapter 12

There was no point going to school. It was more than an hour's walk from Afia's hut to Walumira Primary, and even if she ran all the way, Lilian would only make it in time to hear the final gong. She had never missed a test, even when she'd sprained her ankle she had hobbled to class. *They'll know*, she shuddered, pushing open Nasreen's gate: Wekesa and Thomas and the boys in the back row. They'd call her dirty and when she asked Mr Igbe to catch her up on what she'd missed, they'd call her stupid. Another stupid girl.

Worst of all, Amal would know. He wouldn't say anything, but he'd know her days at school were numbered and he'd pity her. She couldn't stand being pitied. She stopped outside Nasreen's door and wondered if life would be easier if, like Nasreen, she wanted to be married. She was ready to be married. Her mother had been preparing her to be a wife all her life. She could cook and clean, mend fences and herd goats. She'd been taught her body's secrets so she could pleasure a man and now that she'd bled she could have his babies.

Nasreen was in her bedroom, her wedding dress crumpled on her lap.

"He's ugly," she said, not looking at Lilian. "I wasn't supposed to see him but I came home early from the market. He was here with his parents to discuss the bride price." She picked at the beads on her wedding dress.

"Is he smart?" Lilian asked.

Nasreen shrugged. "I don't know. He didn't say much. I served him tea."

"Maybe he likes books?" Lilian persisted, unsettled by the thought that Nasreen's husband might not read, that the husband her parents found for *her* might not read. Nasreen pulled a book from under her mattress. "He thinks books are a distraction. He reads the Koran. Here." She held the novel out. "You might as well have it."

"What if you tell your father it's not a good match?"

Nasreen stiffened. "It is not just my father. I would have to convince my brothers and all my uncles." She lifted her dress from the floor, ironed the creases from the fabric with the heel of her hand and folded it into a neat square. "My mother says I'm being selfish."

Lilian reached for Nasreen's hand and pulled her friend to her feet. The room felt like a coffin. "Let's go for a walk."

"I can't. I need permission to leave the house now that I'm ..." she faltered on the last word, "engaged. Did I mention he's rich?"

She forced a smile. "I'll have everything I ever wanted."

They were quiet for a while.

"I got my P's," Lilian whispered, taking the book. "I'm going to bleed for two days."

"My mother says I'll *stop* bleeding," Nasreen blushed, "as soon as I'm pregnant."

The shadows lengthened across the yard and a yellow moon came up. Lilian readied herself for bed, washing her body and her bloodied rags in a half-filled tub as Afia had instructed. Her nightdress had dried in the sun and she slipped it on, covering the faint pink circle at her bottom with her hand until she was safely in her room.

She'd only missed a day of school, but everything felt strange and different: the dull ache in her stomach, the silent bright blood and the sudden awareness that her shoulder or ankle might drive a man wild. She read Nasreen's book quietly, the lantern's light burning down on the page. She loved the musty smell of books and stepping into worlds bigger than her own, but there was always an ending. She hated the endings, those last words that sent her home, back to herself and the small life she lived.

"Time for bed," her mother said, sweeping the curtain aside to grab the lantern. She took the book from Lilian's hands and set it on the floor.

"Did you ever want to learn, Maama?"

"Learn?" Her mother grimaced. "Learn what?"

"To read."

"And spend my days dreaming?" She busied herself with the lamp. "How would that help? Go to sleep." Her mother wet her fingers with spit and pressed them close around the wick, extinguishing the flame, and their conversation.

Lilian faced the wall. She wasn't angry, just sad. Sad that her mother had never opened a book, never glimpsed the future or relived the past. Never read the Brothers Grimm or any of Lilian's stories. It didn't seem fair that, with a handful of sentences, Lilian could summon Nakato home and bring Sunrise back to life, while her mother remained alone, too angry to speak of the child she'd lost and too frightened to visit the daughter she'd buried.

If her mother could meet the women in storybooks, the smart, strong women Lilian had met, women who climbed mountains and led men into battle, she might understand what was possible for Lilian.

There were only five girls left in Lilian's class. Lilian slipped into the classroom and sat on the rough wooden seat, her legs pressed together, her hands by her sides, waiting for the boys in the back row to point and laugh and say she smelled. She held her breath every time she rose from her seat to read out her work or write on the board, checking her skirt, then the seat.

No one mentioned the blood but Masani guessed, leaning

over to whisper in Lilian's ear. "Bring a jumper to school. If you leak, you can tie it around your waist." At lunchtime she pulled Lilian aside. "What are you using? Leaves? Old clothes?" Lilian looked past Masani for Amal. In class, he'd asked if she needed help with her English and she'd said, *No. Do you?* He hadn't laughed. He'd slunk away, as if wounded.

"Pads are better."

"Pads?" Lilian asked, unsure how a stack of paper would work better than a rag.

"They're made of cottonwool wrapped in gauze. You put one in your underwear and when it is full you fold it, slip it into its bag and throw it out. No washing."

"Sounds expensive."

"Not when there are boys willing to part with their money. Boys like Thomas."

Lilian shook her head.

"You don't have to tell him what the money's for." Masani waved Thomas over. "Just tell him you need a few shillings and make it worth his while."

"You talking about me?" Thomas stepped between the girls.

"Why would we do that?" Lilian meant to sound dismissive but Thomas laughed.

"Maybe because you like me."

"She *might*," Masani said, excusing herself to visit the latrine.

"You want to go out after school?" It was just the two of them and Thomas was standing too close.

"No," Lilian said. She meant to say, *Not today. Not ever.* But then she thought of the extra miles she would have to walk to draw water from the well to wash her rags and how easy it would be to steer him to the back of the library and let him kiss her.

"I can't," she said, allowing for the possibility that one day she might.

Amal handed the maths tests back.

"Mr Igbe said you can do yours tonight and hand it in tomorrow."

Lilian flipped through the pages. "Can you go over it with me?" she asked, not because she needed help but because he liked to give it.

"Sure." Amal's smile stretched from ear to ear. "Maybe we can walk home together and do it then?" He slid Trinah's test onto her desk and returned to his seat.

Lilian waited for Trinah's cry of surprise when she discovered another Division 1. She got Division 1's on all Mr Igbe's papers, which incensed Amal and irritated Masani. Lilian didn't begrudge her that small happiness. Next year, in Senior One she wouldn't be the teacher's pet.

"How did you do?"

Trinah's mouth drooped. "A Division 3," she whispered, sliding the paper Lilian's way.

"Trinah Mutete!" Mr Igbe said her name as if he was spitting it. "Did I call on you to speak? Talk again and you're out." He stopped at her desk and drummed his fingers on the wood. "On second thoughts, get out."

He gave no explanation. "And don't come back after school. I'm appointing another assistant." He turned to Amal as Trinah slunk out of class. "You're the class monitor. Any suggestions?"

Lilian stared into her lap, waiting for Amal to call her name.

Trinah sat outside the library, cross-legged in the dirt. Fat tears rolled down her cheeks.

"What happened?" Lilian touched Trinah's arm and her friend startled. "Trinah?"

"I'm done," she said. "I can't ..." She was quiet, sunk deep in her own thoughts.

"Can't what?" Lilian sat down.

Trinah shut her eyes. Her face was wet from crying. "Mr Igbe ..." She stopped and began again. "I didn't know ... not at first." She lifted her head and stared into the distance, picking at a scab on her knee. "He'd rest a hand on my arm or tell me to come sit close, but we were working together." She forced the words out. "He said he chose me because I showed ... potential." She clung to the word. "And when he held my hand ..." Her eyes grew misty. "My father used to hold my hand." She watched the children file out of class and the yard empty. The sore on her knee bled and she wiped at the blood with the hem of her dress.

"I was scared if I said no, he'd leave, just like Taata …"

"No to what?" Lilian wasn't sure that she wanted to know, just knew that the words had to be said.

"Yesterday, after school, he locked the door." Trinah's eyes were enormous. "He'd never locked it before. He told me not to be scared, that it was okay. He asked me to sit on his lap. I shouldn't have." She screwed her eyes shut and Lilian waited. "I shouldn't have sat on his knee." She shrugged. "But he'd been so kind. He gave me a paper and pen and told me what he needed for class, a duster, some pins … I took notes." Her eyes fell to her lap. "And then he slid his hand up my skirt and started pulling down my–" Her mouth trembled. "I asked what he was doing and he got angry." She sucked in air. "He said I *knew* what he was doing, what we'd been doing all along, but I didn't," she said, and Lilian believed her. "So I ran." Trinah's voice dropped to a whisper. "I unlocked the door and I ran."

"I'm so sorry," Lilian said, drawing Trinah into a hug. "That must have been awful." Lilian closed her eyes and thanked God she wasn't Igbe's assistant, thanked God Amal had suggested Douglas Natembo instead. "What he did was wrong." Lilian loosened her grip so she could look at her friend. "I'll come with you to Mr Okurut." She wiped Trinah's eyes. "He can call your mum."

"I can't tell my mother. If she finds out what I did …"

"You didn't *do* anything." Lilian took Trinah by the shoulders. "It's not your fault; she'll understand."

"No," Trinah said, swatting away her tears. "Mr Okurut won't do anything and Maama doesn't need to know."

Amal was waiting outside the gate. Lilian didn't feel like talking so she was glad when he took the algebra test from his bag to run through the equations. He seemed content to talk and have her listen.

Lilian walked home thinking about Trinah. She stuffed her fists into her pockets and willed the beating of her heart to slow.

"He won't marry you," Wekesa said, when he caught up with them. "His family eats money. They own a car. They will choose him a girl from a rich family. You'll just be a side dish."

"A side dish?" Lilian stared at her brother, confused. "What are you talking about?"

"Thomas." Wekesa stopped her, his narrow face serious. "I saw you talking to him. Be careful." His threat was softened by worry and she remembered a time when he used to keep her safe, from spiders and snakes and their mother's quick anger.

"Thomas?" Lilian said, pretending surprise. "He's spoilt and stupid and—"

Amal butt in. "She needs someone smart."

"She doesn't get to choose." Wekesa stopped a bull ant with his heel and ground it into the dirt. "She'll leave like the others, soon as she's old enough." He directed his words at Lilian, his face hard. "Maama will choose your husband, like she did for Goodness. And you'll leave like Goodness did." He kicked at the dirt. "And then it will just be me."

Chapter 13

Lilian's father was waiting for her in the yard. She ran towards him, careful to hide the shock of seeing him so altered, his face sunken, the skin loose as elephant hide.

"Taata!"

"Tiny Mosquito!" He pulled her close, his thin arms circling her waist. She felt the bump of his ribs through the thin weave of his cotton shirt and his stubble against her skin.

"Are you hungry, Taata?" It was hard to look at him, knowing she was the reason for his jutting bones, knowing he could work less if he didn't have to pay her school fees.

"I'm fine." He brushed a mosquito away. "Just here for the night to see about the cassava."

"Kimanje!" Lilian's mother hurried into the yard to take his bag. "Come, I'll make a fire and Lilian will make you tea."

Her mother grabbed six small, plump green bananas from

the trunk and wrapped them in leaves, setting them to steam in a pot. Lilian hadn't eaten *Matoke* in weeks, hadn't peeled a banana or bitten into its yellow flesh. Every morning she skipped breakfast to pull food from the ground, which she sold for small change. She sold every last passionfruit and banana, packing up whatever couldn't be off-loaded for sale at the Sunday market. *If you eat it, we can't sell it, and if we can't sell it, you won't go to school,* her mother had said. *Your father pays the fees but this garden pays for pencils.*

Lilian didn't mind being hungry if it meant staying in school. She cut the green bananas into cubes and sliced the tomatoes. When the food was ready her mother served the *Matoke* fresh from the fire so they could eat it before it cooled. She piled three spoonfuls onto her husband's plate and three for her son. There was only a smudge of *Matoke* left in the pot. "We'll share," her mother whispered, passing Lilian a plate. Lilian scraped the *Matoke* into her mouth and watched Wekesa eat.

"How about I tell you a story?" Lilian's father smiled, his teeth a bright white against his black skin. "One of Jjaja Olufeni's." He folded his leathery hands across his chest.

"What was Jjaja like before he came to Walumira? Before he had you?" Lilian shuffled close to her father while her mother cleared the plates.

"He was *omulwanyi.*"

"A warrior?" Lilian's eyes grew wide.

"The smartest and strongest in the *Kapchebasa* clan. The bravest too. A storyteller and a fighter." Her father stoked the fire. "You remind me of him."

Lilian's heart ballooned in her chest.

"You will be the first girl in our family to finish primary school."

Lilian's smile vanished. "I want to be the first to finish secondary school too."

Her father was quiet. They sat under the huge moon, the fire sizzling and spitting.

"Taata, will I go to school next year?"

"Leave your father alone." Her mother stepped from the shadows. "He is tired. Even the mightiest eagle must come down to the treetops to rest."

Lilian bent over the basin to wash herself clean. She knew she should trust that her father was doing all he could to keep her in school, but she couldn't sit there and do nothing. She had to convince him. She closed her eyes and rubbed her temples. *I'll read him a story.* Her eyes flew open. *I'll show him my report.* She slipped a dry rag inside her underwear to catch the last of her blood, threw on her nightdress and ran outside, stopping at the sound of her mother's voice.

"She should have more respect."

Lilian stepped behind the mvule tree and watched her father's black shadow.

"She is hungry to learn."

"We are *all* hungry," her mother said, growing bold under the dark cloak of night. "*You* especially. Look how your clothes hang on you. When did you last eat a hot meal?"

Her father opened his mouth to speak but stopped.

"You are a bag of bones. I won't have you or Wekesa starve so she can sit at a desk."

"*I* make the decisions for this family." Lilian's father stood up. "And she'll go to school as long as I can afford to send her."

"And what if the next cassava crop is infected?"

Lilian's father held up a hand to silence his wife.

Lilian crept from behind the tree and snuck into the hut.

"She'll marry, sooner or later." Her mother's words seeped through the walls. "What use will books be to her then?"

Lilian pressed her ear to the wall and waited for her father to tell her mother she was wrong, but there was no sound outside, just the hoot of an owl and the wind tossing the trees.

"Tiny Mosquito, are you awake?" Her father poked his head into her room.

Lilian shifted over so he could flop down beside her, like he used to when she was small.

Her father lay on his back and crossed his arms over his chest. "I should fix that," he said, looking up at the roof.

"No, don't," Lilian said, staring at the blistered sky through the holes in the thatch. "The light, it's almost silver." She put her head on her father's chest.

"Douglas Natembo is Mr Igbe's new assistant," Lilian whispered, hoping her father would ask about Trinah. He'd know what to do. He'd know how to help.

"I thought your friend Trinah was Mr Igbe's assistant."

"She was but she wouldn't …" Lilian searched for the right words. "She wouldn't do what he asked."

Her father faced her, a worried groove between his brows. "What did he ask?" He spoke slowly. "Lilian?" His eyes searched her face. Lilian's stomach churned. She felt her anger ebb away and fear takes its place. *If I tell him what Mr Igbe did, he'll pull me out of school.*

"Lilian?"

"It was nothing." Lilian's face blazed with shame. "She was meant to clean the board. She forgot."

"So you see, a thing as small as a bee or an ant," her father held his fingers a whisker apart, "can be more powerful than an elephant."

Lilian was thankful for the distraction of a story, even one she'd heard before. "My turn." She settled her father's lantern on the floor and dug a story from under her mat. Her father lay on his side, his elbow crooked to support his head so he could watch her.

Lilian slowed her reading when she got to her favourite part. "The young girl climbed the hill and saw the golden orb nestled among the twigs, but as she walked towards it, another hill sprung up. She clambered up but every time she drew near, it hurtled away. The young girl knew her life would change if only she could reach the orb. She walked for seven days, growing weak and faint with hunger, never losing hope that one day the orb would slow."

Lilian's father was so quiet that she looked up from her story to check he wasn't sleeping. His eyes were gleaming but there was something else in his expression too. A deep sadness, Lilian thought. She put down the page and scooped her report from the floor.

"It's my best yet." She handed it to her father.

"All Division Ones," he said, his dark eyes misting.

"Wekesa says Maama will marry me off like Goodness. Goodness was fifteen," she whispered into the dark. "*I'll* be fifteen in a year. Promise you won't find me a husband until I finish school?"

Her father sighed and stood up. "I am working as hard as I can," he said, sounding old and tired, "but I can't promise anything." Outside the hut, the trees moaned and the warm wind sang. Her father lifted the curtain strung between their rooms and disappeared behind it.

Lilian could hear her parents undress behind the thin, moth-eaten fabric. She heard a shoe drop to the ground, then another and after a few minutes she heard her father's moans and her mother's sad whimpering.

You need to understand your own body before you can hope to please a man, Afia had said, before she left Lilian to become acquainted with her body. Lilian's mother had always taught her that food was the way to a man's heart, but Lilian knew her aunt was right. She'd never heard her father moan when he ate her mother's *Matoke*. Lilian flushed with embarrassment remembering all the times she'd fallen asleep to the sound of quickened breathing. She turned to face the wall and clamped her hands over her ears.

The black sky had emptied of stars by the time Lilian stepped out into the pink morning. She'd run most of the way to the well so she could visit Dimple before school without her mother finding out. She mopped the sweat from her face and knocked on the door.

"Sorry," Dimple said, when she finally opened it. She held the doorframe to steady herself. Her skin was pasty, her eyes dull. "I've been sick."

"Do you have a fever?"

"Tell 'em we open at ten." The garbled words belonged to Dimple's father. "Unless they want to buy a dozen." He weaved his way to the front door, talking into the open top of a bottle of *Waraji*. "Oh, it's you," he said, looking disappointed.

"I would invite you in," Dimple said, "but I don't want you to catch it." She lifted a hand to her mouth, as if she was going to be ill. "I'll see you at the market on Sunday. It's just a bug. I'll be better by then."

When Lilian returned home from the well her father was gone. She hurried to school, slid into the last empty seat and raised her eyes to the words Mr Igbe had scratched onto the board. Ten new words she had to learn by next week. Lilian flipped her exercise book open to the last page and ran her fingers down the faint blue lines. Fifteen … sixteen … seventeen. She counted seventeen empty lines before her book would be used up. Lilian copied the first word onto the page, small as she could, the letters butting up against each other.

They'd been working in silence for most of the lesson, when Mr Okurut rapped on the wall. "Excuse me, Benjamin, can I have a word?" The head teacher stood at the door, sweat at his underarms. Mr Igbe put down his chalk and asked Amal to take over. The last time Mr Okurut summoned Mr Igbe from his room it was to tell him that Tracy Namuddu's parents hadn't paid her fees.

"I told him."

Lilian swung around at the sound of Trinah's voice.

"Told who?"

Trinah's eyes darted to the door. "I told Okurut what happened. He said he'd deal with it. What do you think he'll do?" She chewed on her lip.

"Probably throw him out," Lilian whispered, leaning forwards to get a better view of the men. The police wouldn't do anything; Lilian knew that. She remembered their neighbour Madam Tumeetu walking into their yard with a black eye and a broken arm. The police didn't take her statement. They wanted to know what she'd done to upset her husband. *Just as well*, Lilian's mother had said, tearing an old shirt in two to make her a sling. *How would you feed five children with a husband in prison?*

"Thank you, Amal, you can sit down," Mr Igbe said when he returned to class. He picked up the chalk and faced the board. "Who has a sentence for the word *unfortunate*?"

Chapter 14

The dry season ended and the clouds flung down water, turning the playground to mud. Mr Okurut didn't call Trinah's parents to school or sack Mr Igbe. It was as though nothing had happened. Mr Igbe went back to teaching and Trinah to struggling to understand what was being taught. She sat silent at her desk, too scared to open her mouth or raise her hand. Whenever he could – when he found she'd spelled a word wrong or failed a test – Mr Igbe would send her outside to sit under the Shame Tree and so she fell further behind, until Mr Okurut had no choice but to transfer her to a lower grade.

I don't want that girl stepping foot in our home, Lilian's mother had said. *People will talk*. They did. Word of Trinah's reputation trickled through the schoolyard and seeped into town until she couldn't walk to school without men calling out to her and women whispering behind their hands. And then one wet, grey morning Trinah hugged Lilian goodbye. Her mother had learned of her reputation and was sending her away.

A few weeks after the first rains fell, Lilian and her mother planted the cassava stems Lilian's father had bought them. They prayed to the Lord every Sunday that the cassava would flourish and when it didn't, consulted *omusawo-wekinasi*. Lilian followed her mother through the soaked bush, holding a limp chicken by the neck. Her mother placed the chicken on an altar, dropped a handful of fifty-shilling coins in a basket and lifted the brown cloth strung over the doorway of a small windowless hut. An old woman with a circle of plaited roots at her neck and another at her waist, raised a veined hand against the spill of light and beckoned them in, handing Lilian a small pair of rusted scissors.

"I want all ten," she said, holding the basket out. Lilian peered inside and saw, among the broken shells and coffee beans, a smattering of toenail clippings, yellowing crescent moons.

On the low table in front of the woman was a square of black cloth littered with corked bottles of coloured powder and a jumble of twisted roots.

The curtain dropped behind them.

"Your *omukono*."

Lilian's mother lay a clammy hand on the table and the witchdoctor's gnarled fingers closed over it.

"Bad things have happened in your life." The witchdoctor's voice was grim. "Parents dead, a child underground and another missing." Lilian drew in a sharp breath. "Now, hard times."

"*Yee nyabo*," Lilian's mother whispered.

The woman released her grip to tear at the twisted roots on the table.

"Soak this in boiling water and drink the tea before it cools." She closed Lilian's mother's fist around a stick of herbs. "Do not speak until you have emptied the cup." In her mother's other hand the witchdoctor placed a drawstring pouch. "Crushed rhinoceros horn," she explained. "Scatter a third on the cassava stems at dusk, the rest in a high wind."

Lilian's mother did as she was told, sprinkling the powder and whispering the incantation the witchdoctor promised would bring them good luck. But it didn't. The cassava grew out of the ground stunted and sickly.

There was no money for shoes or skirts but a package arrived from Kampala during the long rains in May. It contained three shirts for Wekesa, a work dress for Lilian and a pale blue shirt with pearl buttons and a matching skirt. Lilian's mother wouldn't wear her sister's hand-me-downs – though they couldn't have been worn more than a dozen times – so she gave them to Lilian.

Standing in front of her mother's mirror, with her shirt open at the neck and her belt cinched tight to show off her waist, Lilian had seen a woman staring back at her, a woman with a body like a guitar. A woman with a body Amal might like. *You can wear it to church.* Her mother had appeared behind her, her eyes climbing from Lilian's waist to her neck, taking in what Lilian had absorbed just moments before, the curves, the hips, the boobs, the legs. *Do your top button up*, she had said, as though being born a girl, Lilian was already guilty of something.

Dimple didn't return to school at the end of the wet season and with Trinah gone and Nasreen about to be married, Lilian's only female company was Masani, who spent her lunchtimes emptying boys' pockets of coins. Thomas still tried to buy Lilian with pencil sharpeners and cold drinks but his greasy smirk made her skin crawl. Sometimes she wished she were more like Masani. All it would take was undoing a top button to feel the jangle of coins in her pocket, one visit to the back of the Primary Two classroom and she'd have a red pen as well as a blue.

She'd come close once. Thomas was sitting behind her in class, his breath hot on her neck. She was on the last line of her exercise book, writing as small as she could, when he leaned in to ask if she needed a new one. She'd nodded and he'd found her at lunchtime and held out a book. She'd stood there for the longest time thinking about what she could give him. Her first kiss? A peek down her shirt? *I'm not giving you anything*, she finally said. *If you want to give me the book, give it to me*. He did, and every time she opened it she felt dirty.

It was different with Amal. Amal's smile made her body sing and though he'd stopped their friendly classroom rivalry and never picked her for a study partner, she knew he liked her too. She saw the way his face reddened when she squeezed past him to get to her seat. It was strange, this new heat between them, the way his eyes travelled across her body when he thought she wasn't looking. And how it separated them. It had been months since he'd doused her with water at the well or tackled her at dodgeball. She missed their easy friendship.

While Amal played soccer, Lilian spent her lunchtimes in the library, learning about her body. She read biology books and learned why Goodness had bled on her wedding night. She uncovered things Afia had not taught her about wombs and embryos and sperm and eggs and learned that if a woman didn't want to have babies there was a pill she could take. All she found on the topic of marriage was a picture book filled with blissful brides with painted lips and floor length dresses but nothing, not a word, about how to avoid it.

Mr Okurut stood under an umbrella in the lashing rain talking to Mr Igbe.

Lilian's stomach was in knots. Three students in her class had already been asked to leave Primary Seven. First Tracy Namuddu, who pleaded and begged, then Akram Leku, who punched a hole in the door, and finally Ryan Nansinkombi who hid under his desk until Mr Igbe dragged him out. Lilian crossed her fingers and waited for Mr Igbe to return to his desk.

"This is becoming tiresome," he said, stalking into the room. He scanned the rows of bug-eyed students and found Lilian.

"Lilian Chelangat."

A sliver of cold moved down her chest.

"Your father hasn't paid your fees." Lilian's face blazed with shame.

"But, sir ..."

"I have a class to teach Miss Chelangat. A class you haven't paid for." He stepped away from the door and pointed to the yard.

"My father works, Mr Igbe. He is in Mukono. As soon as he–"

"If your father had money, he would have paid when the fees were due. Go home," he said. "Maybe you'll come back in a few weeks, when he's scraped a few shillings together," he sneered, "or maybe you won't."

Lilian didn't make a scene. She collected her books and slunk out the door. She imagined her classmates, washed with relief, lifting their pens, and Wekesa in the back row, a smug smile on his face. She bolted to the gate. Only when she was swallowed by the bush did she stop at a cluster of acacia trees to catch her breath. She leaned against a quiet tree and pressed her cheek to the peeling bark. She'd never finish school and become a teacher or a writer. She'd sleep under a thatched roof and eat porridge for breakfast till she was bent like her mother. She'd hear stories about people who lived in the city in houses made of bricks but she'd never see a light bulb or sleep on a bed. Not unless she made some money.

She stopped at the open door of the pink-walled church.

"Please, Lord, help me," she said, stepping into the cool darkness. "I only need a few shillings. Just enough for next term."

"What are you doing home?" Lilian's mother looked up from the cook fire. "Did something happen on the way to school? Did someone–" She leaped up and circled her daughter, searching for bruises and broken skin.

"I was chased from school." Lilian shook off her mother's concern. "Taata didn't pay the fees."

"Didn't pay or *couldn't* pay? I thought you were smart." She lifted the cook pot onto the fire and reached for a hoe. "The money's run out."

Lilian searched her mother's eyes for an apology but they were empty.

"Wekesa's in school so we must have *some* money."

"Enough for your brother," her mother said without blinking.

Lilian stared into her mother's pebble eyes. "Wekesa will get half this land and Jjaja's hut when he marries. He doesn't need to study. If I'm going to be a teacher, I need to finish school."

"*Need.*" Her mother spat the word. Her voice was low, her eyes flaming. "Need. Need. Need." She threw the hoe at Lilian's feet. "I'm sick of hearing what you need. We don't all get what we need. Did I *need* to lose my mother and sister?" She didn't wait for an answer. "Did I *need* to be sent away because my father couldn't afford to keep me?

"You think you know so much because you can read and write. I know what it takes to survive and it is not books." Her face blazed. "It is knowing how to build a fence strong enough to keep hyenas out and knowing where to hide if someone comes for you at night. *That* is what I am teaching you and it is all the school you need."

Lilian lay on her bed and wept. She'd mapped her life on three sheets of paper, from beginning to end, from birth to escape. She took a pencil from her pocket and rewrote the story, adding a chapter about the time she was yanked from school, like a tooth from its gum, before her father returned to Walumira to set things right.

"It is time you learned how to mend holes in the roof," Lilian's mother said the next morning. She stood on an upturned box and Lilian balanced beside her, watching her mother's thin fingers knot stalks of grass.

Working seemed to still her mother. Her face would grow soft, and sometimes, when she was weaving a mat or grinding millet, she'd tell stories. It was during these quiet times that Lilian learned her mother had her first baby at sixteen and her last at forty-one. One time, when they were collecting dung, her mother had talked of her own birth, mumbling something about Lilian's grandmother herding goats when the pains came and cutting the cord with her knife. *Her parents weren't impressed,* her mother had said. *She was only bringing home a girl.* Lilian had overheard her mother talk of children turned into soldiers and raindrops that turned into floods and the beautiful serenity she felt sitting outside a hut she'd built with her own hands.

"It is for the best you are home," her mother said, stepping off the box. "The long rains are here and there is a lot of planting to do. Don't let what you cannot do rid you of what you can."

Lilian knew she was lucky to have a home and a garden. She loved the big sky and the green and brown bush. But there were other colours her mother hadn't seen, colours you could only see in books. Lilian missed the sound of turning pages and the ticking of the clock. She missed the noise the lessons made in her head and the stillness of the hushed library. She missed opening a book to the first page and the smell of wet jumpers and how all of it – the rough wooden seats, exams and assemblies – kept her hunger at bay.

When her father didn't return at the end of the month, Lilian put on her uniform and snuck to school.

"Did your father find some money?" Amal asked when he saw her at the gate. Lilian shook her head.

"Then why are you wearing your uniform?"

"I like it," she said. It reminded her of who she was, and who she might be. "I haven't got long before Maama comes looking for me," she said, navigating her way through the bush to stop at a mossy log. She opened her exercise book and pulled her pen from behind her ear, scribbling on the page to encourage the ink. "So, what have I missed?" Amal took the pen from her and held it up to the light. Only a few drops of blue ink remained in the chamber. He removed the small plug from the clear plastic barrel and tipped the ink chamber into Lilian's hand.

"Find a lukandwa tree – there are lots by the church – pick the balled fruit and squeeze it into this hole. The juice is blue." He sat down next to her, not so close that they were touching, but close enough, and told her what she'd missed and let her copy his notes. If he'd asked for a kiss in return, she would have said yes.

When her father finally did return, shuffling up the path, Lilian didn't run to him.

"You lied," she said, when he found her behind the house. "You said you'd try. You said you'd work hard so I could go to school."

She had studied hard. She had kept *her* part of the bargain. He'd broken his, and later, when he drew aside the curtain to say goodnight, she lay curled, facing the wall, and pretended to sleep. She knew it wasn't fair to blame him. *Kimanje is not a young man anymore, it is hard to get work*, her aunt had said. But she needed to blame someone for her ruined life. If there was someone to blame, there was someone who could fix it and Lilian needed to believe her life would be made right.

"Make your father some tea," her mother said the next morning, disappearing into the hut to wake Wekesa for school.

Lilian poured her father a cup of boiling water. "There's no *mujaaja* to flavour it."

Her father took the cup and sat down beside her. "I'm sorry for the tea, and for having you chased from school. I never got to senior school." He smiled weakly. "I wanted better for you."

"Then why send Wekesa to school?" Lilian stared into the fire. "He'd be just as happy milking the cows."

"Wekesa has to go to school," her father said softly. "He'll need a good job. He'll have a wife to support."

"And I'll stay home and get married?"

"Yes, when you are older. Don't you want that?"

Lilian pictured Amal and their home in Walumira with a chair by the window and wall full of books.

"I do," she said, "but I also want to be a teacher and have enough coin to flavour my tea." She knew the words would hurt, but she was hurting too. "If you want more for this family, more for *me*," she said, "let me learn." She reached out and touched her father's arm, the skin loose on his bones, and her anger burned out, quick as dry leaves.

"Please, Taata ..."

Her father lifted her chin so there was nowhere to look, but into his narrow face.

"Don't worry, Tiny Mosquito, I'll make things right."

Chapter 15

A car door swung open. A fat man sat in the back seat. His face was crisp from years of sun and the hair on the back of his head was swept forwards to disguise a bald spot. Lilian, Masani and Dimple stood in the front yard of Nasreen's home as her family packed up the food and decorations. The girls hadn't been asked to the *okuwoowa* and Lilian had been relieved not to receive an invitation; there was nothing to celebrate.

Nasreen dragged her bag to the waiting car. Her *gomesi* was beautiful, the colour of the sky at sunset, but all Lilian could see of her friend were her fidgeting hands and dark eyes. Lilian ran to hug Nasreen but she didn't congratulate her.

"I'm sorry," Lilian whispered.

"Don't be sorry; I am marrying well." Nasreen's mouth was hidden behind an orange veil, but her eyes betrayed her. Her lashes were heavy with tears, her lids swollen. She heaved her bag into the boot and climbed into the back seat. Her father hurried after her with another bag and a rug.

"She's your responsibility now," he said, leaning into the car to shake the man's hand. "Take care of her."

Nasreen blew her nose and waved at her mother, her eyes crinkling at the corners in an attempt at a smile.

"Did you see the size of his stomach?" Masani said, watching the car recede into the distance.

"At least she's getting out of here," Dimple muttered. She cupped her hands to her mouth and ran to the gate. "I have to go," she said when Lilian caught up to her. She rose from her knees and wiped flecks of vomit from her cheek.

Lilian shielded her eyes from the sun with the palm of her hand and watched Dimple recede into the distance.

"When are you coming back to school?" Masani appeared beside her. "Thomas keeps asking. He misses you. He said if you need anything ..." She threaded her arm through Lilian's. "Amal's good looking but he can't pay your fees. Thomas doesn't mind throwing his money around, especially if he wants something." Her face grew serious. "He'll get bored of waiting. If you want money for school, do something now. Oh, look!" She pointed further up the path. "What a coincidence. It's Thomas."

Thomas walked toward them, studying Lilian with a predator's unwavering gaze. "Masani said you'd be at Nasreen's," he began, but Masani cut him off.

"Got to go, sorry, just remembered my aunt is expecting me." She hurried up the path.

"I brought you something." Thomas held a dictionary out.

"I thought you could use it when you come back to school." Lilian stared at the book. She *wanted* to take it. She wanted to write her name in capital letters on the cover and open it to the first page but she didn't know what it would cost her. Thomas shoved the book back into his bag. "I can give you money for next term, if that's what you want."

Lilian shook her head and turned for home.

"It's really not a big deal," she heard him say. "You can come to my house." He followed behind her. "We can watch TV." Lilian's father had watched a movie once, on his brother-in-law's TV in Kampala. *It is a story in pictures*, he'd tried to explain, drawing a square in the dirt.

"You ever watched a movie?" Thomas caught up to her, his gaze tracking down her face to her neck. "My parents are going to Kampala next week. No one will be home."

Lilian's mother was waiting for her at the gate when she returned from Nasreen's.

"*Obweddaoliwa nyabo.*"

Start lunch? Lilian quickened her pace. They hadn't eaten lunch in months. She broke into a run, throwing her arms around her father as he stood to greet her. "Tiny Mosquito," he said, burying his face in her hair.

Lilian tugged at his pocket like she had when she was small to reveal a groundnut or a pencil, or a shiny silver coin.

"They're empty," he whispered.

A tall man wearing leather shoes stepped out of the shadows. His shirt was tucked into trousers held up by a leather belt. He seemed out of place. Everyone Lilian had ever met looked like they were in need of something: a hot meal, a shower, a pair of shoes. Not this man.

"Lilian, meet your Uncle Beneh." Her father's smile dimmed. "Beneh, meet Lilian." *Beneh*. It took Lilian a while to place the name. Everyone – her mother and father, Uncle Lwanga and Afia and all of their cousins – called him The-Rich-Uncle-From-Kampala. *So that's what rich looks like*, Lilian thought, dropping to kneel before him. *A pair of shiny sunglasses and a wristwatch with a metal strap.*

"*Kiluungi okusisinkana.* Nice to meet you," Lilian said, glancing at the car sleeping outside their gate. "Is that yours? Can I see it?"

Her mother threw her a disapproving look but the man grinned, his teeth a white gash in his hard face.

"Stand up so I can see you," he said, motioning her to rise. "She is strong," he scrutinised her, "and you say she is smart?"

"Very smart. Hardworking too." Lilian's father gazed at her with crinkle-eyed affection. "And she can cook. Lilian, go help Maama with the Posho."

Lilian knew that her father and Uncle Beneh weren't close. She had heard her father call him a pig and yet here he was, about to eat the last of their beans.

"Your father could have warned me we had a guest for lunch." Her mother hauled Lilian to the fire and handed her a knife.

Uncle Beneh waved a mosquito away and rubbed his spoon on his trouser leg. He examined his plate, brushed an ant from the plastic and passed the plate to Lilian.

"Your uncle is a very smart man," Lilian's father said, adjusting his face into a smile. "Made his money from coffee and used it to buy land. First one property, then another. How many is it now?" He glanced across at Uncle Beneh, who sat uncomfortably on a log.

"Twelve, thirteen," he said, drawing a checked handkerchief from his pocket. "It is getting harder all the time. The government wants a piece; the police want their cut. Still, it is better under Museveni's rule. Things are stable. The economy is on the rise. You can make money if you know how." He spat a mouthful of food into the handkerchief. "Kampala is where the action is."

"I've never been," Lilian said, sinking onto her knees a second time.

"It is a fine place." He dabbed his lips. "We have roads and proper buildings." He didn't tell her to rise, so she stayed kneeling, her knees steeped in mud. "*Akasozi K'empala.* That's what the British called it when they arrived. The Hill of the Impala. It was the King of Buganda's favourite hunting ground. He–"

"Do you sleep on a bed with legs?" Lilian interrupted. "And eat at a dining table? Is that a phone?" Lilian had seen posters of mobile phones plastered to the backs of buses but had never held one.

"No reception," he grumbled, shoving the small black rectangle into his pocket.

"Your uncle returns to Kampala tonight." Lilian's father raised his hand to silence her. "We have a lot to discuss. Leave us to talk."

Lilian washed the dishes and swept the hut. When she returned to the yard her uncle was at the fence, wiping the mud from his shoes on a wooden post.

"Is he leaving?" Lilian asked her father. "I wanted to sit in his car."

Her father winced as he bent to sit on a felled tree. "Come, Tiny Mosquito," he said, patting the log. "It took a little longer than I'd hoped, but I kept my promise."

"Am I going back to school?" Lilian's heart beat hard. "Can I go tomorrow?"

"You'll need to settle in." Her father glanced at the gate where her uncle stood.

"Beneh has agreed to take you. You will live with your aunt and uncle in Kampala and go to school there."

"Kampala?" Lilian leaped to her feet. "Madam Charity told me they have bookshops in Kampala."

"Bookshops and movie theatres and buildings tall as the sky." The words seemed to drain him. "He will pay your fees and buy your books, but you will have to work to pay your board."

"Of course," Lilian said, ignoring his frown. She was going to school! Her heart lifted. She was going to live in the city! No more hikes to the well or making Wekesa breakfast. Just bookshops and cinemas and ice cream on sticks. She spied her father's drums and her smile wavered. No more drumming lessons or fireside stories. No more Dimple or Amal.

"*Jaangu*," her mother said. "We should pack."

Beneh walked towards them. "Don't bother," he said, glancing at Lilian's bare feet. "We'll buy what she needs. Lilian, say goodbye to your parents." Beneh lowered his sunglasses onto his nose.

When Lilian's father took her by the shoulders, the last of her fear fell away. "Tiny Mosquito, you are going to be the first in this family to finish primary school. Study hard and make a better person of yourself. Soak everything in. I know you'll make us proud." He took her face in his bony hands and planted a kiss on her forehead.

"Who's going to take care of her? Who'll stop her from getting spoiled?" Lilian heard her mother ask as she hurried to the car. "Don't walk the streets after dark," her mother called after her. "The men will eat you for dinner."

Lilian didn't turn to wave at her parents; she was too busy imagining her life in the city and the dress Uncle Beneh would buy her and the shoes she would wear.

"Climb in," her uncle said, stopping in front of the car. Lilian peered through a window and saw plump leather seats and a carpeted floor.

Beneh sniffed at her as if she were a pile of dirty laundry and took a towel from the boot.

"Try not to touch anything," he said, spreading it over the seat.

Chapter 16

"Welcome to Kampala!" Beneh swung the car onto an asphalt road, leaving behind the dirt roads and the huts smeared with dung and the big open sky. Lilian poked her head out the window. There were so many people. The smooth tarred road was choked with cars, the concrete footpath swarming with bodies. Girls in high heels with long hair spilling down their backs stood on street corners. Men in suits swung briefcases. Women wore pants. *It's me!* Lilian wanted to shout, sitting up in her seat so they could all see her. *Me. Lilian Chelangat. In a car. In Kampala!*

The car shuddered to a stop at a blinking red light and a flimsy boy with sweat at his underarms reached into the car with a plastic cup. Lilian heard Beneh curse and saw the boy wrench his hand away before Beneh's window slithered shut. Lilian hadn't touched her window but it too emerged from its hiding spot, closing with a soft click when it met the carpeted roof.

Beneh cranked the stick at his side and the car lurched on, past towering concrete boxes lit from inside and buildings made of stone with coloured doors and glass windows. Lilian pressed her nose to the glass. She couldn't imagine a more dazzling city. The colours were different here, sharper and brighter. There were no fields of cassava or vegetables sunk into the ground. There were carts weighed down with papaya and meat hanging from hooks. There were couples seated at tables scooping food with forks and men sleeping in doorways on flattened boxes. The street lamps flickered on, bathing the road in a white light. Lilian's stomach rumbled.

"Uncle Beneh." She rested her chin on the front seat. "I was wondering, have you seen Nakato?" She forced the words out. "She hasn't been home in a long time and I think she may have come to Kampala." Nakato had loved to draw, dresses mostly, and Lilian liked to think of her sister in the city sketching patterns for rich women who lived in houses made of bricks.

Beneh lit a cigarette. He turned a knob near the steering wheel and a woman's voice snaked through the car.

"Uncle?" Lilian spoke louder.

Beneh twisted the button again and the music rose to fill the back seat.

The car swerved onto a smaller road and the windows sank down into their metal sleeves. Beneh drew on his cigarette and let the smoke escape from between his teeth. Nakato was close, Lilian could sense it. Maybe in the next street or around the next corner. She stuck her head out the window and stared at the darkening sky. As soon as she knew her way around, she would search for Nakato. She hoped her sister wanted to be found.

She's probably looking at the same silver moon, Lilian thought, tilting her head to gaze at the sky, a different sky to Walumira's. The moon was dimmer here, the stars less bright. *It doesn't matter*, Lilian thought. In Kampala she wouldn't need the moon's bright beam to read a book or find the *toyii*. Beneh would have light bulbs and an inside toilet, in a room of its own.

They sped through the streets, Beneh humming aloud to the music, Lilian hypnotised by the strange sounds and fluid rhythms, so different to her father's drums. Lilian blushed at the song's words: a girl describing the man in her bed. It made her think of Amal and the time they lay side by side in the forest, recounting their favourite lines of their favourite books. He'd turned to her and told her she was smart, the smartest girl he knew. "I'm going to be a doctor," he'd said. "We can work together. You'd make a great nurse." She didn't want to be a nurse, but he believed she *could* be, and that was something. She'd listened to him speak, swept up by his stories of Kampala and the house he would build and the money he'd make and the lectures he'd give and the lives he would save. He was so certain of his place in the world, so sure he'd make something of his life. She'd listened, lost in the warmth of his smile. His optimism was infectious and when she was with him, she felt the possibilities too. When she was with Amal she could be anything: a teacher or a doctor, a writer or a wife. All of them, or none of them. It was up to her.

And when she went to him in tears after the stories she kept hidden under her bed went missing and railed against her mother, who she was sure had incinerated them, he had calmed and comforted her. *Start again*, he'd said, tearing a sheet from his exercise book for her. *The second telling is always better than the first.*

She'd wanted to tell him how she felt. She'd wanted to kiss him, but he was so earnest in his lessons, so serious about numbers and equations that he barely paused for breath. And she was glad. She'd promised her father she'd make him proud. Best to wait until they were both finished school.

Lilian sat forward in her seat. The houses had become smaller and meaner with each side street they took. Lilian's palms prickled with sweat. Beneh was rich. *He couldn't live here*, Lilian told herself. The narrow grey streets were adrift with rubbish and mothers picking nits from their children's hair.

"Do you live around here?" she croaked from the back seat.

Beneh swung around to face her, his mouth curled into a smile. "This dump?"

The slums gave way to tree-lined streets. Beneh lifted a small black box from the dashboard and pressed a button. "*This* is where I live," he said, swerving into a driveway. Lilian watched the gates open. "*This*, and another bigger home near the Jinja Road." Beneh parked the car under a sprawling acacia next to another shiny car. Lilian narrowed her eyes and read the silver letters glued to the boot. Mercedes-Benz.

Lilian opened her door and stepped onto the gravel drive.

The house was beautiful. She searched for the word which had won her the Primary Five spelling bee – mansion. It was just like the English mansions she'd seen in picture books with their rectangles of green grass and flowering bushes.

"Anyone home?" Beneh tucked his shirt further into his trousers and pushed the door open. Lilian wiped her feet on the doormat and followed him in, her eyes lifting to the light bulbs dangling from the ceiling.

"I wasn't expecting company for dinner." A woman wearing elegant black pants took Beneh's briefcase and pecked him on the cheek. Her hair was black and fell in waves onto her shoulders. Lilian drank her in. Her long fingers sparkled with jewellery and her nails were painted. Amara was taller than Maama. She had better clothes and blacker hair but they shared the same black eyes, the same long fingers with their nails bitten down to the quick. Should she kiss her aunt or shake her hand?

"She's not here for dinner." Beneh handed Lilian to his wife like a pile of washing. "She's here to stay."

Amara's eyebrows knitted together. She looked Lilian up and down. "You didn't mention you were taking another ..." Her eyes hovered at the scooped neck of Lilian's shirt.

"This is Lilian," Beneh said thickly. "Your sister's girl."

"Nnalongo's child?" Lilian's aunt looked relieved. She gave Lilian a small smile and returned her attention to her husband.

"She'll help with the housework so you won't be so tired. Maybe this time next year I'll have that son you promised me."

Lilian followed her uncle through the house, padding along the cool concrete floor in her bare feet, reaching out with her fingertips to touch the smooth walls and the filmy curtains that danced at the windows.

When the hallway opened into a room big enough to sleep an elephant, Lilian's mouth fell open. The room held a world of things – a clock and a tap and glass container filled with flowers. Beneh grinned.

"You're impressed with the kitchen?" he said, not expecting an answer. "So was I, when I first built it. My other one is bigger."

Lilian wondered how long they'd let her stay. She spied a paperback lying open on a side table. If there was one, there'd be more. She turned to look for the shelves she imagined were sagging with books, but the white walls were bare, except for a flat black rectangle fixed to the wall.

"We have seven channels." Her uncle pressed a button and the box lit up.

Lilian drew closer to the tiny dancers who leaped and spun inside the frame. "How do they get in?"

Beneh ignored the question. "I'll eat my dinner at the TV," he said, dropping onto the couch.

"He likes the meat swimming in sauce and the potatoes burnt, but just a little." Lilian's aunt aimed a bottle of lemon-scented spray at the bench and Lilian lifted her elbows so that her aunt could trap the flecks of dirt with her rag.

"Your kitchen–"

Her aunt pressed a finger to her lips.

"He can't hear the TV if you run your mouth." She folded the rag into a neat square. "We can talk later, when we eat." She lifted a wedge of meat from a pot and, dousing it in sauce, arranged it on a plate beside an army of potatoes and a hill of beans. Lilian watched her set the heaped plate on her husband's lap and scuttle back and forth between the kitchen and TV, proffering a fork and knife, a napkin and a glass of beer, speaking in hurried, half-statements so as not to pull his attention too far from the TV.

Her uncle hacked the slab of meat into smaller pieces and shovelled them into his mouth. Lilian stared at the wasted sauce blotted on his napkin and the mountain of lamb that could've fed her whole family and wondered if she'd ever be able to eat her dinner without feeling that she was taking more than her share.

"It's late," her uncle said, sucking his fingers dry. He switched off the TV and grabbed his wife by the waist, his hands like paws. "Show Lilian around. I'll wait for you in bed." Lilian's Aunt nodded, but she didn't soften at his touch, and when she turned her back to him, her smile had vanished.

Lilian stepped into the glass-walled shower and closed her eyes, letting the cool water chase the dirt from her body. She dragged her fingers over her stubbled head to unpick the dirt from her nails and wondered how it would feel to comb her fingers through long hair. Her aunt had left a soft pink towel folded on a stool. Lilian wrapped it around her body and stared at the toilet. She knew from books that you were supposed to sit down so she lowered her bottom onto the seat. Her aunt had shown her the roll of paper she was to use instead of leaves and the button she must press once she was done. Lilian stood over the bowl and watched the gushing water swallow the paper, before turning to the door.

She was used to ducking under a sisal sack to enter a hut and lifting sheets to move between rooms. She pressed down on the metal handle and the door swung open. Her aunt was waiting in the hall, her long hair plaited into a rope that fell down her back

"This way," Amara said, rushing down the darkened corridor, her high heels clicking on the concrete floor. "I remember my first day in the city, my head full of all the things I wanted to do." She reached for a doorknob. "This room is yours. The other one is bigger." She glanced at the door to her right. "But there's no point having you move when the baby comes." Lilian's eyes flew to her aunt's belly.

"Oh no, I am not ..." Her aunt's hands sailed to her flat stomach. "Not yet." She was quiet for a while and Lilian imagined her reaching into a cradle to soothe a baby. Lilian breathed in a forest of wildflowers and understood why a rich man from Kampala might choose Amara for a wife.

Her aunt threw open the door. There was a bed and a rug and a cupboard with doors.

"The bed will have to be made each morning." Her aunt looked tired. "See how the edges are tucked in?"

Sheets. A pillow. A bed, with legs. Lilian's heart thumped against her chest. Her aunt opened a cupboard door and lifted out a pale blue nightdress, turning away as Lilian dropped her towel to put it on. "We'll go shopping, tomorrow. You'll need clothes for church and a uniform. You can use the table as a desk."

Lilian glanced at the wooden table. Even with the bed, the desk, the chair *and* the cupboard, there seemed too much space.

"*Alyta maama woo?*" Lilian's aunt tried to sound breezy but her voice was strained.

Lilian shrugged. "Maama is fine." She sat on the bed, hoping her aunt might sit next to her. She had so many questions, but before she could ask the first – why her aunt had only been home once since she married – her aunt whispered goodnight and closed the door.

Lilian climbed onto the bed and reached for the light bulb. She cupped her hands around the warm glass, careful not to shatter it, and when the heat grew too scalding she leaped off the bed and searched for the switch. On and off, she plunged the room into darkness then filled it with light, imagining it was how God must feel at dawn and at dusk.

The room was quiet, the curtains drawn. No whispering insects, no tossing trees, none of the familiar night sounds that would lull her to sleep. Lilian's stomach rumbled. Her aunt had forgotten to feed her. Remembering the cook pot large enough for a small child to climb into, she opened the door and crept through the house.

The kitchen bench was bare and the stovetop mopped clean. Her uncle's plate had been washed of scraps and sat drying on a dish rack, the sponge beside it, rinsed of crumbs. A door opened spilling light into the kitchen. Lilian dropped to her knees. Over the bench top, she saw her uncle move into a room, loosen his bathrobe and let it fall to the floor.

Lilian didn't dare move. The bedroom door was open and if

she could hear the sharp intake of her aunt's breath, then they would be able to hear her too. When the grunting stopped, Lilian wrapped her fingers around the refrigerator's metal handle.

"Don't leave, Beneh." Lilian froze at the sound of her aunt's voice. "She has you *every* night. She won't mind if I keep you tonight. I can make you breakfast in the morning. Go back to sleep."

Lilian peered over the countertop to see her uncle pull on his pants and reach for his wallet.

"This should last you a while," he said, flinging an envelope on the bed.

Lilian watched him leave, a memory surfacing: Lilian and her mother sorting through a parcel of clothes. *Look at this*, her mother had said, holding up a silk *gomesi*. *Brand new, and she throws it out. My sister has too much money.* Lilian had taken the dress from her mother and held it against her small body. *Does Aunt Amara work?* she'd asked her mother, hoping to hear that life was different in the city. *Beneh visits her once a week with a bundle of cash and bulging pants,* her mother had said, snatching the dress from her. *I guess you could call that a job.*

Chapter 17

"You ready?" Her aunt poked her head around the door. Her black hair fell like a curtain around her face. Her lips were painted pink and her eyes dusted with powder and Lilian wondered if she slept like that, or rose before the sun to apply her make-up. *Always be ready for your husband*, Afia had said, showing Lilian how to wet her lips with gloss. *Don't force him to look elsewhere.*

Lilian rubbed the sleep from her eyes and lifted her dress off the floor. Her aunt frowned. "There are hangers in the cupboard." She threw the curtains apart and light flooded the room. "Fix your bed and meet me outside. I want to get to the shops as soon as they open."

Lilian climbed into her dress and hurried out.

"We are not driving?" she asked, trying not to sound disappointed when her aunt strode past the car.

"That's Beneh's car."

"You don't drive?"

Her aunt closed the gate behind them. "He never taught me."

They walked to the main road, past women in short skirts wearing strappy sandals and men in suits drinking coffee from plastic cups. And *mzungu*! Pink-skinned, barelegged, *mzungu* with small, slender noses and ocean eyes. They held cameras and carried backpacks and the girls had glossy hair swept into ponytails. Lilian's mother had told her that white people brought good luck and all the stories Lilian read about white-skinned girls had happy endings, but they were just stories. The things her teachers had taught her about the slave trade in America and apartheid in South Africa had actually happened, not far from Uganda and not that long ago.

"It is rude to stare," Amara whispered.

"Sorry, Aunt. Please forgive me," Lilian apologised, remembering her mother's warning, delivered with a slap. *If an elder tells you that you did something wrong, you don't keep quiet like you didn't hear.*

They stopped at a hair salon and Lilian's aunt scanned the price list painted on the door.

"I will bring you when it grows." Amara frowned at Lilian's stubbled head. "Beneh will expect us to look our best for church." She stepped towards a shop with big glass doors and the panels slid open, stealing Lilian's reflection. Lilian had only glanced at herself for a moment before the glass doors parted but she saw, staring back at her, a girl in a tattered work dress with a shaved head and bare feet. All the women in the shop were dressed like her aunt, in colourful dresses or elegant pants. They wore shoes with high heels and coloured stones threaded around their necks. They seemed to be from a different planet, their skin lit from inside. Even the girls Lilian's age seemed to breathe a different air.

Lilian stopped at a row of floor-length gowns, hoping to see her sister's name, *Nakato Checkwech*, in looping gold script on the tags.

"They're too expensive." Amara directed Lilian's attention to the discount racks.

"I didn't want to buy one," Lilian apologised. "I was just looking for my sister's dresses."

"Your sister?"

"Nakato. She left home just after she turned fifteen. She didn't say goodbye or tell us where she was going but she always talked about the city. She wanted to be a dressmaker."

"I know. I saw her."

"Here? In Kampala?" Lilian brightened.

"She came to us years ago." Lilian's aunt busied herself with a rack of dresses. "I answered the door. She didn't want to come in. She said she needed money." Amara slid a dress from the rack and held it to Lilian's chest.

"Did you give her any?"

"Beneh said if she chose to leave home she had to stand on own two feet." Amara plucked another dress from the rack.

Lilian touched her aunt's arm. "How was she?"

"Nakato? I don't know. Tired maybe."

Nakato was in Kampala. Lilian brushed her fingers along the rows of silk dresses and cotton shirts. *In Kampala!* It was only a matter of time before they found each other. She tried the dresses her aunt had pulled from the half-price rack. She liked the pink dress with the square neck best, but her aunt didn't ask which was her favourite. She scanned the price tags and chose the cheapest one, counting out three notes from the thick fold of bills she kept in the blue wallet buried at the bottom of her bag.

They spent the morning shopping. They bought a second-hand uniform, which was two sizes too big, three pairs of underwear and a pair of black shoes Lilian could wear to school and to church. They bought two pairs of socks, a toothbrush and toothpaste, but best of all was the leather satchel Lilian proudly swung by her side, its bulging pockets crammed with books and pens.

"We'll have one of those too," Amara added, pointing to a red plastic lunchbox on a shelf behind the cash register. She emptied the contents of her wallet onto the counter so the woman could take what was owed.

Lilian threw her arms around Amara's waist. "*Webaule*," she whispered, burrowing into her.

"Don't thank *me*." Amara pulled away from her. "Thank Beneh. It's his money." She returned the empty wallet to her handbag and stuffed the change down her bra.

They walked home in the muggy heat, Lilian's arms laden with bags. The hot tar burned her soles, but she didn't care. Tomorrow she'd wear shoes to church and on Monday, she'd go to school.

Amara unlocked the door and disappeared into her room.

Lilian slipped into her uniform, slung her schoolbag over her shoulder and stood in front of her mirror, turning circles in front of the glass. She'd seen her forehead, a shoulder, a thigh, in her mother's cracked hand mirror, piecing the parts of her body together like a puzzle, but here she was ... *all* of her: the shirt and the skirt and the socks and shoes. She didn't want to take the uniform off, but her aunt was calling. She peeled off her old underwear and slipped a new pair on. There were no holes at the crotch and the elastic was tight. And she had two more. When she washed one at night, there would be a dry pair to pull on. She stared at the plastic bag her aunt had left for her. *It is for your old underwear*, she had said. *The rubbish bin is outside*. Lilian lifted her old knickers from the floor. If she could get her hands on a pair of scissors she could cut them into rags. She heaved the corner of the mattress up and slid her frayed underwear between the bed's soft mattress and its base, then slipped the plastic bag in too.

"Let's eat," her aunt said, when Lilian joined her in the kitchen. She wrung out her mop, set it against the wall and emptied the fridge, sweeping her husband's leftover dinner scraps onto two plates. Lilian demolished the wilted beans and cold potatoes, wondering why her aunt hadn't used her spare change to buy a shoulder of pork from the butcher on the corner.

They spent the afternoon cleaning. As soon as Lilian finished one chore, her aunt set her another, but she didn't mind. The house smelled of lemons and her aunt's perfume, and if she wanted to wash out her rag, she only needed to turn on the tap and watch the water pool in the sink. She wasn't allowed into Amara's room, under any circumstances, and was escorted to another room, with strict instructions not to upset anything on the desk.

"Beneh's books are ordered alphabetically by author," her aunt opened the door, revealing a room lined with books. "You can dust them, but put them back in the same spot. The same spot," she repeated, waiting for Lilian to nod. She watched through slitted eyes as Lilian cradled a book to dust its spine.

Only when her aunt left, did Lilian dare take it all in, the wooden stepladder standing quietly in a corner, the small window spilling light onto a leather armchair, the heavy desk with carved wooden legs and the worn paperbacks clinging to the walls. There were books on music, business and farming, a dictionary crammed with words and an encyclopaedia, its leather-bound volumes embossed with gold letters. Lilian reached up to pull an atlas from the shelf to check it was real. She fanned through the pages, countries – whole continents – opening up to her.

She slid the book back into place and continued her dusting No one in Walumira had a library or a study. Her father kept a bible by his bed and Afia had a hymnbook, but nobody Lilian knew, not even Nasreen, had an encyclopaedia or an Oxford English Dictionary . Lilian dusted the tops of the books, *Oliver Twist* first, then *Great Expectations*. She'd need to prove herself useful if she wanted to stay long enough to read all of Charles Dickens.

"I *had* to take her," Beneh said, as if he owed the woman sitting next to him in church an explanation. "Her parents have no money. I'm her only hope. She'll help around the house. If you need her to watch Shanitah ..." The woman was squeezed into an emerald-green suit. Her hair had been smoothed and her lips painted. She looked like the pictures on the shampoo bottles Madam Kiyonga kept on a high shelf in her shop.

"You're a generous man, Beneh. Always helping those who can't help themselves." She leaned forwards and regarded Amara with distaste.

A small girl in a white dress climbed onto Beneh's knee and poked her tongue out at Lilian.

"Aunty, who's that girl?" Lilian asked. Amara pressed a finger to her lips. The priest was readying himself to speak.

Lilian hoped his words would reach the back row. The room was much bigger than the pink-walled church in Walumira. The ceiling was higher, the stained glass brighter, the congregants better dressed. God had been kind to them. Lilian stared at the woman's fingers threaded through Beneh's, dripping with coloured stones big as orange drops.

The priest started thundering his sermon and the room fell silent. He cursed the congregation's bad luck and blamed the devil for their empty cupboards and broken-down cars. Men nodded in agreement and women listened through half-closed eyes, rising in the name of Jesus to ask for forgiveness. The priest sprinkled holy water and then everybody sang, "Glory, Glory". Lilian sang and swayed. Next to her, Amara moaned.

"God, big as the sky," Lilian heard her say, "can't you do this one small thing for me?"

Lilian sang the last verse of "Jesus Loves Me" and then the service concluded and the congregation spilled outside.

"*Jangu wano*, Lilian, come!" Beneh waved Lilian over to where the woman in green stood.

"Go," Amara said, shunting Lilian forwards. "He wants to show you off." Lilian's cheeks lifted. She smoothed her dress and walked towards them, smelling of toothpaste.

"Lilian, I'd like to introduce you to my wife, Joyce Perembata."

His wife

Lilian's smile came unstuck.

Uncle Beneh had another wife. Uncle Lwanga had two wives, but Lwanga lived in the bush. Beneh lived in the city.

Lilian felt a flare of anger, then, remembering her manners, sank to her knees.

"Pleased to meet you," she lied.

The woman glanced down at her. "You're a lucky girl, having such a generous uncle." She looped her arm through Beneh's. "How's your aunt? Poor thing." She replaced her smile with a pout. "Still no babies, after so many years. What a waste."

The little girl who'd poked her tongue out, bounded up to them, her shiny braids swinging from side to side. She whispered something to her mother and pointed at Lilian.

"She's not from here." Beneh's second wife looked bored. "She lives in the bush."

"With the monkeys?"

Beneh laughed. "She lives in a village." He swept the girl

onto his shoulders. "Her name is Lilian. Lilian, this is Shanitah, my little princess." He lowered her to the ground.

Shanitah didn't say hello; she asked if Lilian ate bananas for breakfast.

It started to rain, fat drops which spattered the pavement and soaked their clothes. The woman's hand flew to her hair. It wasn't kinky like Lilian's mother's, or thick like Afia's. It waved gracefully around her face and fell in drifts around her shoulders. Beneh handed her an umbrella.

"Time to go, princess." He grabbed Shanitah's hand and sprinted to the car.

"Beneh!" Amara called after them, slipping a plastic bag over her hair. But Beneh didn't hear her. He closed the car door for his second wife and walked to the driver's side.

Chapter 18

Lilian's heart thumped under her blue collared shirt. She pulled up her socks and straightened her skirt. A throng of boys pushed past her. Buoyed by the weight of her bag and the books buried inside it, Lilian stepped through the school gate. The yard swarmed with students, all of them hurrying past her to disappear into classrooms.

"We've been expecting you." The principal's assistant introduced himself, before ferrying her through the grounds. "Your uncle said you'd be starting today." Lilian hurried after him, past the library and a sports oval where meaty-faced boys lobbed balls in the air. Lilian's stomach heaved. At Walumira Primary she knew everyone, if not by name, then by clan. Her throat closed over. Nobody here knew her. Her shirt gaped at the neck and her skirt was too long; that's all they'd see. They didn't know she was smart. Lilian's eyes widened. What if she wasn't? There was so much she didn't know about the city. So many things she'd never seen: the white sheen of a dinner plate, the inside of a car, the metal box above the stove that sucked the steam from the cook pot.

"The next door on the left is the Primary Seven classroom." The principal's assistant motioned to the door. "Your uncle has taken care of the term's fees and your meal card." He handed Lilian a slip of blue paper and swung the door open on her future. "Welcome to Namugongo Primary School."

"Come sit." A tall woman with gold hoops in her ears patted an empty seat in the middle row. Lilian's eyes darted across the room, saw the boys hunched in their seats, and the girls, squeezed between them, their hair trimmed like Lilian's or knotted into braids.

"I'm Madam Kyobiggya, your English and literature teacher. You are?"

"Lilian. Lilian Chelangat, but my friends–" Lilian stopped. Lala was a barefoot girl in a ragged work dress who lived in a hut smeared in dung. Lilian lived in Kampala with her rich uncle. She squared her shoulders. "My friends call me Lilian."

"Lilian, perhaps you can tell us a little about yourself. I believe your uncle is Beneh Bukulu?"

The room was still. A few students swivelled around to gape at Lilian. The girl beside her beamed.

The teacher lifted her coffee cup from her desk and took a sip. "Best coffee in town," she said, swivelling the cup so the class could see the words *Bukulu Coffee* emblazoned on it.

Lilian blushed and then, because they were all waiting, added,

"I've moved to Kampala to live with Uncle Beneh so I can finish school and go to university." The teacher turned to a stocky girl with beads worked into the knots in her hair. "Grace, will you show Lilian around at break time?" The girl smiled her assent and the teacher's gaze returned to Lilian. "Grace Nampewo will familiarise you with the school. If you have any questions go to her, and if she doesn't have the answers," the teacher rested her hands on Lilian's desk, "come to the staffroom and ask for me."

Lilian pulled an exercise book from her bag and opened it to the first page, her panic giving way to excitement.

"We're studying *Romeo and Juliet*." Madam Kyobiggya placed a book in front of Lilian. "If you haven't read it, start tonight."

Lilian's eyes grew wide. "Excuse me, madam, am I allowed to take it home?"

The teacher nodded and Lilian slipped the book inside her schoolbag, the smell of ink and glue chasing away the last of her fears.

"So, is it true your uncle has four houses and a cook?" Grace Nampewo looped her arm through Lilian's and led her to a spreading acacia to shelter from the rain. The yard was loud with chatter. Girls huddled under trees while the boys held their mouths open to catch the rain.

"I'm not sure about the cook but I know he has two houses."

The girl's smile emptied. "I heard he had an aeroplane, but if he only has two houses, he probably can't afford ..."

Lilian had a choice – she could write the next page of her story or close the book. "He's building a third home. It will be bigger than both of them. I just haven't seen it because," the words spilled out, "I only got here a few days ago and I've been too busy shopping."

Grace cast a wary eye over Lilian's faded shirt and worn skirt.

"So, if he is eating money, why didn't he buy you a new uniform?"

Lilian had asked herself the same question. Her aunt had plenty of money. "He wants ..." She scrambled for an answer. "He wants me to focus on what's important."

Grace fingered the beads worked into her braids.

"Uncle Beneh chose this shirt for me to make a point," Lilian said, warming at the memory of her father's whispered farewell. *Soak it up, Tiny Mosquito,* her father had said, *and come back a better person.* "I'm here to study." She held up her shabby skirt. "This is a reminder not to get swept up in the cars and clothes."

When the rain abated, the girl offered Lilian a tour of the school, pointing out the sports field and the library, the toilets and the water fountain.

"This is the canteen." Grace's eyes lit up. "They have *kaloddo*, *lumonde* and *muwogo* but the *namagoddi* sells out first."

Lilian dug out her meal card.

"That only covers lunch. You need money for snacks." Grace waited for Lilian to retrieve a wallet from her bag.

"Who are those girls?" Lilian tried to distract her. She

pointed to a group of older girls in long sleeves and long socks.

"They're the Senior Sixes. Namugongo Secondary is next door. We share the canteen and the oval. The one in the jacket is head girl."

A smile lifted the corners of Lilian's mouth.

"If you want to be head girl of Senior One next year, you'll have to fight Kamali for it." Grace pointed to a girl with rebellious hair hammering a piece of paper to a tree. "If you get the boys' vote, you might have a chance. They don't like her much. She helps run Empowerment Club." Grace's lip curled. "They meet once a month. It's a "girls only" thing. She's a feminist."

Lilian didn't know what a feminist was but she could tell from Grace's sour mouth that it wasn't a compliment. She stole another glance at the girl. Her eyes were closed, her face tilted up at the clouds.

"They talk about how to manage your P's, what to do about bad touches, blah, blah, blah. We've already learned that stuff from our aunties: don't talk to boda boda drivers; don't walk alone at night; no boyfriends at school. You don't mind if we skip the science lab?" Grace sailed past a room full of microscopes and beakers. "We have to do chemistry this year, but don't worry," she said, stopping at the oval to watch the boys play soccer, "girls are allowed to drop it in Senior Five. Maths too. I mean, it's like putting us on a soccer field and expecting us to compete."

Lilian walked home at the end of the day ducking questions about the size of her bedroom.

"Okay, enough," Grace said, batting the other girls away. "She doesn't like bragging. Once she is settled in, I am sure she will invite us over."

The girls drifted off, one by one, as they neared their homes.

"This is my street," Grace said, hesitating. "But I can come over to watch TV if you want?" Lilian shook her head. She wanted to search for Nakato. "My aunt wants to take me out for dinner," she lied. "I better get ready."

As soon as Grace turned the corner, Lilian read the first item on her list: *clothing stores*. She would search for Nakato in the dress shops along the main road and then work her way through the smaller streets. The hunt could take months but eventually she'd find her. Lilian ran her finger down the list: *clothing stores, dressmakers, hat shops, movie theatres.*

Lilian scanned the teeming streets for her sister's face. When she reached a clothing store with sliding doors she splayed her fingers on the glass and peered inside. She didn't look for a skinny girl with a shaved head and big ears. She looked for the woman her sister must have become: a woman with hair spilling over her shoulders, wearing high heels and a dress of her own design.

"Nakato?" Lilian whispered, her eyes finding a girl Nakato's height, with the same wide shoulders. Lilian pressed her nose to the glass. The girl was bent over a box of scarves, her black hair spiralling down her back. Lilian couldn't see her face, but she was wearing a red dress, Nakato's favourite colour.

"Nakato!" She rapped on the window. "Nakato!" She pushed her way inside. "Nakato!" She ran to the back of the shop and lunged at the girl.

"Oh." Lilian slumped when the stranger swivelled to face her. "I'm sorry. I thought you were my–" Tears clouded her eyes.

The shop next door was a dressmaker. "Maybe she is working from home," the woman behind the sewing machine suggested. Lilian hadn't thought of that. She closed the door behind her and headed back to Beneh's, searching the leafy yards and silent houses near her uncle's home.

I'll find her tomorrow, she told herself, adding *Put up posters* and *Knock on doors* to her list.

The front door was open, and on the floor, in the hall, was a note from her aunt. Lilian scanned the list of chores: wipe down the gate, wash the car, sweep the driveway. Lilian peeled off her uniform and slipped on her work dress. She heaved a bucket of water to the gate and lifted a sopping rag to a metal post.

"Lilian?" A girl in school uniform stopped at the gate. She lowered the ice block that had stained her lips orange. "I'm Hope. From your class." Her forehead creased in confusion. "What are you doing?"

"I can't stand spiders and the fence is crawling with them." Lilian pretended to shiver. She dipped a rag into the bucket and swiped at a spider web.

"Doesn't your uncle have someone to do that?" The girl stared at Lilian's bare feet.

Lilian counted out three beats. "*Nzijaa*, I'm coming! Sorry, my aunt's taking me out for dinner. I have to get dressed." She hurried to the house, creeping back out when Hope had gone.

Lilian worked quickly, sweeping the path of leaves and dousing the car with water, returning to her room to empty her bag of books. She plucked Shakespeare from the pile and curled up in bed.

"Lilian, wake up!" A rough hand shook Lilian awake. The room was dark, the sky at the open window, black. "Where's dinner?"

"Dinner?" Lillian sat up and rubbed her eyes. "What time is it?"

"After six!" Her aunt whipped the blanket off the bed. "Beneh will be expecting dinner. There was a list on the kitchen bench ..." She fled the room and Lilian ran after her.

It took them an hour to roast the sesame and pound it into a paste for the bean stew. Lilian prepared bamboo shoots to accompany the beans and Amara steamed the fish she'd bought fresh from the market. She heaped the vegetables around the fish and set the platter on the bench, with a piece of buttered bread, scooping the leftover beans onto two smaller plates. Lilian's stomach rumbled.

"We should wait for him," Amara said, wiping down the bench.

When the last of the pots had been washed and dried, Amara stood by the open window and stared at the bright stars. When the clock struck nine, Lilian tapped her on the shoulder.

"Aunt, can I go to my room and do some homework until uncle comes?"

Amara nodded, her eyes settling on the sad plate of food on the bench, the heat lost from the fish, the beans limp. Her fingers found the small leather pouch at her waist and unpicking the clasp, she reached into the bag to steal a pinch of fine powder. Lilian saw her lips move as she sprinkled it over the fish whispering words to charm her husband, and a memory bubbled up: her mother and Afia huddled by the fire. *It is a terrible destiny*, she remembered Afia saying as she fed the fire with scraps of bark. Lilian had thought they were talking about her mother's little sister who had died in the tin drum, but it was Amara they'd spoken of. Amara's curse.

When the clock struck ten, they ate their wilted beans. Amara covered the fish with foil and slid it into the fridge.

"Shanitah likes him to read her bedtime stories," she said in a small voice. "He probably fell asleep. Things will change," she said, fingering the leather pouch at her waist, "as soon as I give him a son."

Chapter 19

Lilian walked to school, stifling a yawn. She had woken early to prepare breakfast for her uncle, though he never came. Amara had sat with her head in her hands, her body crumpled over the plate of cold eggs, and Lilian had felt at first a black sadness and then a spark of hate, but then she'd put on the uniform Uncle Beneh had bought her and her anger had loosened. And walking through the front gate of Namugongo Primary, she found her exhaustion lifting too, so that by the time she stepped into the schoolyard, her mind was less foggy.

Lilian searched for a familiar face. She missed Dimple's clammy hands dragging her to the swings and sitting on the oval reading romance novels with Nasreen. She missed Amal's wide smile and the heat that came off him when he sat beside her.

The girls in Primary Seven were hunched together on the

hot concrete, their voices quiet in conspiracy. Grace lifted her face from the gossip.

"Do you think we're idiots?" she said, her voice hot with anger. The boys playing soccer stopped the ball and shifted closer. "You can't put on hand-me-downs and expect us to believe–"

"You were washing your uncle's fence," Hope interrupted. "You pretended you were on your way to dinner." She faced her friends. "Penina saw her an hour later washing his car."

"So?" Lilian said, glad to be free of the lie. *There's no shame in being poor.* Her father's words pulsed in her head. "My uncle pays for school and I help around the house."

"How do we know he's her uncle?" Grace questioned her friends. "He's probably her boss."

An older boy spoke over them. "He wouldn't pay for his maid to go to school. She must be doing something else for him." He winked at Lilian and reached for his crotch.

"I'm his *niece*," Lilian bit back. "Why would I lie about that?"

But she *had* lied. She'd made up a story about Beneh and Amara and her place in their home, and none of it was true.

Grace's eyes were fierce slits. "Why would you lie?" She shrugged. "I don't know, maybe to make out you are better than the rest of us. Maybe to impress us." She turned her back on Lilian. "It didn't work."

"I'm sorry," Lilian said but no one was listening. The boys had gone back to soccer, the girls to gossiping.

"Ignore them." The voice belonged to the girl who called herself a feminist. Lilian had found the word in her uncle's dictionary. *Feminist – a person who advocates for equal rights for women.* Lilian liked her already. "They want to put us into boxes; you're either a good girl or you're spoiled. A rich kid," she tossed Lilian a grin, "or a maid. Why can't we be all those things? Or none of them?" She stuck out a hand and Lilian shook it. "I'm Kamali." She handed a pamphlet to Lilian. "I help run the girl's Empowerment Club. It's mostly senior girls but if you're in Primary Seven you're allowed to join."

Lilian scanned the pamphlet. "Grace said we learn all this stuff at school."

"At school they tell you how to behave and what to think. At Empowerment Club they give us the facts and then it's up to us. We get to choose." Her face lit up as she spoke. "You can't choose how to live your life unless you know what's out there. Like sex. Everyone tells us not to do it." She didn't lower her voice. "But girls do it and we need to know how to stay safe." Kamali pointed to the sweaty pamphlet in Lilian's hand. "The next session is on leadership."

Lilian stared at the girl. She'd seen the same fearlessness, the same conviction and unwavering confidence before – in Amal and in Beneh – but never in a girl.

"I'm going to run for information prefect next year. What post do you want?"

Lilian blinked. *What post did she want?* As if wanting was enough.

"Maybe class monitor," she said, feeling emboldened by the girl. "I heard being a prefect helps if you want to get into university. Are you planning on going?"

"I don't know," Kamali said, and Lilian's smile faded. "I used to want to be a scientist." She chewed on her lip. "Now I'm thinking, maybe a judge."

Lilian studied the crumpled list in her hand. She'd searched the clothing stores and seamstresses on the main road, asking everyone she met whether they knew of a girl called Nakato. *She looks like me, except her ears are bigger. She might have been asking for work?* No one had seen her.

Lilian stabbed the next entry. *Hat shops.* She'd visit hat shops tomorrow. She walked home searching the streets bordering Beneh's home looking for a businesswoman in a suit or a woman carting bolts of cloth, but she also gazed at the faces of the maids in starched uniforms and the nannies pushing prams. Just in case.

"Oh, it's you." Amara seemed disappointed when Lilian appeared in the kitchen. She pulled a slab of meat from the fridge and set it on the bench. "I thought you were Beneh. He's coming for dinner. Pass me an apron?" She pointed to a drawer and Lilian opened it.

"Would you mind?" Amara said, holding her arms out. She was wearing a pink sleeveless shirt and a billowing skirt, her face masked by make-up. Lilian slipped the apron over her aunt's smoothed hair and tied a bow at her back.

"You must be missing home," Amara said, her mood lightened by the impending arrival of her husband. "There's nothing to be ashamed of. I wanted to go home, at first." She tucked a wisp of stray hair behind her ear. "That was years ago. And Beneh's coming for dinner," she smiled nervously, "so things are good. Things are great." She sawed the meat. "Do you want to call your parents?"

"They don't have a phone."

"Of course," Amara said, her eyes on the door. "There's paper in Beneh's study if you want to write them a letter and you can dust while you're in there." Amara pressed a rag into Lilian's hand.

Lilian raced to the study and flung the door open. She grabbed a sheet of crisp white paper from the pile on Beneh's desk and sat down.

Dear Taata.

She set her pen down, wondering what to tell her father first. That she was looking for Nakato but had failed to find her? Or that Uncle Beneh preferred the wife who bore him a child? Telling him the girls at school were mean would only upset him. She thought about introducing him to Shakespeare but then she'd have to tell him she hadn't finished *Romeo and Juliet*, and she was so far behind she might never catch up, not with all the cooking and cleaning she had to do. *I made a new friend today*, she wrote instead. *Her name is Kamali. You would like her.*

Lilian wrote about the school canteen and the library, the grassy oval and her teacher, who hadn't laughed when she got an answer wrong, but said even wise men didn't know everything. *Take your time*, Madam Kyobiggya had said. *He who goes slowly goes far.*

Lilian filled three pages writing herself back together, back to the person she'd meant to become, a girl like Kamali, humming with energy. *How's Maama*? She wrote. *Has she planted more cassava?* She signed the letter *From your Tiny Mosquito* and picked up the dusting rag, her guilt about leaving her mother alone in the garden waning as she read the titles of the books displayed on the shelves. She stopped at a hardback volume with green lettering on the spine. *Agricultural Innovation and Transformation.*

Lilian didn't know what *innovation* meant but if she could find the reason the cassava was dying from a *book* – not a witchdoctor or a neighbour – maybe her mother would encourage her to stay at school. She tipped the book from the shelf and flicked through its pages until she found a table of contents and, running her finger down the list, stopped at chapter twenty-two, "Principles of Plant Disease".

There was a knock at the front door. Lilian heard her aunt's clattering heels, crammed her father's letter into her pocket and slid the book back onto the shelf.

"You're still in here?" Amara poked her head into the study. She looked panicked. "Take this." She hauled the apron from her neck and hurled it at Lilian. "And get the meat out of the oven." She ran her fingers through her hair and swung the door open.

"Beneh!" She fussed about her husband, taking his umbrella and his hat. "Come in, you must be exhausted. Would you like a drink before dinner?"

"A scotch would be good," Beneh said. "I'm not eating."

Amara's smile dissolved. "But you said–"

"I said I'd come over." He smiled as though he'd bestowed a gift. "And here I am. As promised."

Amara's lip quivered.

"What?" Lilian's uncle stopped in the hall and Lilian flew past him on her way to the kitchen.

"You going to make a scene again? No tears. I've had a shitty day and I don't come here–"

"No, Beneh, please. I'm not upset," Lilian heard her aunt say. She balled her hands into fists, imagining her aunt hanging off Beneh as she begged him to stay.

Beneh stalked to the kitchen, his face crowded with contempt.

"See?" Amara said, flashing her teeth at him. "I'm happy. Sit down. I'm sorry."

Beneh picked up a fork and prodded the meat. "Smells good," he said. "Cover it with foil and I'll take it home."

Home. Amara reeled as though she'd been slapped. Beneh plucked a cigarette from a thin silver case and Amara snatched a lighter from the coffee table and tilted it towards him.

"I can't stay long," he said, sliding a hand under her shirt.

Lilian woke for the toilet in the middle of the night. Beneh had left an envelope of money on the side table in the corridor and she'd picked it up, just to feel its weight, but in the morning it was gone. She made herself breakfast and ate in Beneh's study, her uncle's book open on the desk. She read five pages on the principles of plant disease but found nothing about cassava.

She walked to school alone and hid in the library at lunchtime, reading *Romeo and Juliet* and thinking of Amal.

"Hey." Kamali stopped at her desk. "You coming to class?"

Lilian grabbed her bag. "What are you reading?" She pointed to the worn paperback tucked under Kamali's arm.

"Dr Nambooze's biography. Madam Cherop, recommended it."

Lilian stared at her blankly.

"Madam Cherop runs Empowerment Club."

"And Dr Nambooze. Who's he?"

"*She* ..." Kamali corrected her, "was the first female doctor in Uganda. Studied right here in Kampala."

Lilian had read about Marie Curie who had won Nobel Prizes in Physics and Chemistry. She'd learned about Cleopatra in history class and Joan of Arc who'd burned at the stake: women who'd defied history, but here was a woman with brown skin like Lilian's, a doctor who'd walked the same red dirt paths and slept under the same yellow moon.

The girls walked to class together and met again at the gate at the end of the day.

"Why so quiet?" Kamali asked when they neared Lilian's home.

"I'm looking for my sister. She left home when I was young." Lilian's shoulders sagged.

"What happened?"

"She disappeared before my sister – her twin – got married. They were close; they did everything together. They were going to marry cousins and live in the same village."

Kamali was quiet. She didn't fill the silence with a story of her own, like Amal, or pull a face to make her laugh like Dimple would have. She didn't tell Lilian that Nakato was wrong to have left, like Nasreen had done or change the topic like her mother always did when Lilian spoke of her sisters.

"She didn't say goodbye, didn't even leave a note," Lilian continued. "I think she's in Kampala."

"Here?" Kamali frowned. "In the suburbs?

Lilian was confused.

"Well, if *I* was a runaway, I'd be looking for a cheap place to stay."

Kamali nudged Lilian in the opposite direction. They turned a corner and walked past elegant houses, until the trees grew scrappier and the streets more pocked. The houses slouched and the streets smelled of exhaustion.

"Nakato won't be here. Not in a slum." Lilian tried to keep the panic out of her voice. She'd been through these sad streets before. Beneh had driven through the neighbourhood on the way to his house.

Surely, her sister wouldn't have left Walumira to live in streets strewn with broken glass, in a house made of rotting wood and rusted metal. The shops were little more than blankets on the dirt and the smell ... Lilian pinched her nose and sidestepped a pile of discarded fish heads, almost trampling a small child who sat on the roadside begging for change. He was thin with hunger, his empty grey eyes sticky and crawling with flies. Three old men dressed in rags stood around a burning metal bin warming their dinner. Lilian's stomach heaved and she felt like she might be sick. "She's not here," she said again, pulling free of Kamali.

Lilian ran all the way home, but returned the next day and the one after that. On her seventh visit to the slums Lilian found her sister. Nakato stood leaning against the wall of a small tin shack, a cigarette dangling from her fingers, her lips full and red, her nails painted to match. She wore a short black skirt, like the models in the fashion magazines and had grown out her hair. Her heels were high, her legs bare. She looked out of place in these streets of barefoot children and ragged men. She sparkled. Lilian swelled with pride. Her sister didn't live in the best suburb but Nakato had done this all on her own: found a house and a job, made a life in the city. Lilian stood across the road from the house and beamed.

Nakato smiled too, but it wasn't at Lilian. A man in a blue suit had stopped to talk to her. He took the cigarette from her lips and let it fall to the ground, then he leaned in to kiss her. Nakato turned her face so that his stubbled lips grazed her cheek, but she was smiling. She threaded her fingers through his, and slowly, hips swaying, pulled him through the door.

Lilian stood under the white sky, wondering why Nakato hadn't brought her husband home to meet them. Her husband. Nakato had chosen her own husband! The thought warmed her. Her sister had a job and a house *and* a husband. Maybe it didn't have to be a choice – a career or a man. Maybe Lilian could have both: a job *and* Amal.

The sky darkened with rain clouds and when the first fat

drops fell, Lillian took shelter under a stubby tree to wait, like Afia had taught her. *Cover your ears when the moaning begins and keep your hands from the curtain*, Afia had warned after Lilian had barged into her parents' room to discover her father lying on top of her mother.

The rain spattered Lilian's clothes but she didn't move, not until the door swung open and the man slunk out, stopping at the door to zip up his fly. Nakato stood in the doorway in an unbuttoned shirt waiting as he pulled out his wallet. Lilian turned up her collar and stepped onto the road an icy chill travelling through her.

A long black car stopped and the window rolled down. A small, beakish man poked his head through the window. His eyes travelled over Lilian's wet dress. "The room's booked for the day," he said, tilting his head towards Nakato's door. "This is *my* street, *my* girls. You want to wait for customers here, you work for me."

Nakato sold her body to strangers.

   She was a prostitute.

Lilian felt like she'd been kicked in the stomach. The tight skirt and high heels were for the men who paid to climb into her bed. A wave of nausea ripped through her and Lilian closed her eyes and tried to catch her breath. When she opened them again, she saw a dark shape follow her sister through the door to an unmade bed. A pair of worn knickers lay splayed on the floor, surrounded by empty bottles and discarded cigarettes.

Lilian steadied herself against the tree and fought the urge to be sick. Awful tears rolled down her face. Nakato had had so many dreams, dreams Lilian had weaved into stories to allow her to forgive her sister for not saying goodbye. *She had to go*, Lilian told herself whenever the anger pricked. *She had to forge her own path*. Nakato had left in the dead of night, deserting her twin, wounding Lilian and embittering their mother. "And for what?" Lilian blinked back her tears. "This?"

Chapter 20

"You haven't been crying, have you?" Amara pounced on Lilian as soon as she entered the kitchen. "No crying, not tonight." She frantically reached for the tissue box. "I'm expecting Beneh and he can't stand–"

"I saw Nakato today." Lilian waved away the tissue box. "It was from across the street. She didn't see me, we didn't talk, but I saw the men. I know what she does." Lilian blinked back her tears. "Nakato came to you. You told me she asked for help and you sent her away," Lilian gulped. "You told her to stand on her own two feet and now she's flat on her–"

"I didn't know what she was doing, not then," Amara said.

"And when you did know, you still did nothing. Why didn't you help her, Aunty? Why didn't you let her stay?"

"He wouldn't allow it."

"Wouldn't allow it?" Fury rose at the back of Lilian's throat.

Amara had two spare rooms, one for a maid and one for a baby she'd probably never have. "Why not?"

"His reputation. He has a hundred employees. He owns half the street. He can't have people talking behind his back." She pressed a tissue into Lilian's hand. "Beneh told Nakato to clean up her mess and leave us out of it." Her eyes flickered towards the door. "Please. He'll be here soon." She pressed her palms together as if in prayer.

"You have money. He gives you money every week." Lilian remembered the blue wallet swollen with cash and the sharp point of her anger found its target. "You could have given her some."

Amara's eyes darted to her bedroom. "Have you been in my room?"

Lilian shook her head and Amara breathed out. "It's complicated," she said. "I tried to help. I went to see your mother." Amara eyed the front door.

"I told her I saw Nakato. She said she didn't have a daughter in Kampala. She said she only had three daughters and knew where all of them were: Sunrise was dead, Goodness was married and you were in school."

So her mother knew? Lilian fell onto a chair and buried her face in her hands. Her mother knew where Nakato was and had done nothing to save her.

The next day, Madam Kyobiggya asked Lilian to stay back after class. "You were quiet today, Lilian. Is everything all right? I know you have a lot of catching up to do–"

"I've finished *Romeo and Juliet*," Lilian rushed to reassure her. "It's not that."

"Then what is it?"

"I don't know, Madam." Lilian hesitated. "It's just ..." She looked around the room, at the bookshelves crammed with books and the posters on the wall. "I'm not sure I can do this."

"Do what?"

"Pretend that I'm going to finish school." Lilian picked at her hem. "Pretend that my life is going to work out." She lifted her shoulders and let them fall. Maybe Mr Lwere had been right; maybe she did belong at home in the garden. Dreaming about university only made things more difficult. "Sometimes, I wish I wanted less. It'd be so much easier."

"What does less mean?" Madam Kyobiggya asked.

"A life like my mother's. A husband, a garden."

Madam Kyobiggya squeezed into the seat beside her. "When I was younger than you, and living in Wantete, I told my father I wanted to be a teacher. He laughed at me. So did my brothers." She flinched at the memory. "But my maama, she gave me a scrap of paper, a pen and a tin. She told me to write down my dreams and bury them."

"Bury them?" Lilian's mouth fell open.

"She passed me a shovel and watched me dig. And when I was done burying the tin, she told me that if I really believed in my dreams, if I watered and fed them, they would grow."

"What were they?" Lilian asked, her mouth growing dry.

"I had four," Madam Kyobiggya said, holding up four fingers. "The first was to get my A levels." She lowered a finger. "When I did that I dug up the tin, pulled out the scrap of paper and drew a line through *Finish School*."

"And the second?" Lilian held her breath.

"My second dream was to finish university."

"Did you dig up the tin?"

"Absolutely." Her eyes crinkled. "My third dream was to get a job in the city, which I did."

"And your fourth?" Lilian whispered.

"I'm still working on it, but when it's done, I'll dig up the tin and add another one." She looked Lilian in the eye. "Don't ever stop dreaming."

Lilian spent lunchtime in the library. The librarian, a woman with wiry hair pulled into a bun, sat her in front of a computer and showed her how to search for information. Lilian typed the words *Cassava Disease* and when she pressed the arrow button, pages of information pulsed onto the screen. Her heart lifted. If she found out why the cassava was dying, her mother would change her mind. She wouldn't marry her off for a goat or a cow; she'd want her at school. And with the money the new cassava crop brought, they'd have enough to pay the fees at Walumira Secondary. Lilian stared at her reflection in the silver-blue glass of the computer screen and wondered if Amal would find her changed. Would he look into her eyes and see the barefoot girl he helped with maths, or the woman she hoped to become?

She skimmed the page then scrolled through another and stopped. Their garden wasn't cursed. She scanned the bright paragraphs. The cassava had been struck by a virus! Lilian grabbed a pen and wrote it all down in words her father could read and her mother might understand.

It is called Cassava Brown Streak disease, she wrote, underlining the impressive name. *Maama must have planted cuttings from a diseased plant.* Lilian copied a diagram of an infected plant, pointing out the mottled yellow leaves, rotting roots and streaked stems, which mirrored her mother's crop. *You will have to destroy any plants showing signs of the disease and replace them with cuttings from a healthy plant. And tell Mamma to sterilise her knife in the fire.*

Lilian reread her notes, feeling full of power. She'd send the letter to her father and they'd be burning off the cassava in a week. In a month they'd replant and in six months they'd have a line of customers at their fence and Lilian would go home.

"I should have guessed you'd be in the library." Kamali pressed a flyer into Lilian's hand. "Can you stay back after school for Empowerment Club?"

"Sorry." Lilian stood to leave. "I promised my aunt I'd come straight home." She hated lying to Kamali but she wasn't ready to tell her about Nakato.

She glanced down at the crumpled brochure Kamali had given

her: *The Dangers of Wonsetibik*. Lilian knew about circumcision. She knew that her father had been cut when he was seventeen. Her father had told Lilian and Wekesa about his initiation and shown them the bamboo strips his uncle had given him as a mark of his strength. *I was painted from head to foot in* malwa, *decorated with skins and given two black-and-white monkey tails to wave in the air. We danced for three days*, Lilian's father had told them. *Every village we visited welcomed us with gifts. I came home with enough money for your mother's bride price.*

Will I be cut? Wekesa had asked, hopeful.

Becoming a man is your choice. Lilian's father had rested a heavy hand on Wekesa's shoulder. *Your great-grandfather, your grandfather and I, and all the great men in our family, chose to be initiated. If you want to inherit your grandfather's spear and his hut, you will too.*

If he gets the hut, what do I get? Lilian had asked and her father had laughed. *You get to dance with your brother and help brew the beer.*

Lilian didn't know any girls who had been circumcised. She had heard that some of the clans up north cut their girls but things like that didn't happen in Walumira. The Baganda taught their daughters to stretch their *enfuli*. Lilian thanked the spirits she wasn't raised on Mount Elgon and aimed the pamphlet at the bin.

The children in the slums stared at her – a girl in a uniform, wearing shoes. Their eyes were too large for their faces, their legs too thin. Lilian had grown up hungry, but slum poor was different to village poor. Slum poor held out plastic cups and waited for change by the side of the road. Slum poor had bellies rounded by hunger and girls who took strangers into their beds. Lilian's thoughts travelled back to Walumira's wide brown land and the trees shedding fruit and the bush where she played hide-and-seek with Nakato.

Now she stood across the road from her sister, separated by a rusted tin door and a string of men. Lilian pictured Nakato hired by the hour and the men who crept into her bed: drunk men with sour-smelling breath and pimply boys damp with sweat.

They came to the small room at the edge of the slums, one after the other, she scribbled as she waited. *Princes and Kings and clan chiefs from far-flung tribes. They had heard of the girl's magic and arrived carrying sacks of gold thread and bolts of silver cloth and animal skins and buttons made of bone. They laid their offerings at her feet and waited while she worked, stitching wisdom into their cloaks and lining their boots with courage. She buttoned patience onto shirts and stitched wealth into collars. Every piece held her initials and a little stroke of luck.*

Lilian glanced up from her story at the sound of a fist pounding on tin. A woman was rapping on Nakato's door. On her back, asleep in a sling, was a small boy of two or three. Nakato opened the door and pressed a fold of bills into the woman's hand. A truck rattled past and when the dust settled Lilian saw her sister had taken the child and settled him on her hip. The little boy stirred and Nakato's mouth lifted into a smile, a blur of red lipstick. She pulled a blanket over the child's head and disappeared into the room.

Lilian crossed the road, stood at the door, took a deep breath and knocked.

"Who's there?" Nakato peered through a crack in the open door. Her eyes were narrowed, her voice hard.

"Nakato." Lilian's voice was hoarse. "Nakato, it's me, Lala."

Nakato's eyes grew round and her mouth fell open. She shoved the door open and, grabbing a fistful of Lilian's shirt, yanked her inside. The room smelled of ashtrays and sweat.

"*Okolakiwaano?*" Nakato poked her head out the door, searching the street. "How did you know I was here? Is Maama with you?"

"No," Lilian shook her head.

"Are you okay?"

"I'm fine."

Nakato reached out and, with trembling hands, touched her fingers to Lilian's face. "You've grown," she whispered, her eyes drifting to Lilian's uniform. "You're in school!" She flung her arms around Lilian and pulled her close. Her breath smelled of cigarettes. "You're in school," she said again, her body shuddering. "I thought Maama might have–" She stared into Lilian's black eyes. "Come." She sat on the edge of the bed and patted the empty space next to her. "Tell me everything. How did you get here?" She swatted away her tears and Lilian saw under her make-up a bruise flowering under her eye.

"You didn't say goodbye." Lilian jerked her hand from Nakato's. She wanted to cry. But she was angry too. Angry Nakato had left her.

"You just left. I was ten. Ten," she repeated, "and when I asked Maama where you were …" Lilian felt the rip of her sister leaving. "We weren't allowed to use your name. Wekesa searched for days. If you'd just said something, we would have known you were okay."

"I *am* okay." Nakato reached for Lilian's hand.

"Are you?" Lilian shrunk from her sister's touch. "How can you be … doing this?"

The child cried out and the two of them turned to the cardboard box in the corner of the room where the little boy lay on a mess of blankets.

Nakato sprang from the bed to rest a hand on his chest. Soothed by her touch and her warm breath on his skin, the boy quieted.

"This is Joseph," Nakato whispered, "your nephew." She bent over the box and planted a kiss on his cheek and Lilian's anger bled away. What was it Kamali had said? *They want to put us into boxes; you're either a good girl or you're spoiled.* Lilian kneeled beside Nakato and peered into the box.

After Sunrise had died and their mother stopped smiling at them, stopped bathing them and kissing them goodnight, Nakato had taken over. It was Nakato who sheared off Lilian's knots with a razor blade when her hair grew too long, Nakato who pulled the jiggers from her feet and scratched the mosquito bites in hard to reach places, Nakato who lay with her when the hyenas howled.

"He looks just like Taata." Lilian reached into the box to touch the soft skin of Joseph's cheek.

"He looks like his father." Nakato's mouth sloped downwards.

"Who is he?"

"It is a long story." Nakato scooped a pair of knickers from the floor and shoved them under the bed. "You go first."

"There's not much to tell. I'm living with Uncle Beneh and Aunt Amara. Beneh pays for school and I help them around the house. What happened, Nakato?" She couldn't rein the questions in any longer. "Why did you leave? It couldn't be for *this*?" She stared at the bed. Nakato pulled on a pair of dirty white sneakers and a faded jumper. She lifted her sleeping son from the box and settled him on her hip. "Walk with me?"

They stepped into the violet light of dusk, Nakato stripped of her make-up, her hair mussed from the bed. Her earrings, which had looked expensive from across the street, were cut glass, her pantyhose torn. She was thinner than Lilian remembered. Quieter too. It took her a long time to talk.

"I couldn't do it," Nakato whispered, once her son was asleep. "I couldn't marry a man I didn't know, sink things into the ground and pull them up again. I didn't want that life." She looked up at the clouds and lifted the blanket over her son's head. A light rain descended and her hair, which had been ironed straight, began to frizz. "I would have had to give up everything I'd worked for, all my dreams." Nakato shivered though the night was warm. "The Sabiny way is the only way Maama knows." She turned to Lilian. "But if you're in Kampala, studying, maybe my leaving made Maama think."

They walked under the fading sky in silence.

"What about Goodness? Why didn't *she* leave?"

"Goodness was ... good." Nakato shrugged. "She always did

what Maama told her to. I couldn't, so I ran."

Lilian thought of Thomas and his slippery hands. He was tall and well made, but if her mother had told her to marry him, she would've run away too.

"I didn't plan on working the street." They walked past men selling second-hand mobile phones and shacks selling spices, past dull-eyed fish in baskets and discarded car parts.

"What happened?" Lilian worked up the courage to ask. Nakato nodded as if she'd been waiting for the question.

"I got a sewing job. The woman I worked for let me stay in a room behind her house. She had a son." Nakato stared into the distance. "He was tall as a spear, always dressed smart. We were going to open a shop together." She lifted the corner of her son's blanket to wipe her eyes. "He said he loved me. We talked about marriage." Blood drummed in her face. "And then I got pregnant."

"You didn't use a ... condom?" Lilian blushed.

"He didn't want to. *You can't eat sweets with the wrapper on.*" She looked down at her sleeping son. "He wanted me to get rid of him. When I refused, he told his mother I was pregnant." Nakato slumped to the gutter and Lilian sunk down beside her, suddenly bone-tired. "She threw me out."

"But it was her grandchild, her *muzzukulu wange.*"

"He told her it wasn't his." Nakato touched Lilian's arm. "I'm fine, Lala, really. I have a room. It's not much but it's big enough for both of us and I make enough money so we don't go hungry."

I'd rather be hungry, Lilian thought.

"There must be other jobs? Safer jobs?"

"You think I didn't try?" Nakato's anger flared. "No one

wants a girl with a reputation or a baby. They're scared I'll snatch their husbands."

"So you went to see Uncle Beneh to ask for money but he wouldn't give you any ..." Lilian tried to make the story more palatable.

"He took one look at my stomach ..."

"And sent you away. Why didn't you come home, Nakato? It would have been better ... better for Joseph."

"I wanted to." Nakato lowered her head and Lilian could feel the shame coming off her. "I wanted Joseph's backyard to be a banana garden. I wanted him to hear Taata's stories and climb trees with his cousins, but Maama wouldn't have me back."

"You came back to ask?"

"Not me. Aunt Amara. She told Maama I wanted to come home, that I had a boy who needed family. Maama told her we weren't family." A bright hurt spread through her cheeks. "She said the day I left Walumira was the day I stopped being her daughter."

"Aunt Amara has money," Lilian said, her voice hardening. "I know. I've seen it."

"Aunt Amara has been good to me. She does what she can." Nakato stood up. "When Beneh is away on business she watches Joseph so I don't need a sitter."

"Amara knows what you do," Lilian said. "Does Maama?"

"She knows she has a grandson." Nakato wrapped the blanket tight around her son. "She doesn't know what I do to pay the bills."

Chapter 21

You have to go, Nakato had whispered as the two of them stood, collapsed into each other. Lilian had refused. She'd just found her sister and wasn't ready to let her go, but Nakato wouldn't listen. She'd dragged her arms from Lilian's waist, her face full of despair, and begged her not to come back or tell Beneh they had met. *Don't insult the alligator until you've made it across the river. Do everything Beneh says until you finish school*, she'd whispered. *I'd never forgive myself if he threw you out because of me. You'll see us again*, Nakato had said. *I promise.*

Lilian replayed the conversation in her head. It had been twenty-two days since she'd seen Nakato; twenty-two nights she'd lain in bed imagining her sister sprawled on a damp sheet, the men who visited her slippery with sweat. June had chased away the month of May. The wet season was over and the puddles had dried up, turning the damp ground to dust, but Nakato was still for sale and Lilian had done nothing to help her.

Your sister doesn't need your pity, Kamali had said after Lilian told her about Nakato. *She needs your help.*

Don't you think I'd help if I could? I don't have anything to give. Lilian had thrown up her hands. *You wouldn't understand. Your family has money.*

But Kamali *did* understand and her family weren't rich, they were as poor as Lilian's. Lilian had sat under the dim shade of a mango tree and listened to Kamali talk of her twelve siblings and their house on the hill and their mother whose legs had stopped working so she couldn't walk or work or feed her children. Kamali was only at *Namugongo Secondary* because when she was eleven, a priest had climbed the hill and offered to put her through school.

Do something, the voice in Lilian's head needled, *Nakato needs you.* She pushed the front door open, tangled in shame. She was no better than Amara and Beneh. She knew how her sister made a living and she'd done nothing, said nothing because if she demanded that her aunt and uncle do something to help Nakato – if she made things difficult for them – they might send her home.

Lilian dumped her schoolbag in her bedroom and kicked off her shoes. She was living in a house with running water and a toilet. She slept on a soft mattress under a roof that didn't leak while Nakato slept on the floor of a shack. If Nakato had money, she wouldn't need to work. Amara had money – a big stack of it. Lilian's hands formed fists, her fury driving her down the corridor to Amara's lonely room. The envelopes of money Beneh left weren't Amara's to keep. The money was for both of them.

I'm just taking my share, Lilian convinced herself, as she let herself into her aunt's room. She worked quickly, listening for the front door, rummaging through drawers and tipping shoes upside down. In the small table by Amara's bed, Lilian found a worn plastic bag and inside it, folded in two and bundled with string, the stories she had written for her father.

She batted away the plastic and riffled through the pages she'd suspected her mother of burning. How had they found their way into Amara's home? She clutched the pages to her chest and closed her eyes. Images of Walumira skittered across her lids: her father at the fire spinning stories, the rock she used as a desk.

Lilian's breathing slowed. Her mother hadn't destroyed her stories. She had saved them. Maybe she'd been proud. Why else give them to Aunt Amara? Lilian's grip on the papers tightened. *Don't be stupid*, she told herself. *Maama can't read.* She looked down at the stolen pages. *The Land of Forgotten Girls, The Golden Orb, The Snake Charmer*, they were *her* stories, her way of making sense of the world and finding her place in it. Her mother had no right to give them away and Amara was wrong to keep them. Lilian smudged a tear from the corner of her eye and scanned the room, searching for something she could snatch, something to even the score.

Her eyes slid over the side table, the chair, the perfectly made bed. There was nothing of Amara's in the room, nothing to hint at her childhood or her Sabiny ancestors, no framed photos of family, no paintings on the walls, nothing to indicate that a person lived here. It's all *his*, Lilian realised, all these things are for Beneh. There was the bed he visited when he was in the mood, a chair he could throw his pants on when he undressed, and everything else – the side table heaped with combs and curlers, the rainbow of lipsticks and cupboard full of clothes – they were no more than stage make-up and costumes, bought so Amara could play the part of a pretty wife.

Lilian steadied herself against the wall. She and her aunt were both in Kampala to fulfil a role. Amara played the glamorous wife and Lilian – she searched for the right words – Lilian was the charity case, the poor relative from the bush, brought to the city to be schooled. When Madam Kyobiggya gave Lilian a book of poetry to take home, a book with impossibly long words, she'd told Lilian to try to read it. She'd said *just try, trying is enough* – but it wasn't. Trying wasn't enough. Passing wasn't enough. Lilian had to get Division 1s, had to give Beneh something he could take credit for, something he could boast about. Lilian had to make it easy for him to reach for his wallet and pay for her school fees.

Lilian slipped the stories into the plastic bag and returned them to the bedside table before hurrying to the kitchen to start on dinner. Amal would hate this silent house, Lilian thought as she emptied the fridge, letting her thoughts return to the boy she'd grown up with, a boy who enjoyed being questioned. He wouldn't want a partner who was a pretty show thing. He'd want a wife who challenged him and made him think, who demanded he try harder, as he'd demand of her. Amal wouldn't try to muzzle her.

Lilian's anger uncoiled. Amara hadn't stolen the stories – she'd been given them and she wasn't to blame for Nakato's life. She had tried to talk to Maama. Lilian's thumping heart slowed. Amara could keep her stories. Lilian had written dozens of new ones since coming to Kampala, most of them about Amal. In her favourite, he was a doctor and she was the principal of a school where students who wore shoes had to leave them outside. Amal had helped paint the sign strung over the front gate *The Barefoot School – No shoes. No fees.*

Lilian often reread those stories, especially the ones describing the long evenings Lilian and Amal shared. Amal would wait for her outside the Barefoot School and they'd walk home together holding hands. He'd tell her about his patients and the complicated surgeries he performed. She'd tell him about her students and they'd kiss in the dark, laughing as they pulled their front door open. In Lilian's stories, they owned a big brick home, with light bulbs bright as the sun. Nakato lived a few streets away, above her dress shop and Wekesa, Goodness, Afia and all the cousins would gather around the fire pit in their big backyard and dance to the drums under the smiling moon until, one by one, their eyes would droop and Amal would lead them to one of the spare bedrooms and insist they stay. And then it was just Amal and Lilian, their bodies pressed together, his breath on her lips. *I don't want anyone else, I never will*, he'd whisper.

Lilian had written Amal and he was nothing like Beneh.

Lilian left the dirty breakfast dishes on the kitchen bench and rushed outside. If she hurried, she'd make it to the slums before school, and if she ran straight home after the final bell she would have time to wash the dishes before dinner. She clutched the bag she'd filled for Nakato and turned down the crooked street that would take her to the slum. She'd promised her sister she wouldn't return but leaving a gift at Nakato's door wasn't the same as visiting. A month had passed and Lilian's guilt sat heavy as a stone inside her. She had done nothing to help her sister escape the line of men who waited at her door and the days had grown muggy and the insects loud. Nakato would be sweltering inside the tin shed.

Lilian knew the present wasn't enough, but it was a start. Nakato could take the scissors, needle and thread Lilian had stolen from Amara in exchange for her stories, and offer to repair clothes for her neighbours. She could take the scraps of cloth and torn shirts Lilian had found at the rubbish dump, and sew them into stylish designs she could sell on the street.

It had been Kamali's idea to scour the rubbish dump. *If you make some money, you can buy things for Nakato*, Kamali had suggested, rummaging in her schoolbag for a toy car she'd made out of a soft drink can and icy pole sticks. *Tourists love this stuff.*

She'd dragged Lilian to the dump on the edge of town to wade through festering garbage. Lilian decided on dolls. She'd make dolls out of plastic water bottles and sell them on the street. *This place is a gold mine*, Kamali had laughed, climbing a hill of bulging rubbish bags and greasy lunch wrappers. *Last week I found a pair of Converse.*

Lilian held her nose and pulled a plastic water bottle from the mountain of waste. She would need buttons for the eyes, some yarn for the hair. She tried to calculate how many dolls she'd have to sell to pay Nakato's rent.

Kamali kicked aside a broken jerry can and hoisted a grubby T-shirt from the mountain of waste. *Here*, she said, grinning, *you can dress the dolls.*

Fabric. Lilian chewed on her lip, her eyes narrowed. *What did Madam Cherop say? You can give people money or empower them to make their own.* The senior teachers were always saying things like that. Astounding things that no one, not even Afia, had thought to teach Lilian. She'd started bringing a notebook to Empowerment Club so she could get it all down.

Your body is yours. You can always say no.

Education is your ladder out of poverty.

Don't rely on a man to give you money.

Kamali had dragged Lilian to her first lunchtime session, but she'd gone willingly, hungrily, after that, listening with rapt attention to the teachers who talked about child labour laws and children's rights. There were laws against female genital cutting and domestic violence, Lilian learned, and shelters where battered women could hide from angry husbands. *If you have your own money, you'll never be at the mercy of a man*, Madam Cherop had told them. *You can make your own decisions.* Lilian hung off her every word. Madam Cherop's sentences were like thunder rattling through her, like bolts of lightning. She felt as if she'd slumbered through her first fourteen years and had only now been shaken awake.

It had been two weeks since Lilian had taken the grubby T-shirt from Kamali and unearthed a wardrobe of stained clothing in the piled-up junk. She had emptied her bag of bottles and filled it with fabric. Nakato had wanted to start a business. She didn't need money. She needed material and Lilian could tell her where to find it. *I'm not going to give Nakato money*, she'd yelled to Kamali across the wasteland of garbage. *I'm going to help her make her own!*

When she reached Nakato's shack, Lilian lowered the bag onto the footpath. She yawned. It was hard to wake early after so little sleep and so much studying, but the thought of Nakato's face when she opened the bag made it worthwhile.

"*Yingila*," a voice purred from inside. "Come in. Don't be shy." The door creaked open. A girl wearing a black bra and purple shorts stood in the doorway.

"Who are you?" She lifted a cigarette to her lips, and then, seeing the bag, reached down to grab it.

"That's for my sister." Lilian snatched the bag from the path, panic creeping in. She stepped around the girl and peered into the dark space. "Where is she? Where's Nakato?"

The girl dragged on her cigarette. "I don't know any Nakato," she said, eyeing a man in the street.

A reedy man stopped at the door, his eyes travelling from Lilian's legs to the girl's black bra. "How much for both of you?" He reached for his zipper.

Lilian ran, past men sucking the last drops from their *Waraji* bottles and boys playing cards, past a blind beggar and a young boy playing the drums. Past a woman hanging her husband's wet underwear on a line and two barefoot girls braiding each other's hair. Nakato could be anywhere – a different part of the slum, a different city.

Lilian slowed to a walk, still clutching the bag. Maybe Nakato had left the slum for a fresh start. Lilian weaved the idea into a story. By the time she had Nakato seated at a sewing machine, Lilian was on the main road where the houses were bigger and people wore shoes. This was the Kampala she had dreamed of, the Kampala she'd hoped Nakato was a part of, a city of women in colourful wrappers and restaurants with tables spilling onto the road. A city with a thousand burning lights and a university and a cinema. A place where girls had jobs and chose their husbands. And people brought their biggest dreams.

"I'm sorry. I was going to wash the dishes as soon as I got home. I shouldn't have left them piled by the sink." Lilian dropped to her knees to pluck the shattered china from the kitchen floor. Amara stood over the mess of broken breakfast dishes.

"*Sorry* is no good to me," she said, looking from the jumble of broken plates to the clock on the wall. "Beneh is coming so I tried to hide them and …" She grabbed a dustpan and dropped to her knees. "We need to clean this mess." She was shaking like a hen after a rooster's visit and Lilian saw, in her clenched jaw and the hard line of her lips, not anger, but fear.

"He might not come," Lilian said to calm her, but Amara

wasn't listening. She dragged a clump of Posho from her hair and a limp bean from her sleeve. "I have to get changed." She reached for a mop and passed it to Lilian. "I don't want to see any sauce on the floor and not a sliver of glass." A light sheen of perspiration beaded her lip. "Run your hands along the floor, just to be sure. I'll leave the bin out for you. Knot the bag twice." She stared down at her spattered skirt.

"He might not come," Lilian said again. "It's been weeks since we've seen him."

"He might," Amara said, her face bright with hurt. She peeled off her shirt and stood in the kitchen in her skirt and bra, her loneliness terrible, and Lilian saw at her neck, not her usual thin gold chain but a small glass vial hanging from a leather cord. A charm to plant a baby inside her, Lilian guessed, staring at the cloudy green liquid.

She wanted to tell Amara that she was wasting her money. The broken pot by the door hadn't chased away the spirits who had made Amara barren and the frayed banana leaves she wore belted at her waist hadn't made her belly swell.

You're lucky you haven't given him a child, Lilian wanted to say. *You can leave*.

Amara wiped the sweat from her face with the back of her hand leaving a smudge of sauce across her cheek. Lilian lifted her hand to point to the muddy smear when a memory bubbled up: Amara in a flaming red dress at their fence and Nakato in the doorway bent over an exercise book, trying to capture the sheen of the silk with a stubby black pencil. Lilian remembered both of them lifting their heads from the page at the same time and gasping as the stranger pulled off her dark glasses to reveal a bloated left eye, purple as a plum.

Mwattu, Please, Nnyamba, Help me, they'd heard the woman whisper, but Lilian's mother hadn't picked up her suitcase or invited her in. She'd folded her arms across her chest. *Your husband will be expecting his dinner*, she'd said. *Go home.*

Chapter 22

Mwattu, Please, Nnyamba, Help me. The words haunted Lilian. She imagined Amara's thin lips shaping the words as she stood over the kitchen sink. She pictured Nakato whispering them as she lay pinned under a man, and Sunrise calling from deep underground, the words muffled by all that red dirt. *Mwattu, Please, Nnyamba, Help me.*

Lilian didn't know how to help, so she went to church to pray for guidance. Back in Walumira, church had meant spending time with her father in the pink-walled quiet and conversations with God. Her prayers had been simple. All she'd wanted was an extra helping of Posho and a book. It hadn't crossed her mind that once she had a book she might want a desk and that once she had shoes, she'd long for socks.

Lilian asked God to give Nakato and Amara the courage to escape. She asked him to watch over Sunrise and fix her father's stooped back. She asked for a good crop of cassava and Division 1s on all her tests, but she wasn't sure God was listening. Why would he look her way when he ignored the whispered prayers of prostitutes and childless women? All God and the priests seemed to care about was sin – the sin of sex before marriage and dressing immodestly. It was like Lilian lived in two worlds: the world the senior teachers talked about at Empowerment Club where women wore business suits and took part in the world; and the caged world her mother and the priests lived in, a world you couldn't escape unless you had money or white skin.

It was hard for Lilian to see her aunt so powerless. With each passing week Beneh grew more distant. He would stay away for weeks and then, when he did come, would find fault with the food or the way she kept the house. He took his meals in front of the TV, as if she wasn't there, and then, one day in the middle of the dry season, he brought a hamper of laundry – his business shirts and a pair of grey trousers and a purple dress and silk pantyhose. Amara had lifted a small pink dress from the pile.

It's Shanitah's, Beneh had said. *Joyce is too exhausted to do the washing. She's pregnant again.*

Amara had buckled and Beneh had watched her sourly. *I came here to celebrate*, he'd said, taking a cigar from its case. Amara had let him lead her to their bed. Lilian had watched Beneh unbutton her aunt's shirt before he closed the bedroom door.

It had seemed like a punishment, his mouth at her neck, his hands on her body. A punishment for not giving him a child.

At church that week, Amara congratulated Joyce and sat beside her, her mouth bent into a smile. Joyce rested her hands on her belly, her fingers filthy with jewels, and asked Amara if she was still trying for a baby. *It must be hard*, she whispered, *seeing the disappointment on Beneh's face.* Lilian had taken Amara's hand and held it tight until she was sent outside to push Shanitah on the swing.

The sun was high, the heat suffocating as a blanket, but Lilian couldn't refuse. She wasn't the older cousin. She was *the help*, as Joyce had made clear at Shanitah's birthday party. *Shanitah doesn't need your help opening presents*, Joyce had said, pointing to the crumpled wrapping paper. *The bins are outside. When you're done tidying up, bring in the cake.* Lilian hadn't minded. She'd kept some of the wrapping paper and tasted the icing.

She hadn't expected to be called back the next afternoon. Joyce greeted her at the door wearing a red dress that hugged her hips and bottom. *Beneh eats with us every night*, Joyce trumpeted as if she'd won a prize, *and I have a baby on the way so I need your help. You'll make the beds, clean the house and help prepare dinner.*

Lilian was exhausted. She had stayed up late the night before helping Amara empty the baby's room of toys and baskets of nappies. Amara hadn't said why she wanted to collapse the cot and pack away the clothing, but Lilian guessed the teddy bears and small blankets were a daily reminder of how she'd failed Beneh. The next morning, her aunt was still asleep when Lilian sat down to breakfast, so when the doorbell rang, she ran to answer it before the buzzing woke her aunt.

It was Beneh. He wore an elegant cream suit, a newspaper tucked under one arm.

"Morning," he said, looking past Lilian for Amara. "I was around the corner, thought I'd stop in for breakfast. Where's your aunt?"

"Asleep," Lilian said, forgetting herself.

"Asleep?"

"I'm sure she'll be up soon." Lilian threw him a nervous smile.

"It is after seven." Beneh pushed past her. "I have a meeting in twenty minutes. Why is she asleep?"

Lilian's stomach shrunk fist tight. "She must have forgotten to set her alarm." She followed him down the hall, wondering if Amara's door had a lock.

"Forgot?" Beneh's voice blistered with anger. He stared at the bedroom door as if planning his next move.

"I can wake her?"

"No. Go to school."

"I can make you something? Some eggs?"

"Go to school," Beneh said, sharp as a slap. "You don't want to be punished for being late."

Lilian sat through maths, but she didn't hear a word the teacher said. She stared at the blank page in front of her, wondering how Beneh had woken Amara. She pictured him standing over her sopping body with an upturned bucket and a bloodless smile. He liked to call her a whore. The walls were thin, even in expensive houses.

"Anyone know the answer?" Madam Kyobiggya pointed to the problem on the board. "Lilian?"

"I'm sorry," Lilian said, fear churning inside her. "I don't feel so well." She rose from her seat. "Can I be excused?"

Beneh's car was gone by the time Lilian got home. She flung the gate open and ran down the path. The door was unlocked, the corridor dim.

"Aunty?" Lilian dropped her schoolbag and raced to the kitchen. It was just as she'd left it, her bowl on the bench, a dirty spoon beside it. Lilian's heart sank. "Aunt Amara!" She hurried to her aunt's room and pressed her ear to the door. The room was too quiet, the house too still. She knocked twice, then let herself in.

Amara was in bed, under a mess of blankets. It was the middle of the dry season and the middle of the day. The room was hot and smelled of sweat.

"Aunty, are you sick?" The blankets were tucked into the mattress and hoisted up under Amara's chin so that none of her, not her legs or feet or fingers, poked from under the wool. A fly crawled over her lips and Lilian shooed it away. "Do you have a fever? Are you cold?"

She kneeled beside the bed and rested the back of her hand on Amara's wet forehead.

"Maybe we should take the blankets off?" Lilian reached for the covers but Amara grabbed her hand.

"When he woke me he said if I wanted to spend the day in bed, that's what I'd do." She lifted her eyes to the door. "It is my fault. I slept in."

"What about a glass of water?"

"No!" Amara lifted her head from the pillow, her eyes wide with fear. "No water or food. He'll know."

"He's not here," Lilian said, lowering herself onto the edge of the bed. "Please, just one blanket? It's so hot."

Lilian slid her hand under the blanket and threaded her fingers through Amara's.

"I can help you dress and get you some food. We can talk while you eat."

"He'll be back." Amara glanced towards the door again. "He'll know if I moved. I haven't got up, not even to-" She closed her eyes and Lilian felt the shame coming off her. The stench that had struck Lilian when she walked into the room hadn't been sweat. It was the smell of urine.

Amara rolled over to face the wall. "He didn't say when he'd be back. You should go."

Lilian scooped two handfuls of water from the basin and splashed her face, then grabbed a towel from the wall and plunged it into the sink.

"I'm not going," she said, returning to mop Amara's face. "Not until you've taken something to drink." She passed Amara a glass of water and sank down beside her. "You have to report him to the police."

"They won't do anything. He gives the station free coffee."

"Then go to another station. I'll come with you."

"No one is going to arrest him, not once he opens his wallet. Money turns heads." Amara's voice was apologetic. "It turned mine. He told me I'd never go hungry. He promised I could finish school. When we fled Mount Elgon I was in Primary Six and—"

"Primary Six?" Lilian's brow furrowed. "But Maama can't read."

"Your mother was the oldest," Amara explained. "After our mother died, she stayed home to help raise us."

"And Maama blames you." The puzzle pieces fell into place. "That's why she sent you away, when you came home with a black eye."

"She sent me back to Beneh because that's where I belong." Amara sat up slowly. "*A wife belongs with her husband ... to her husband.* Your mother's words. *You may not love him.*" Amara affected her sister's clipped sentences. "*You may grow to hate him – but you'll do what he says because you need him.*"

"You can leave. I'll help you," Lilian begged.

"I have nowhere to go."

"You have money."

"Not enough. I didn't finish school or learn a trade. I wouldn't survive on my own." Her voice dropped to a whisper. "Don't look at me like that."

"Like what, Aunty?"

"Like you feel sorry for me." She snatched the silver frame from her bedside table and stared at her wedding photo. Beneh's meaty hand was wrapped around her waist.

"This is as good as it gets for women like us. You enter your husband's home in a wedding dress." She laid the frame facedown on the wood. "But you leave in a coffin."

Chapter 23

Lilian lifted her head from the kitchen table to read the clock. It was two am. Outside, the insects whispered and the warm wind sang, but inside the house was quiet. Beneh hadn't come back, had probably never planned on returning, knowing his threats were enough to keep his wife in bed and teach her who's boss. At Lilian's urging, Amara had finally thrown off her blankets, changed the wet sheets and swallowed some food. *I'll wake you if I hear the car*, Lilian had promised as her aunt crawled back into bed.

A hard lump formed in Lilian's throat. She'd complained to Kamali that her aunt was cold and treated her like a servant. Now she understood why. When Amara demanded Lilian scrub the bathroom tiles until her arms ached, it was fear of ending up on the street that drove her, not anger or spite. Lilian saw Amara teetering around in high heels and a cloud of perfume and judged her vain, but it was self-preservation, not vanity, which drove Amara to the hairdresser. The house was Beneh's showpiece and Amara just another pretty thing he liked to show off. Her aunt knew, Lilian realised, that if she didn't conceal the dark circles under her eyes or disguise her slack mouth under a sheen of pink lipstick Beneh would leave her. Just as he would dump her if she didn't, eventually, produce a son. She wasn't self-centred or spoiled or mean. She was a survivor.

The last vestiges of Lilian's anger towards her aunt dissipated and pity welled in its place. What would it have been like to marry a man twice your age? To speak only in the silence between his sentences? To watch him climb out of bed for another woman's body?

Lilian unfolded the letter she'd written to her father and read it a third time. She hated bothering him, but she didn't know what else to do. She loved Namugongo Primary. She loved her smart uniform and her long blue socks. She loved maths and English and dance class and sport. She spent every lunchtime with Kamali, the coolest person on earth, and once a week, in Empowerment Club, the senior teachers showed her glimpses of a world they promised was within her grasp. *I don't know what to do, Taata.* Lilian reread the first line. She wanted to go home, but she couldn't leave Amara to bear her pain alone. Lilian knew her mother wouldn't take Amara in, so there was no choice but to stay. At least when Lilian was there, Beneh checked his anger. *I know how hard it must have been to ask Uncle Beneh to pay for school*, she read on, *and I'm happy to be here. Please don't think I'm ungrateful. I just need your advice.* Lilian hadn't been able to save Sunrise or help Nakato. She'd said nothing to defend Trinah and she'd lost touch with Nasreen. She had to do something to help her aunt.

The letter revealed everything: the fat veins that stood out on Beneh's forehead when he screamed and the names he called Amara and the things he made her do. Lilian had wanted to ask her father if what Amara said was true. Was this as good as it gets for girls like them? Was marriage just cooking and cleaning, sharing your husband with a second or third wife and tending to your bruises? Was love a ridiculous dream? *Do you love Maama?* She almost wrote. *Did you ever love her?*

Beneh visited twice that month. The first time he came after midnight. Lilian heard the front door creak on its hinges and Amara's light footfall coming down the hall. *Look at you.* Lilian recognised the sound of Beneh's anger. *I don't know why I bother.* Lilian heard Amara apologise and offer to fix her hair. *I can switch off the light*, Lilian heard Beneh grunt. The second time he came, Lilian had been at Joyce's changing the bedsheets. When she returned home and headed to the kitchen, she saw them: Amara on all fours licking dust from the floor and Beneh above her, bellowing and pointing.

Something shifted in her aunt after that. When Amara closed the door behind Beneh and threw the umbrella stand across the hall, it seemed to Lilian, she'd thrown something else off too. The next day, when Lilian returned home from school, she found Amara in the kitchen, her springy hair pulled back in a black elastic.

"I'm tired of stretching it," she said when she caught Lilian staring at her badly behaved curls. "You know how many times I've burned my fingers on those hot combs?" She was also done with make-up, it seemed. Lilian stared at her aunt's naked face, saw for the first time the dark freckles on the ridge of her nose and her short brown lashes.

"Sorry about the mess." She pointed to the clothes line sagging with wet bedsheets and the dresses flung over chairs. "I'm going to be doing the neighbours' laundry. I do Beneh's so what's a few more shirts?"

Lilian helped Amara prepare Beneh's dinner but when he didn't show up, instead of wrapping it in tin foil and sliding it into the fridge, Amara poured herself a glass of red wine and pushed the plate towards Lilian. Neither of them mentioned Beneh's name. He didn't show up the next night or the one after that and the days turned into weeks, then months, in which they held their breath and willed him not to come. His absence felt like the lifting of a storm cloud and the house grew brighter and their conversations easier. One night Amara switched on the TV and they sat together in its technicolour glow. The next morning Lilian heard her aunt playing music. Not quietly in her room with the door closed, but in the kitchen, swaying to the beat.

She suggested Lilian bring her books to the kitchen at night – the table was larger and she could spread out her work. If Lilian left a story open on the bench, Amara would read it and once, when Lilian left flyers from Empowerment Club lying about, she saw Amara read those too. It was good to see her aunt's white smile. It felt good to talk out loud and tell stories again.

It happened gradually, this thawing between them, but when Lilian wrote of it in *Return of the Stork Princess* she described it like the sudden opening of a door. One day the house was silent and full of fear, and the next, they were dancing side by side, the music blaring and the two of them laughing and shaking their hips.

Their laughter made them bold, and Amara suggested Lilian invite a friend for Christmas dinner. *The one who helps run that Empowerment Club.*

Lilian invited Kamali and Amara peppered her with questions about life in the dormitory and the work she did at the women's shelter. "I felt so low when I first came to Namugongo Primary," Kamali told them. "The kids said I was dumb, because I couldn't speak English. To be real, I didn't like the language at first. The teacher would beat me for speaking Luganda, and then in Primary Three," Kamali smiled at the memory, "I wrote a perfect composition and the teacher made me stand on my desk and read it to the class. They all clapped their hands and the teacher bought me breakfast. I loved English after that. I especially love speaking it back in the village. When I speak even the men listen."

After dinner Amara turned the radio up loud and let Kamali choose a station. A woman with a honeyed voice was demanding to know who ran the world.

"Girls!" Kamali shouted, throwing a fist into the air.

"Girls," Lilian joined in the chorus. "Girls."

Kamali showed them a picture of the singer – a women called Beyoncé – in a tattered magazine. Lilian's mouth fell open. She was brown, like them. An African woman who sang about women doing whatever they wanted. Lilian stared at the singer's fierce eyes. She wanted to believe her but Lilian had grown up listening to her mother sing *Omuwala omuto, owempiisa, ya awuliriza ... A good girl always listens to her mother*. What universe did this girl with one name live in, where girls ran the world?

The next morning Lilian woke to find breakfast waiting for her. And when she opened a drawer to choose her underwear, she discovered a pink plastic packet of *Stayfree* pads, a gift of twelve small cotton cushions to soak up her blood. There were other gifts too, spread across the weeks: a bar of soap, a hair comb, three dresses left on her bed. *Beneh doesn't take me out for dinner any more so I don't need them*, Amara had said, and she hadn't looked sad.

Beneh didn't leave envelopes of money on her dressing table either, but Amara had plenty of laundry work to do, so there was always enough to eat, and on Sundays at church he would hand her a fistful of cash and wait for the priest or a neighbour to commend his generosity. Lilian didn't know what her aunt did with the money and she didn't try to find out. Her spare time was better spent searching for Nakato. Amara had promised to keep an eye out too.

"Did you ever love Beneh?" Lilian asked one night, early in the new year, as they were shelling peas.

Amara laughed a short, barking laugh. "What's love got to do with marriage?"

Lilian reddened. She supposed *Nothing* was the correct answer, the answer her mother and Goodness and Nasreen would have given. "Why did you marry him?"

"Your maama and I, we came to Kampala on our own," Amara relented. "Our taata sent us here to keep us safe after Baako was killed. Your maama married first. We had no money. She didn't love your father – she barely knew him – but he was Sabiny and had a job. He turned out to be a good man," she said, "but he didn't have enough money to support both of us, so I had to get married. I was thirteen." She rinsed the peas under cold water and set them on the stove in a pot. "The first time Beneh hit me I ran home to tell your mother. She told me it is better to cry in a Mercedes than on a bike." Amara slumped in her chair. "Maybe she is right. Why leave a dog only to fall into the arms of a wolf?"

They're not all wolves, Lilian thought. Well, maybe the man with the caterpillar eyebrows who only let Goodness come home once a year. And maybe Nasreen's husband who hadn't reached for her hand as their car sped away from her childhood home. Uncle Beneh was a wolf ...

"Why do you let him touch you?" Lilian wanted to understand.

Amara struck a match and held it over the stove. "I thought if I gave him a child ..." She lit the gas and set the pot to boil. "I thought if I was pregnant, he might be kinder. I thought if I gave him a son, he might love me and if he didn't, it wouldn't matter, because I'd have someone to love."

"The *omusawo's* herbs won't help," Lilian whispered. She had read about it. She'd searched the library computer and found dozens of entries on infertility. There were doctors who could help, tests they could do.

Amara's gaze dropped to the glass vial at her neck. "I know," she said wrapping her fingers around the small bottle. Lilian heard the snap of leather as the cord came away from her neck. "Anyway, it doesn't matter. I don't want a baby. Not anymore. Not if it's his."

Amara unfurled her fingers and the bottle slipped from her grasp, splintering on the floor into a thousand silver shards.

Chapter 24

Things were better now that Beneh rarely visited and Lilian almost wished she hadn't confided in her father. She had started Senior One at Namugongo Secondary and her studies were going well. She'd sent another letter telling him so, but hadn't received a reply. She lifted one of his letters from under her pillow, her favourite. She had read it so often she knew it by heart.

Tiny Mosquito,
Do you remember how I taught you to spell your name?
I drew L-I-L-I-A-N in the dirt and handed you the stick.
Your face lit up like a firefly. You covered the front yard
with L's, I's, A's and N's. You wouldn't go to bed. 106
Lilians. Remember? We counted.
I wonder how many words you have collected now and
how many stories you have written. I always loved reading
them. You have your grandfather's talent.

I am proud of you, Tiny Mosquito. The men here are tired of hearing me boast. The school report your aunt sent me is fixed to the wall of my room and I pass around your school photo whenever I get the chance. I think your mother might even be convinced she did the right thing in letting you go. Last week she burned off the cassava just like you told her.

Be good, Tiny Mosquito and study hard. I can't write often; the stamps cost me dinner. I don't tell you this to hurt you. I tell you only to stoke the fire that burns inside you. My dreams have been snuffed out but there's still hope for you. Study hard and build a better life for yourself.

Her father had dreamed of studying in the city long before Lilian was born and now he was living the dream through her. So she studied hard, and when she wasn't at school or folding washing for Joyce or scouring the streets for Nakato, she read. She brought home books by women and books about women, books whose heroes were girls who refused to do as they were told. Books that revealed the type of woman she could be. And as she read, her writing changed. No more stories about lonely girls locked in towers or women married to wolves masquerading as men. She wrote powerful women onto her page, women who ran their own households. Doctors and poets, engineers and inventors, both white and black.

In Lilian's stories Amara always escaped. Sometimes Lilian had her slip away in the dead of night. Sometimes she confronted Beneh, but she always left, landing up in Walumira, where a bed was made up for her, next to Nakato's. Lilian didn't accompany Amara in these stories. She was studying in the city and Amal had joined her. Not as her husband. Lilian wouldn't give that power to any man, not until she'd been to university and made her own money. He was her lover; her bright light in a black sky.

Lilian was tying her school shoes when the doorbell rang. It was seven am. Her aunt was dressed and preparing a plate of fruit in case Beneh came. It had been months since his last visit and Amara's dark eyes were ringed with blue circles from lack of sleep, but it wasn't fear that kept her awake. It was laundry. She travelled further than the houses bordering her suburb. She now walked miles every day to collect dirty washing. When Lilian asked what Beneh would do if he found out she was running a business, Amara's eyes grew steely. *He won't*, she said, anger edging out fear.

"I'll get the door," Lilian called. It wasn't Beneh. It was his driver, the man who picked up his dinner when Joyce didn't want to cook. Katonda bent his long, bony body and tipped his cap. "Would you like help with your bag, Miss?"

"My bag?" Lilian asked, curious why Beneh wanted her driven to school. She passed the old man her satchel.

"Is that all you have?" He scratched his forehead. "No clothes?"

"Clothes?" Lilian said, turning at Amara's approach

"Clothes, a suitcase ..." He tipped his cap and bid Amara good morning.

"Why would she need a suitcase?" Amara's hand flew to her mouth.

Lilian grabbed the old man's sleeve.

"Is something wrong? Has there been an accident?" She pictured her father's body being lowered into the ground and her legs buckled. "Has someone died?"

The old man reached out to steady her. "No, Miss, your family are fine. They are well."

If everyone was fine, then why was he here? Lilian searched the old man's eyes.

"The boss wants me to take you home."

"Home?" Lilian grew panicked. "To Walumira? Why?"

Katonda dragged his cap from his head. "The boss didn't tell me Miss, and I don't want to bring trouble but I did hear him talking to Madam Joyce." He lowered his voice. "He said he was finished with your family and Madam Joyce said it was about time."

"Is Uncle Beneh angry with me?" Lilian lunged at Amara. "Did I do something wrong?" She searched her aunt's face. "I'm doing well at school. I'm getting A's."

"He doesn't need a reason." Amara's voice was flat.

"So that's it?" Lilian asked, her voice hot with anger.

Amara didn't meet her gaze.

"Boss said you can keep your clothes," Katonda offered. "Except for the red dress. Shanitah wants it."

Lilian pulled her stories from the bed and shoved them into her bag. She wrote a note for Kamali and a letter to Nakato, which she left on Amara's bed with a story she'd begun the previous day. She hoped Amara would like it, would see herself in the trapped bird who flew to freedom. In the first draft, a kind servant boy snuck into his master's study to prise open the cage door and set the bird free, but in the final draft the boy had vanished and Lilian had crafted the bird a golden beak to peck the lock open.

Lilian stepped into the hall lugging a bag of clothes.

"Let me help," Katonda said, lifting the bag from her arms. Amara passed him a cardboard box crammed with books. "Beneh hasn't been in his study for months," she told Lilian. "He won't miss them." She slipped her wedding band from her finger and pressed it into Lilian's palm. "Sell it if you have to. Don't stop school."

Stop school? Lilian sucked in air. It hadn't crossed her mind.

"What if I tell Uncle I'm sorry? I'll work harder. Eat less." Her eyes widened as a thought struck her. "Maybe if we both apologise?" Lilian said, hating herself for it. "He might let me stay. We can go there now."

"It won't make any difference." Amara wrapped her arms around Lilian. "Once Beneh has made a decision, you can beg as much as you like. He won't change his mind."

Lilian lowered the car window and let the rush of air dry her tears. She sank back into the car's soft seat but took no pleasure in the electric windows or carpeted floor. The stories that had found their way into Amara's bedside table lay on the seat beside her, stupid and childish. There were no golden orbs or happily-ever-afters, no hidden cities ruled by women.

Lilian tipped the stories from their plastic bag. Her father had given them to Beneh, Lilian had discovered, and she didn't know whether she should be angry or flattered. *Your father didn't betray you*, Amara had said, handing them back to her as she packed. *He gave them to Beneh to prove you were smart. He knew Beneh wouldn't put you through school unless it reflected well on him. I found them in the bin, in his study. I should have given them back to you.*

Lilian looked up from the pages as they wound through the slum, the streets packed with beggars holding their hands out for coins and barefoot children washing windscreens. Leaving the city meant ending her search for Nakato. Now all Lilian could do was hope Amara would find her and give her Lilian's letter begging her to come home. Lilian pictured Nakato at their gate and Joseph sleeping in her arms, thick black lashes fringing his eyes and skin soft as butter. Surely Maama would take one look at him and change her mind.

Chapter 25

"So this is Walumira?" Katonda's words woke Lilian. He dragged his eyes from the dung-covered walls of the little round hut. "Welcome home."

He helped her with her things and climbed back into the car. "I have to fetch Madam Joyce from the hairdresser," he apologised through the open window. "Your parents will be home soon?" He scanned the empty yard.

"I will be fine," Lilian said, forcing a smile. She slid her bag from her shoulder and settled the box of books on the dusty ground.

Home, she thought, squinting at the splintering fence and sagging clothes line. "I'm home," she said as the car sped away and the yard grew silent. She stabbed the dying embers of the fire with a branch and inhaled the lingering smell of roasted groundnuts. If her father couldn't afford to send her to school, she'd be forced to spend her days in the garden until she got married. Lilian shuddered at the prospect.

"I'll work," Lilian said to the trees and the sky. "I'll wash clothes for our neighbours and sell cassava chips by the roadside and save for my school fees. I can catch up a term."

Cassava! Lilian dropped the stick and ran to the garden, past the jackfruit trees her grandfather had planted and the towering sugar cane, until she reached the small plot her mother had sown. Lilian stared at the green-leaved bushes pushing out of the soil. Her mother had followed her instructions – the instructions from a book – and it had worked! Lilian crouched down to touch the leaves.

She would be glad to yank the cassava from the earth now: pound it and sell it in sacks to pay for her schooling. Lilian dropped to her knees, dug a cassava from the ground and shook it of dirt. The fruit was plump with no sign of disease. Lilian's smile widened. She walked to the banana garden and tore a banana from its bunch, peeled away the skin and took a hungry bite. She had everything she needed: bananas and cassava, groundnuts and maize, a mat to sleep on and a thatched roof to keep her dry. She didn't have a desk or a lamp but she had a flat rock on which to rest her books and the moon to light her page. *We don't need Uncle Beneh's money*, she decided, *I can finish Senior One here.*

She grabbed a knife from beside the wall and cut a piece of sugar cane from its jointed stalk, sawing off the green bark to gnaw at the stick, the sun warming her face. In Kampala she hadn't allowed herself the luxury of missing home. To pine for a stick of sugar cane or a crackling fire on a cold night only made it harder to be away. She spun around and saw the blinking cows tearing the grass with their curling tongues. She saw the garden that fed her and the ring of flat stones circling the fire pit where her father, and his father before him, had talked of Mount Elgon. She was rich, she realised, crouching to sit in the shade of an acacia tree. She had to chase rats from the *toyii* before she could squat over the pit, but what good did a flushing toilet do Amara or Beneh? None of it, not the clothes or the TV or the cars seemed to make them any happier. All Lilian needed was enough money to pay for the next term of school.

"Maama?" she called, returning to the yard to check if anyone had come home. She scratched Moses under the chin and ducked her head under the hut's low door. Her parents' room was empty but her father's bag sat open on the floor. He was home! She lifted the sheet dividing the hut in two, half expecting to see Wekesa asleep on his mat but the room was deserted. The sheet Wekesa had strung up between their mats had been taken down and her brother's sleeping mat dragged into the middle of the small space. Lilian's mouth fell open at the sight of a splintering desk. Its legs were uneven and its timber gouged but it sat upright in a corner, begging for books, an old metal chair pushed up under it. Lilian swept her brother's crumpled clothes from the desk and laid out her things, books stacked in a pile, pens and paper beside them.

A gust of wind stirred the branches of the tree and a flurry of yellow flowers tumbled onto Lilian's head. She shook them from her hair, which now sprung from her head in short black coils, tucked her stories under one arm and set off to see Sunrise. The sun hung in the sky, a red ball flaming. Lilian wished Sunrise could see it. She stood over her sister's grave and mopped her face with her sleeve.

The dirt her father had shovelled onto Sunrise's coffin was littered with leaves. Her mother hadn't been to clean it. "She feels bad," Lilian explained to her sister. "That's why she doesn't come." A memory floated up from the grave: Maama's hands linked with Lilian and her sister's, the three of them dancing circles around the fire. Their mother had been a different person then. Before Sunrise died she used to laugh and sing them to sleep. An idea lit Lilian's face. *I'll go to the library.* She flicked a bug from the dirt. *I'll find a name for Sunrise's illness and prove to Maama it wasn't her fault.* Lilian smoothed the ground above her sister's small body and drew a sheet of paper from her pocket.

"I thought you might like a story," she whispered to the dirt.

"*Okomyewo?*" Lilian's mother dropped an armload of firewood, her eyes travelling from Lilian's dress to her shoes and back up her long body. "You've grown. Must be all that good food." Lilian couldn't tell whether her mother was pleased to see her, or disappointed.

"I'm sorry, Maama." Lilian rushed towards her. "I don't know what I did to make Uncle Beneh angry. I was doing well at school. I helped in the house."

Her mother stepped back and held up her hand. "Beneh did not send you away. Your father fetched you back."

"Taata? No. You must have misunderstood."

"Your father wrote Beneh himself." Her mother picked a broom from the ground and rested it against a wall. Lilian's future flashed before her: brooms and buckets and cook pots and dung.

"Why, Maama? Why would he do that?" Lilian tried to keep the anger from her voice.

"He has his reasons and it is not for us to question them. Come, take some tea." Her mother sat down and Lilian crouched beside her.

"Did he say anything?"

"No." Her mother touched the collar of Lilian's new dress. "Just that there won't be any more parcels from your uncle." She lifted a pot of tea from the fire and filled a cup for Lilian. "Don't make that face. We can use you at home." Her face softened. "Especially now the cassava has grown."

"There she is!"

Lillian swivelled around at the sound of her father's voice. His face was thin and his left leg dragged behind the right but his eyes still sparkled when he saw her. "Lilian!" He shuffled through the gate, easing down beside her. "You okay, Tiny Mosquito?"

Lilian let her father hold her face between his hands but she didn't try to hide her disappointment.

"Why, Taata?" she asked, trying to make sense of the

betrayal. "Why did you make me come home? I just started Senior One and—"

"I'm sorry, Tiny Mosquito." His hands fell to his sides. "I couldn't let you stay in that house, not after what you wrote about Beneh. If he thinks it is okay to do those things to his wife, what's to stop him hurting you? I should have brought you home sooner."

"I'm okay," Lilian said, taking his hand, "but we have to help Aunt Amara. Uncle Beneh treats her—"

"How Beneh treats his wife is none of our business." Her mother's voice was choked with impatience.

"Your mother is right. I'm sorry, Lilian, there's nothing I can do." He took her chin in his calloused hand and lifted her face so she had to look up at him. "Amara is welcome here if she chooses to leave Beneh but *she* has to make the choice." He brought his stubbled face close to Lilian's. "If your husband ever treats you like that, you come home. Don't let him hit you."

Let him? Let who? Lilian's stomach clenched. Was her father planning a wedding?

"Come. I have something to show you."

Lilian followed her father to the back of the hut. Resting against the mud wall was a rusted bicycle. Lilian looked from the faded red bike to her father and back to the handlebars. The rubber was torn and the seat was pitted, but it had two wheels, and neither of them was flat.

"For me?" Lilian ran to heave the bike from the wall.

"Well, if you're going to ride with Wekesa to school ..."

Lilian dropped the bike and ran to her father. "When do I start?"

"Tomorrow," her father said, his face shiny with pride.

"But how? The cassava isn't ready. We can't afford it."

"Don't worry about the money. It is all arranged."

Lilian didn't question her father, though his smile had dimmed. She didn't want to know what he had done to secure the money. All she needed to know was that she was going to school. Tomorrow. In Walumira.

The sun had begun to dip in the sky by the time Lilian filled her jerry can. She brushed a mosquito away, balanced the container on her head and started slowly through the bush to Dimple's house. The sun was a soft orange and the forest full of shadows.

"Dimple?" Lilian called, when she reached the front yard. Dimple's father was snoring on the couch, his enormous belly heaving.

"Lala?" Dimple appeared from behind a tin drum. "Lala! You're back!" She flung her arms around her friend. "Oh, don't worry about him," she said. "Once he's passed out, he's out for hours." She grabbed Lilian's hand and spun her around. "Wo, wo, wo. Your dress!" She stood back to admire the pleated skirt and brown belt. "And the shoes." She clapped her hands on her cheeks. "They must have cost the moon. Are they comfortable?"

Lilian kicked off a shoe. "Best thing is, no more jiggers. Try one. We can share." Lilian remembered her friend's face on the first day of school and that bastard Ephraim Kakooza. *One*

Shoe, he'd called her and the name had stuck. "I don't mean we wear one each." Lilian reddened. "We can take turns. Have you been at school?"

Dimple shook her head.

"And Prosper?"

Dimple's cheeks lifted. "She's in Kampala, on scholarship." Her smile teetered. "They offered both of us, but someone has to run the business." She glanced around the yard, at the tubs of browning bananas and the tin drums and empty bottles.

"Why didn't you write me?" Lilian asked.

"I didn't know what to say."

"About what?"

Dimple narrowed her eyes. "You don't know?"

"Know what?" Lilian's face was a blank.

"The vomiting?" Dimple waited for a reaction. "I got fat ..." Lilian's eyes slid to Dimple's belly and her mouth fell open.

"I'm not pregnant," Dimple said. "I had him months ago. His name is Akello."

Lilian listened for the sounds of a child.

"He's not here," Dimple said and Lilian waited.

"He's in Mukono with my aunt."

"Why?" Lilian had so many questions. Who *put the baby inside Dimple? What did sex feel like? Was giving birth like squeezing a watermelon through a straw?*

"It was either that or visit the woman who helps girls lose their babies. I couldn't ..." Dimple's breath caught. "Chiamaka, that girl two years above us at school? You remember her?"

Lilian nodded. Chiamaka had disappeared when she was in

Senior One. No one knew why, but a rumour went around that she'd had sex with a boy in Senior Six and was going to have an abortion.

"She died," Dimple said, "on the floor of the woman's hut. I told my father if he forced me to see her, I'd run away. We made a deal." She smiled weakly. "I could keep Akello if my aunty looked after him until he was old enough to work."

"What about the baby's father?" Lilian asked. "Do you love him?" The words sounded stupid when spoken out loud, but Lilian hoped Dimple *did* love him, if not now, then at least when he'd lain on top of her.

Dimple screwed up her face. "I liked him, but not like that. He was kind, he listened, he treated me like a grown-up." Dimple gnawed on a fingernail. "He knew about my dad, knew he drank and beat us. He said we could move in with his family if things got really bad." She rocked on her heels. "He fed us," Dimple shrugged, "as many chapattis as we could eat."

Lilian felt sick. "Mr Musoke?"

Dimple stared at the ground. "He took me to a restaurant. I thought we were just having lunch." She sucked in air and continued. "He stopped on the way back, at a room. It was somewhere in a forest ... there was a bed in the room. He told me to undress." She rubbed her eyes. "He said if I didn't let him, he'd leave me there. My father would have killed me dead if I didn't come home in time for dinner." She kicked at the dirt. "'It won't hurt,' he said, 'your father's fist will.'"

"He shouldn't have done that." Lilian's anger swelled. "You know that, right? It's against the law."

"The law?" Dimple stared at Lilian as if she were simple. "He didn't find me on the street and grab me. I escaped from home and took myself to meet him. I went to the room. I sat on the bed. I *let* him touch me."

You can always say no, Madam Cherop had told the girls at Empowerment Club. *If you don't want to have sex or get married, say no*. Madam Cherop should have told them that those words belonged to city girls, not girls like Dimple, who lived in mud huts, and didn't have mothers, just fathers who drank. Lilian pulled her friend close. She thought about the diseases Madam Cherop listed on the board when she warned the girls about unprotected sex. Diseases that made you itch down below and burn when you went to the toilet. Diseases that revealed themselves in blisters and scabs and rashes on your mouth and the palms of your hand.

"Does Musoke still work on the main road?" Lilian imagined standing next to his stall to shoo girls away. She pictured following him home to tell his wife what he'd done and reporting him to the police. Musoke would deny it, but there were tests you could do to prove he was Akello's father. Lilian would write to Kamali. She'd know what to do.

"I don't want to see him," Dimple said.

"You don't have to do anything you don't want." As soon as Lilian said the words she knew they were a lie. Dimple had to stop school to make *Waraji* for her father and Lilian had to wake every morning to make breakfast for her brother and draw water from the well. Every day, girls were forced to do things they didn't want to.

"I should get back to work." Dimple stared at her father, asleep on the couch, a silver trail of spit hanging from his mouth. "Maybe we'll go see Akello next month?"

Lilian pulled her friend into a hug. They wouldn't go to Mukono. Not next month or next year. They didn't have the bus fare. Dimple would see her boy when he was old enough to haul bottles. She would have forgotten what he looked like, and he'd have forgotten the smell of her skin. "You will get your boy back," Lilian whispered into her friend's ear, "and I'll finish school. Everything will work out. You wait and see."

Chapter 26

"I had to guess the size." Lilian's mother handed her a dress and waited for her to climb into it. Lilian stepped into the uniform, fed her arms through the sleeves and fastened the buttons. The dress was pale blue with a white collar and pleats. Lilian fed the thin black belt through the loops at her waist and cinched it tight, wishing she had a mirror to admire herself, to see what Amal would see tomorrow, at school.

"Too short," her mother said, bending to lift the hem. "Take it off. I will fix it." Lilian pulled the dress over her head. *Strive to prosper.* She mouthed the words embroidered on the collar. "Strive to prosper," she said out loud, remembering her mother couldn't read. "It's the school motto. It means *work hard.*"

"Work hard?" Her mother flung the uniform over her shoulder. "Hard work is what *fed* you all these years, not your pens or books." Lilian opened her mouth to speak but her mother waved her words away. "I know your books saved the cassava, but you can read now. It is enough. Your father is tired. He is too old to load trucks." She lifted the sisal sack that hung over the door. "Look at him." She pointed outside at Lilian's father, who stood over the fire, heaping branches onto the flames. His shirt hung loosely, his back was bent. "Senior school costs three times as much as primary. You want your father to work three times as hard?" Lilian didn't want to think about what it cost her father to put her through school but she couldn't ignore his crooked back or the tape that held his shoes together.

"I want to get a job, Taata," Lilian said when her mother was out of earshot. "I can wash the neighbours' clothes."

Her father shook his head.

"I can sell cassava chips."

"The fees are paid," her father said, raising an axe to split more wood. "Just help your mother and do your homework." He brought the axe down hard.

"I will, Taata," Lilian stooped to collect the wood. "But I *want* to work. I need to make my own money." She rested a hand on his arm. "I saw what Uncle Beneh did to Aunt Amara. You said if my husband ever beats me, I should leave him. I'll need money to do that."

"Feed your brother, help in the garden and keep the hut clean." He paused at his work. "And if you still have time after that, you can work."

The world was changing, Lilian thought. *I've changed, but this place is exactly the same as I left it.*

Wekesa came home just as they sat down to eat.

"Lala, you're back!" he said, a smile crinkling his eyes. He snatched a plate from the trunk and held it out. "I'm starving."

Lilian scooped two spoons of Posho onto the plastic and drowned them in sauce.

"So, why are you home?" He pointed to the beans.

"Long story," Lilian said, ladling them onto his plate.

"She belongs here, with us," her father said.

"And she is going to school, so you will ride with her," her mother added.

"Eeeh, but she can't ride," Wekesa complained.

"So teach her," Lilian's father stooped to sit on a sun-warmed stone.

Wekesa groaned. "She won't keep up."

"I will. I'm a quick learner. Do you want to take a drink?" Lilian asked, remembering Nakato's advice ... *make it easy for him*. If Lilian wanted to go to school, she had to make it easy for her family, for her mother and father and Wekesa too. She picked up the jerry can and dribbled water into Wekesa's cupped palms.

He'd grown taller while she was away and his skin had cleared. He had a black mop of hair and two dark eyes dropped into his face. He was handsome but hard.

"Okay, this is how it will work," he said when they were alone. "I teach you to ride and you do my homework. Hope they taught you algebra in that fancy school." He passed Lilian his workbook. "I have to hand it in tomorrow."

"You teach me to ride and then we'll talk." Lilian walked to where the bikes slept propped against the mud brick wall.

"Fine," Wekesa grumbled, grabbing her bike to steady it.

Lilian curled her fingers around the handlebars and lifted her leg over the seat.

When Lilian returned from the well later that night, Uncle Lwanga and Aunt Afia were huddling by the fire. The light had leaked from the sky and a giant moon had come up and three shadowy figures were dancing in the dark: little Norris, sharp-shouldered and legs thin as twigs; gap-toothed MoreBlessing who was still waiting for teeth; and Ajani who was now a head taller than Lilian.

"Lilian! Welcome home!" Uncle Lwanga settled his beer on the dirt and waved her over. The drumming stopped and five sets of arms circled Lilian's waist. Afia peeled MoreBlessing's arms from Lilian. "Look at you!" She spun Lilian around. "You're tall as a jacaranda." She motioned for Lilian to sit beside her, their knees pressed together. "I hear Beneh is eating money. Tell me everything. Did you sleep on a double bed? Is his second wife pretty?" She stopped to suck in air. "I like your hair."

"Did you watch TV?" Norris hopped from one foot to another.

"Did you sit in Rich Uncle's car?" Ajani stood in front of her, his back to the flames.

"Let her catch her breath!" Afia led Lilian to the back of the hut where it was quieter. "How was school? Did you make any special friends?"

"Just one," Lilian said, pretending she didn't understand

what her aunt was asking. "Her name is Kamali. She grew up with her hands in the dirt, like us, but she's sharp as a needle and she knows everything, or at least everything worth knowing. She took me to Empowerment Club and–"

Afia raised an eyebrow. "So, you're a feminist now?"

"A feminist? You know what that is?"

"Of course I do," Afia snorted. "Feminists are women who can't find husbands. But you won't have any trouble," her aunt assured her. "I could find you a rich man like that!" She clicked her fingers.

"I start school tomorrow." Lilian made her voice hard.

"I know," Afia said with fading enthusiasm. "I am surprised your mother agreed. What are you now? Fifteen?" She didn't wait for Lilian to answer. "Your maama won't get as much for you in two or three years. What's that face? You don't believe me?"

"No, I do, Aunt, it's just," Lilian hesitated. "Things are changing. In the city–"

"We're not *in* the city," Afia said. "And your mother is Sabiny. She lived a Sabiny life, still does. Why do you think she married Goodness off at fifteen?" She brushed a leaf from Lilian's hair. "On Mount Elgon, if a girl is young, the bride price is six cows. If she is no longer soft and sweet, if she is old like me, with missing teeth, well, I wouldn't get more than three. You're valuable *now*."

Lilian stiffened.

"If it was up to me," Afia continued, mistaking Lilian's anger for sorrow, "I'd let you finish the year. As you say, things are different, men don't mind smart girls. Another year of maths and you can help balance your husband's books. I'll talk to your mother," Afia said as though she were handing Lilian a gift.

"See if we can put off a wedding until you've done your O levels."

Lilian would be seventeen when she finished her O levels. She turned her back on Afia and walked towards the music so she wouldn't say something she might regret. Her father sat in front of the fire, his thin legs clamped around a drum, his body like a tree bent heavy with fruit. MoreBlessing grabbed one of her hands and Ajani took the other and she let them hurl her into the beat, where she could stamp her feet and shake her fists and stomp on the life her family had planned for her.

Lilian danced with her cousins in front of the flames, lost in the music, until one by one they sunk to the ground to sit cross-legged by the fire.

"Who wants to hear a story?" Lilian's father stopped drumming. The children gathered round, their eyes wide with anticipation.

"It wasn't so long ago, on a night like this," he waited for Wekesa to join them, "the wind was howling and the moon was huge. We sat here, all of us, under the black sky, and I said to you ..."

The children held their breath.

"I said that, just as I took over as storyteller from Jjaja Wange Olufeni, there would come a time when I passed Jjaja's cloak to someone who had new stories ..."

The children swivelled around to stare at Lilian. MoreBlessing's hand shot up. "Can you tell us the story of how the grey parrots got their red tails?"

"No!" Ajani leaped to his feet. "Tell us the one about Mpobe the hunter."

"Or the one about Kasanke the little red bird?" Mirembe

looked up shyly from her father's lap.

"She will do better than that!" Lilian's father crowed. "She will read you one of her own!"

He handed Lilian a crumpled sheet of yellowing paper. "This one is my favourite."

Lilian took the story from him. He'd given Beneh her stories but kept one for himself. She held it up to the fire so she could make out her looping script. The pages were smudged and worn thin where her father had held them. Lilian thought of the novels in the library at Namugongo Secondary. The best books, the ones that were the hardest to get hold of because they were always on loan, were shabby and dog-eared, their pages frayed. Lilian smiled at the coffee stain blotting the title.

"Would you like to hear it?" Lilian's father asked the huddled circle, hammering his drums. Ajani hooted and MoreBlessing clapped her hands. Wekesa sat bent over the maize beer, a straw between his lips, but when Lilian began to speak, he too looked up.

"There once was a wise ..." Lilian paused. The story was about a wise man who'd won the king's favour by taming a snake with seven heads. "There once was a wise *girl*," Lilian held Mirembe's gaze, "who hypnotised a snake ..."

Lilian had been up for hours when Wekesa finally woke. She had finished his homework by the time the sun lit the sky. It hadn't taken long, the maths was basic and she'd filled in the answers;

eight correct and two wrong. If Wekesa got ten out of ten, his teacher would know he had cheated. *I'm protecting him*, she had told herself. But she wasn't. She was tired of washing his uniform and angry that he had swept her books from his desk. She would help him scrape through school but standing on the podium and being crowned Senior One's top student? That was *her* prize.

"Got to go," Wekesa said, pulling on his crumpled uniform and jumping on his bike. "I'll teach you to ride later." Lilian grabbed her schoolbag and wheeled her bike to the gate.

As soon as they turned the corner and their mother could no longer see them, Wekesa sped off, his feet working the pedals. Lilian watched him shrink to the size of a groundnut and then disappear, swallowed whole by the bush. She slung a leg over the seat and rested her foot on the pedal. Wekesa used to like teaching her things – the best hiding spots in Atia's garden, how to scale a tree. If he wouldn't teach her how to ride, she'd have to teach herself. She lifted her foot and rolled forwards slowly. She fell three times, then climbed off the seat and dragged the bike through the bush, on the lookout for men.

No one leaped out to grab her, but there were plenty of men on the main road selling sunglasses and sticks of pineapple. Lilian ignored them when they called to her, and when a young man in a leather jacket offered her a ride to school on the back of his boda boda she shook her head, her eyes on Mr Musoke. She wanted to kick the wheels from under his stall and smash in the hotplates, but that would just land her parents in debt and her mother would force her to marry before she got into more trouble.

"You're Wekesa's little sister," the principal said, when Lilian finally arrived at Walumira Secondary with a bruised knee and grazed hand. He peered at his clipboard. "Lilian Chelangat?"

Lilian nodded.

"You are in Mr Nabbak's class." Lilian's smile emptied. Wekesa was in Senior One with Mr Bugembe.

"Do I have to repeat Primary Seven?" Lilian panicked.

"Repeat it?" The man laughed, his chins wobbling. "No, you'll be in Senior One, same as your brother. Mr Bugembe takes the regular class. Mr Nabbak takes extension."

The principal took Lilian's grazed hand and turned it over. His nails were short and clean, his hands soft. Indoor hands.

"You should go see Madam Namusisi about that," he said, walking her to assembly. "She's a teacher here, but also the school nurse."

"Over here, Lala!" Masani waved Lilian over. "Finally, another girl to talk to." She moved aside to make room for Lilian. "Jemimah is no help." She cocked her head to the right. "She's the principal's daughter, spends lunchtimes in her father's office." Lilian looked past the sweep of boys and saw a tall girl in a neat uniform, and then, Amal.

"Hi," he mouthed, staring straight at her. He was as handsome as she remembered except his face was more angular, his shoulders broader. She swivelled to face the podium, her face burning. *Idiot*, she muttered under her breath. They were friends. Just friends. They'd known each other forever. Why couldn't she have just smiled?

"He missed you," Masani, whispered, her voice honeyed. "If you want, I can arrange for the two of you to meet?"

"I can't believe you still do that."

Masani handed Lilian a pen. It was silvered and smooth and had a button at the tip that released the nib. "I got this from Stephen Kasome last week after Doreen Natembe met him behind the sports shed."

Lilian looked sceptical.

"It's not easy money. I have to talk the girls into it, and when the boys dump them, it's me they come crying to."

"He told you he likes me?" Lilian tried to keep her voice even.

"He's liked you for years, wasn't it obvious?"

"Amal's hard to work out."

"Amal?" Masani gawked at her. "I'm not talking about Amal. I'm talking about Thomas."

Lilian looked back and saw Thomas Kobego, standing slouched at the end of the Senior One line.

"Don't you feel bad?" Lilian handed Masani back her pen. "Setting the girls up, knowing the boys are just using them."

Masani shrugged. "Does the man I buy gum from feel bad for ruining my teeth? It's business."

"Business? If you want coin so bad, why don't you sleep with them?"

"Think they don't try?" Masani's anger crackled. "Only way to stop them is to tell them I have a boyfriend."

"And do you?"

"A boyfriend? At school?" Masani grimaced. "No one is touching me until I turn eighteen."

Lilian stood under the empty sky and willed herself to listen to the prefects' reports: the toilets hadn't been properly cleaned; drama rehearsal for the upcoming school play was starting at four pm; Scripture Club meetings were shifting to Thursdays.

"I wish that were me, up there on the podium," Lilian said, as a peace offering. If she had started Senior One at the beginning of the year with the rest of them, she could have been up there on the podium, telling everyone what to do.

"There's always Senior Two." Masani snuck Lilian a piece of gum.

"What about a committee?" Lilian sunk her teeth into the rubbery sweetness.

"All full. You're not the only one who wants a free meal."

It wasn't the free meal Lilian was after – it was the blazer and badge. She watched an older girl at the foot of the podium pull up her socks before stepping onto the stage. Lilian couldn't wait to get to Senior Five and wear a shirt with long sleeves and white socks that reached her knees. She couldn't wait to take her place on the podium as head girl of Senior Six. She imagined the smile on her father's face when she showed him the gold pin with her name engraved on it. Amal squeezed past her on his way to the stage.

"Information prefect," Masani said, before Lilian had time to ask.

Lilian didn't speak to Amal until much later. He spent break time at his desk drawing up rosters and lunchtime in the cafeteria. "Got a meeting," he mouthed, ducking under the canteen's low door. Three boys filed in after him, carrying clipboards under their arms. Lilian took her bowl of porridge and crossed the yard for Madam Namusisi's room.

"Keep it on overnight," the teacher said, smoothing a white gauze bandage over Lilian's grazed palm. "I can wash it again tomorrow if you haven't got antiseptic."

"Is that yours?" Lilian asked, admiring the small brass trophy on the teacher's desk. "Do you play soccer?"

"Yes. Would you like to learn?"

Lilian laughed, extending her bandaged hand. "I'm having enough trouble riding a bike. I didn't know women played soccer."

"They do." Her teacher grinned. Lilian glanced down at Madam Namusisi's fingers. She wasn't wearing a wedding ring.

"There *is* something I'd like to do," Lilian ventured. "I've started the year late. I was in Kampala ..." The words spilled out. "I want to get onto a committee. Do you know which might need another pair of hands?"

"I'm sorry, they are all full. You'll have to wait until next year."

Lilian's eyes slid to her lap.

"Maybe that's a good thing." Madam Namusisi skirted the desk to stand beside Lilian. "You don't want to be on just *any* committee." Her eyes burrowed into Lilian's. "What is it that needs fixing? When you leave this place, how do you want to see it changed?"

Lilian didn't need thinking time.

"There's no Empowerment Club," she said, meeting the teacher's eye. "In Kampala, we had a club and the senior teachers spent one lunchtime a week with us. We had guest speakers who talked about child labour and women's rights. They told us things like *Be who you are, not what boys want you to be*."

Madam Namusisi's face was lit by a smile. "The principal's daughter is in your class. Get her on board. She's smart and she's driven and Mr Lubega will listen to her."

The gong sounded and Lilian stood to leave.

"And tell him," Madam Namusisi said, tossing Lilian the roll of gauze, "I'm free at lunchtime, Tuesdays and Thursdays."

Chapter 27

Masani reached for Lilian's shirt and unfastened the top button. "That's better," she said, plucking a tube of pink lip gloss from her bag. "You have nice eyes." She peered into Lilian's face. "With just a bit of mascara you could ..."

"I don't wear make-up," Lilian told Masani, thinking of the women she knew who did: Nakato whose false lashes were an advertisement, and Amara, whose make-up disguised her fear.

"I'm not saying you're not pretty. It's just–" Masani dabbed gloss on Lilian's lips, "you could be prettier." She waved Thomas over.

Lilian wiped the pink from her lips. Pretty could help, but it could also hurt you.

"Looking good," Thomas said, as if it mattered. Lilian grabbed her bag and started for the gate.

"So, Kampala's pretty cool, huh?" Thomas's voice followed

her. "I went two years ago, a birthday present from my dad. We went to the swimming pool. You know, the one with the diving boards?"

Lilian didn't know.

"What about that ice cream shop?" Thomas appeared beside her. "They have twenty-one flavours."

"I was there to study. I didn't have time for anything else." Lilian had meant to sound aloof but the words came out sad.

"It's a crime," he said, his voice oily. "You, in the city, looking so fine and no boy to take you out." His eyes slid from her neck to her chest.

Lilian reached the school gate and grabbed her bike, cursing Wekesa for not teaching her to ride. She was about to veer onto the track leading to Afia's home when she spotted Amal sitting on a rock, his bike resting on a nearby tree. She wanted to drop the bike and run to him, but she made herself walk. "Flat tire?"

"Lala!" Amal grinned, getting to his feet. "No, the bike is fine. Wekesa wasn't waiting for you and I figured you might need a lesson?" He rested a hand on her bike. Just him and her and no space between them. "He says you're completely hopeless." He steadied the seat. "Get on."

Lilian had promised to visit Afia. *You must come see me*, her aunt had said. *The boys will be wanting to get into your pants.*

Lilian lifted her leg over the seat, her dress bunching at her thighs.

"Okay, hold the handlebars." Amal slid Lilian's skirt back over her knee. "Now lift a foot, yep, there, on the pedal." He slammed his hand over hers to stop the bike wobbling. She felt the warmth of his skin and the damp sweat at his palm. "Sorry, I just … I didn't want you to fall," he said, shoving his hand back into his pocket.

But she *had* fallen. Hard. Lilian lay on her sleeping mat and squeezed her eyes shut. Amal was different to other boys. They'd been alone in the bush and he hadn't tried to kiss her.

She would have let him. Lilian summoned the thrill of his hand curved over hers on the hot metal handlebar and her body began to hum. He was nothing like Thomas or Mr Musoke. She stared up at the stars through the gaps in the thatch. She knew thinking about Amal was dangerous. She should be thinking about school, instead of replaying their conversation. *What do you want to do after you finish school?* she'd asked him, wheeling her bike next to his. *Study medicine*, he'd said. *I'm going to work in a hospital in the city.* He hadn't asked about Kampala and Lilian had been grateful. She didn't want to talk about Beneh or the girls at school who had nicknamed her "the maid". *I'm going to study too*, she'd said but he hadn't replied. Her mother was at the gate scowling, so he had said goodbye and gone in search of Wekesa.

Lilian imagined his fingers slowly unbuttoning her shirt. *We want the same things*, Lilian told herself. *He finishes my sentences. He likes that I'm smart.* Masani had sworn no one would touch her till she was eighteen. Lilian wondered if she was strong enough to wait.

They bumped into each other the next day in the library after school. Lilian was trawling the internet's medical sites for information about her sister's illness. Amal leaned over her desk and read her notes on whooping cough. "What are you doing studying infectious diseases?" he said, taking the mouse from her. "Library's about to close. Ride you home?"

The first time Lilian fell, Amal leaped off his bike to help her. The second time, she lay sprawled on the ground and he dropped down beside her, so close that she worried he could hear her heart thumping. They lay in the long grass listening to the cicadas. The sky was cloudless above them, the earth warm at their backs. He didn't touch her.

"They have a huge infectious diseases department in Kampala. I'm going to work there one day," he said.

Lilian loved listening to him talk. He did everything with such resolve: studying for exams, riding his bike, even the way he gripped his pen.

"And you?" He propped himself up on an elbow. "You still going to be my assistant?" She would've been mad if it was anyone else, but she was touched that years later, he still recalled one of their conversations.

"Actually, I'm thinking of writing," she said, because when she was with him, she could be anything. "You're the information prefect. I could be your deputy. I could write your newsletters and takes notes at meetings."

He pulled a twig from her hair. "I'll see what I can do."

Lilian waved him goodbye on the main road. Amal had wanted to accompany her home, so she'd had to lie. *I have to visit Afia*, she'd said, pointing in the direction of her aunt's hut. *I'll see you tomorrow*. Instead, she hid her bike behind a tree and watched Mr Musoke sell the last of his chapattis to a girl in a pink singlet, leaning too close as he ladled another spoonful of beef onto her flatbread. Lilian watched him feed the last of the beef into his mouth and pack the onions and oil into small plastic boxes before grabbing her bike and following him home. She had decided to tell his wife what he had done unless he paid Dimple half his earnings. *Child support*. She'd been surprised to learn at Empowerment Club that the law had a name for it – and that fathers were supposed to pay it.

Lilian stopped at Mr Musoke's front gate with her mouth hung open. She'd expected his wife to be wearing shoes. She'd expected his children to be in uniform. She'd imagined a brick house on a giant parcel of land with a door and a tin roof and a grain store and kitchen. What she saw was a tired hut and a skulking dog and a woman bathing a child in a plastic tub. She had a baby tied to her back and children tugging at her skirt. Lilian counted seven as she watched Mr Musoke step from the hut in a pair of faded shorts and a shrunken T-shirt. Lilian backed away from the gate. There would be no money to send Akello to school. No money for Dimple's bus fare. Lilian watched Mr Musoke open his wallet and hand his earnings to his wife. If Dimple took half, the Musokes would starve.

Chapter 28

Lilian's father wasn't there to see her graduate Senior One and he didn't return for her first day of Senior Two, so Lilian wrote him a letter telling him she was studying Swahili and politics and had a job sweeping Madam Namusisi's room. *The heads of each year haven't been announced yet so I'm still hoping for head girl, but I'm class monitor*, she'd written, unpinning her gold badge to run a pencil along its glinting edge. She imagined her father tracing its outline with his finger and hoped he'd be proud.

She would have liked to write more often, but stamps were expensive and she didn't have much time. She spent her days in class and her nights doing homework by the moon's bluish light, forcing herself out of bed when the rooster crowed to make breakfast for her brother.

Her lunchtimes were spent with Amal and the other prefects. She was a rung below them in the school hierarchy, but as classroom monitor, she sat in the cafeteria and ate what they ate – greasy cassava chips and neat parcels of minced meat fried on a hotplate. She sat across from Amal and watched him talk, imagining his cotton-soft lips pressed against hers. It was easy to daydream – he required nothing of her – directing his conversation to the boys who crowded their table. He didn't ask her opinion or seek her advice. He knew, as well as she did, it would only take a look or his hand brushed against hers to start the rumours, and relationships between students were forbidden at school.

They waited instead for the final gong to sound, climbing onto their bikes once the school had emptied. Amal would set off first and Lilian would follow, until he'd slow and then stop at their secret spot. Spreading his blazer for her on the sun-scorched earth, they would sit and study, setting aside their books to lie flattened under the sky. He grazed her bare arm with his fingers once and her throat closed over. The last time they met, he had weaved his fingers through hers to help her up and didn't let go until they reached the road.

She tried to commit their love story to paper, to form words to describe the slope of his shoulders and his cool gaze and what it would feel like when his fingers finally hitched her close. She used to think she wanted to be like Amal. That wasn't true. She didn't want to be like him – she was his equal now – she wanted to be *with* him. She pictured him brushing her cheek with the back of his hand and lowering her gently onto a bed, but every time she tried to paint the story in words, her mind returned to the room where Mr Musoke had undressed Dimple, and the words disappeared. She thought of Beneh's hands on Amara's throat, and Goodness's pregnant belly lifting her skirt, and put down the pen.

She should be focusing on Empowerment Club, not how soft Amal's skin would feel when she finally touched him. As Madam Namusisi had predicted, the principal had given his daughter permission to hold meetings and 4000 shillings to use as she liked. The first meeting was poorly attended, just Jemimah and Lilian and Madam Namusisi, but word got around that they served cake and soon the classroom was crammed with girls. The money had run out and so had the cake but the girls stayed, even Masani, who pretended not to listen to Madam Namusisi tell them they had a right to an education, same as their brothers. *You can have a career and a husband*, she'd said, *if you choose right*. If they *chose*. The girls had tasted the word, rolling it around on their tongues and Lilian had felt hope unspool inside her. *What career do you choose?* Madam Namusisi had asked. Miriam wanted to be a nurse. Mercy hoped to study teaching. Masani wanted to do a business degree. Lilian admitted she wanted to write and no one laughed. *Know who you are and what you want*, Madam Namusisi counselled them. *Don't let anyone dictate what you can be.*

Lilian scribbled everything she heard onto a scrap of paper and slipped it into an envelope, addressing it to Amara Bukulu. She didn't have an address for her aunt. Amara's mail went to Beneh's postbox. Lilian imagined Beneh reading the note meant for Amara, his eyes fierce slits. *Taata said you are welcome to stay with us, but you have to leave*, the note said. Lilian pictured

Beneh's meaty fist crushing the note. She saw the crumpled ball of paper sail through the air and land in a bin, but still she sent it, marking the envelope with the words: *Clothing Sale*, to dampen his curiosity. *I am certain Taata will take Nakato back too*, the last line pleaded. *Amara, if you find her, please tell her to come home.*

The sun was sinking, its orange light flaming the sky. Lilian breathed in the smell of the cooling earth and stepped into the dim shade of Afia's hut.

"About time you come see your *Ssenga*!" Afia said, inviting Lilian inside.

Uncle Lwanga folded his newspaper and rose from his chair. "Looks like women's business." He winked at Lilian and, hoisting Norris onto his shoulders, tramped to the door, trailed by his girls.

"Your button is undone. I can see your bra." Afia waited for Lilian to feed her shirt button through its hole. "I know it is just a bra strap." Afia slid a pipe between her lips. "But men see it as an invitation. So, what were we up to?" She scraped a chair from the table and Lilian sat down.

"We were talking about sex," Lilian reminded her aunt.

Afia eyes narrowed in warning. "Boys are a mess. When I was at school," she confided, "I didn't let them near me. My parents got six cows when I married Lwanga."

"And what if you hadn't been a virgin?"

"He could have beaten me. In your great-grandmother's day,"

Afia said without blinking, "they walked girls to a waterfall and told them to jump. Your mother will find you a good man," Afia assured her.

But Lilian didn't want a husband. She wanted a boy who would steal the moon for her. She wanted Amal.

"How did you know what to do the first time?" Lilian asked.

"My *Ssenga* showed me. After our *Kwanjula* she took Lwanga to a room and they both undressed. She told me to sit in the corner and watch."

Lilian's breath caught.

"We don't do that any more. Pity," she said, winking at Lilian.

Lilian hadn't asked about marriage, she'd asked about Afia's first time, but of course her aunt had waited until she was in a wedding dress. When Lilian pictured herself married she saw Amal slotted into the shape of a husband, but that was after they finished university. She wanted to kiss Amal now.

"It was a valuable lesson," Afia continued, "but even more useful was her advice about how to be your husband's favourite." Lilian sat up in her chair. "Don't lie still or he'll think you're not enjoying it. Tell him you *are*," Afia began. "Tell him how strong he is and how much you love him. Tell him you'll never have a man as good as he is." Lilian slumped in her seat as Afia rattled off a list of instructions. "Don't deny him. Never say no."

Why was it always about the man? Lilian wanted to ask. *He* needs, *he* wants. What about her?

"There's this boy," she ventured. Afia had told her that if she slept with a boy she would get pregnant but that wasn't true. Madam Namusisi had told the girls there were ways to protect themselves. That if they made boys wear condoms the girls wouldn't catch diseases or find themselves with a stomach.

"Have you told him how you feel?" Afia inquired.

Lilian shook her head.

"Don't. If you tell him first, he'll never marry you. A man needs to hunt for a wife. What clan is he from? Grasshopper? Mushroom?"

"*Nkula*," Lilian said.

"The rhinoceros clan?" Afia lifted the pipe from her lips. "Be careful of the boy." She waved away a pale string of grey smoke. "The *Nkula* are skilled hunters and medicine men who use the magic rhinoceros horn to lure women to their beds."

"There are eleven prefects and not one is a girl!" Jemimah Lubega was standing on the library steps, a circle of schoolgirls inhaling her anger.

"Girls aren't as smart."

Lilian swivelled at the sound of scouring laughter and saw Thomas, wearing a mean smile, and next to him, Amal.

Jemimah's face turned purple. "That's because we miss a week of school every month! If we had locks on the latrines–"

"Some things you just don't talk about." Amal cut Jemimah a disapproving look. He slung his bag onto his shoulder and headed for the gate, looking over his shoulder to signal for Lilian to follow him.

"Jemimah is right," Lilian said when they reached the school gate. "More girls *should* be prefects." She waited for Amal to agree. He had silenced Jemimah and she needed him to make up for it.

"Is this about me not making you my deputy?" They made their way through the bush. "There was nothing I could do. The boys on my team didn't want a g–"

"It's fine," Lilian said, and it was, because she was class monitor and had done it without him.

"They didn't want a girl on the team." He climbed off his bike. "So I made Jacob Kwagala deputy on condition the boys vote you in as class monitor."

Lilian rearranged her face to hide her disappointment.

"You know what Jemimah said about girls being invisible?" Amal lifted a branch so Lilian could duck under it. "It's not true. You couldn't be *less* invisible." He shifted closer. "Sometimes I have to force myself to look away."

Lilian didn't want him to look away; she wanted to kiss him. They were in their secret spot, hidden by ancient trees and a canopy of leaves.

"Lala," he said, his face full of wanting. She could feel his longing, and then hers, rise to match it. She closed her eyes and let his lips find hers and his tongue push her mouth open. She didn't tell him he was the first boy to kiss her, but he knew.

"Remember that time you were sitting under a tree reading a book, I think it was *Cinderella*, and I stopped playing soccer and sat next to you?" He untangled himself from her and threaded his fingers through hers. "I knew, then," he said, "You weren't just beautiful. You were smart."

They kissed again, eyes closed, tongues and teeth and lips and skin. It seemed for hours, but it couldn't have been more than a few minutes. When Lilian opened her eyes she was surprised it was still daylight, surprised the trees and the sky looked the same.

Lilian waited for a car to pass so she could cross the street. She'd left Amal outside his house, but she could still feel his fingers digging into her waist, still taste the warm honey of his breath. She didn't feel shame, just a dull ache that he was gone.

"I know you." A woman grabbed Lilian's wrist. She had a sour, wrinkled face and calloused hands. "You're *Nnalongo's* youngest." Her narrow face poked from the folds of her scarf. Lilian had seen her before. At the market, but also at their home. Lilian kneeled before the woman, as her mother had taught her, her gaze dropping to the woman's bare feet and her crumpled black dress. At her feet lay the faded red bag she had dragged into their yard, moons before. Lilian remembered Goodness following her to their grandfather's hut and the man with the caterpillar eyebrows landing on their doorstep a few months later.

"*Olina emyaka emeka?*" The woman eyed Lilian's uniform.

"Fifteen." Lilian's stomach clenched. It was the dry season; the time of her birth. Lilian was closer to sixteen but she wasn't going to tell the woman that.

"Your sister was fifteen when I visited and now she's married with babies of her own. The time has come." She spoke quickly, leaving no space for protest. "When you sleep tonight, lie facing the dawn. At midnight I will come."

Chapter 29

Lilian wheeled her bike home, the thrill of kissing Amal fading to panic. Fear ploughed through her. The old woman would come with a suitor in mind and if the bride price was agreeable, Lilian would be married by the end of the month. Madam Namusisi had told the girls that marriage was a step you took when you were in love with a man. When you could stand beside him as his equal and say *this is what I want my life to look like from now on.*

Lilian didn't want to stop school or start making babies, but the *when* wasn't up to her, she could see that now. Her future had been written the day she was born. She could give in to it, like Goodness had, or run away, like Nakato. Either way you ended up in bed with a stranger. She smudged a tear from her eye. She wasn't ready to be someone's wife, but she didn't want to lose her family and be cut off from her clan. She didn't want to sleep in a box with a tin roof that shut out the stars in a place where no one told stories. If she had to be married, and couldn't choose when, she would choose *who*.

I'll tell the old lady I'm engaged. Lilian's breathing slowed. Amal would agree to marry her. He loved her. He'd shown her with his mouth and his hands. *I'm not messing around,* he'd said, undoing her top button and sliding his hand down her top. *This is forever.*

Lilian hated the idea of binding herself to a boy while she was still in school, but at least she'd get to finish school if the boy was Amal.

Lilian woke with a start. Her mother was dragging off her bedsheet. "Lilian, wake up. We have to go."

Lilian held the sheet tight. The room was black, the moon cowering behind cloud.

"I don't want to," she whispered, burrowing into her bed.

Her mother took her hand. The last time they'd held hands was when Lilian was small and still afraid of the night. "*Oli mukyala*. It is time."

She helped her up and threaded silver loops into Lilian's ears. "The woman who helped Goodness, she's waiting at Jjaja's hut." She tied a blue beaded belt around Lilian's nightdress.

"I'm not ready, Maama," Lilian whispered into the dark. "Can't you send her away?" She couldn't see her mother's face but she felt her body stiffen.

"You can't stay a child forever." Her voice was steely. "You will show her respect." She led Lilian into the black night, keeping her close. "In my day we celebrated leaving our childhood behind. My skin was decorated with *mondet*." She stopped to smear clay on Lilian's face. "And we sang songs to give us strength. We may be far from Mount Elgon," she smeared Lilian's legs and feet, "but we are still Sabiny."

They walked through the bush under a black sky, Lilian rehearsing, in her head, what she would say to the woman. *He can match the bride price. His family have cows*, she would tell the woman when she suggested a suitor, and her mother would agree. She would marry Amal.

When they could make out her grandfather's hut, Lilian's mother took a clump of herbs from a small pouch at her waist. "Here," she said, feeding the bitter leaves into Lilian's mouth. "It will stop the pain."

"The pain?" Lilian stopped at the sagging wood door.

"It will be quick." Lilian's mother swung the door open and pulled Lilian inside.

A mattress had been dragged into the middle of the hut. The room was puddled in shadow, the floor littered with leaves. Lilian felt as though she were stepping into a grave. A candle sat on a battered timber table and in its slanting light Lilian saw the old woman crouched on the ground scraping a hole into the earth. She wore the same black rags she'd worn the previous day but her shoulders were swathed in animal skin and her neck was strung with beads. Two dark shadows stood in the corner of the room.

"Good, you are here," the old woman said, rising to drape a

shawl made of cow skin over Lilian's shoulders. "It will be light soon. We have to be quick." She fetched four strands of rope from the table and picked up a knife.

"Lie down," she told Lilian, "and open your legs."

Lilian staggered backwards. "The Baganda stretch their *enfuli!*"

"I am not interested in your *enfuli*. Baganda women waste time on the skin that hangs between their legs. You are not a Muganda," the woman spat. "You are Sabiny and Sabiny girls have their *kintir* cut."

Kintir! Lilian had heard the word before, in Empowerment Club. Madam Namusisi had written the word in capital letters on the board in Luganda and English: *Kintir*/Clitoris. *It's not a dirty word*, she had said, drawing a diagram on the blackboard and circling the nub of flesh. *It's there for your enjoyment.* She'd handed the class a pamphlet about genital mutilation but Lilian had only glanced at it before burying it in her bag.

"Maama?" Lilian searched the room. "Maama are you here?"

The woman caught her by the arm and dragged her from the door. "Don't make me use these," she said, dangling the ropes in front of her.

"She won't need them," Lilian's mother stepped into the pool of light cast by the candle. "She is brave." She bent over the mattress and draped a rag over a dark, purple stain. "I bore it silently," she told the woman. "So did her grandmother."

Lilian's heart hammered in her chest. The blood she'd seen all those moons ago wasn't Goodness's period. "You bore it silently but Goodness didn't, I heard her," Lilian said, remembering her sister's strangled screams. "So did Nakato. That's why she left."

She reared on her mother. "She knew what you did to Goodness; what you planned to do to her!" Lilian stared into the yellowed whites of her mother's eyes. "Nakato knew what you were doing and she ran away." Lilian backed towards the door.

"Nakato was foolish," her mother said.

It happened quickly after that. Her mother glanced at the old lady, someone dragged Lilian onto the mattress, her arms were tied with rope and her legs pinned down. The candle was moved from the table to the floor.

Lilian tried to sit up but someone forced her head down. She bit a hand and someone swore.

"Tell your girl her ancestors will haunt her." The woman nudged Lilian's legs apart with her bony elbows. "Tell her it's for her own good."

Lilian's mother stood in a dark corner, her head bent as if she were praying.

"Please, Maama," Lilian begged. "Please. Don't let them cut me I'll do anything you want. I'll work hard. I'll be good." Someone gripped Lilian's ankles and her legs were spread wide. "Tell me what to do, Maama," Lilian whimpered. The old woman crouched between her legs and Lilian felt a rush of water, then the woman's cold hands. It was going to happen. She'd be cut and then married.

"STOP!" Lilian bucked, as the woman took hold of her. She felt a dark tug of pain. "I'll do it," she said, hot-faced and stammering. "On one condition." If she was going to be cut, she wanted her pain to be worth something.

"I'll lie still, if you promise I can go back to school."

Lilian's mother nodded.

"Say it!" Lilian shouted. "Promise me, Maama."

The heel of a hand forced her head back and someone stuffed a rag into her mouth. The candle flickered and shadows danced on the walls.

"I promise," she heard her mother say as blood spattered the mattress. And then the candle went out and the room spun away.

A terrible pain ripped through her, dragging Lilian back to the black room. She let out a roar, like an animal in a trap, startling the old woman. The room smelled of blood.

"Do not speak of this to anyone," the woman warned, kicking dirt over the small grave she'd scraped into the earth where Lilian's childhood was buried. "If you do, white ants will crawl out of your head."

Lilian felt as though she'd been split open like a cassava. Her ankles were tied together with sisal and the mattress was wet. A dark string of blood seeped from between her legs.

"Why?" Lilian whispered, when she had the strength. The women had left and her mother sat beside her spreading balm on her ankles where the rope cut her skin.

"People around here want to destroy our traditions." Her mother narrowed her eyes. "Your cousins, Afia, your friends at school," she hesitated, "even your father, they think because we live among the Baganda we should take on their ways. But I am still a daughter of the Sabiny. And you," she said, "are daughter of the same tribe."

"I don't need to be cut to know who I am." Lilian closed her eyes and clawed the mattress as pain jagged through her. "You *know* how much it hurts." Her mother knew how it felt to have her skin sheared away, and yet, she'd paid someone to do the same thing to Lilian.

"Yes. I know the blade of a knife," her mother said, her eyes dark and unblinking, "and I saved you from the worst of it. When the cutter finished with me, my maama handed her a blunt needle and told her to sew me up tight. I didn't do that to you." She pulled her eyes from Lilian's dark shame. "It was only the *kintir*. It is a stubborn thing and only gets you in trouble. It is my job to tame you."

Lilian tried to sit up but a searing pain pressed her to the mattress. "Afia said ..."

"Afia grew up here. She married a Muganda from the Mbogo clan. What does she know about our people?" Her mother's voice was hard. "Does she know what happens to girls who aren't cut? They can't care for the sick and no one will marry them, except old men. Their ancestors haunt them." She crouched close to Lilian and kept her voice low. "And wherever they go they bring bad luck."

Her mother pushed open the door and a grey light seeped in. It would soon be morning. Lilian reached down and felt the blood running thick between her legs. If her mother had lain beside her and wept, or held Lilian until she cried herself to sleep, maybe Lilian's resentment wouldn't have run as deep, maybe she would have tried to understand. Instead she was left alone, with her pain and anger.

"I hate you," Lilian hissed, as the door slid shut.

Exhaustion brought on sleep. Lilian dreamed of blood and woke to find it wasn't a dream. She'd been split in two. She lay in bed, too scared to move, the blood frightening, the pain worse than any she'd known. *Please don't let me die*, she begged the spirits when something dark slithered out of her and the purple stain spread. She needed to pee but she had to wait for her mother – her legs were bound and it hurt to move. She thought she might die there in that lonely hut.

"I could have died." Lilian told her mother when she returned to wash her. She knew it would hurt her mother to think of another child underground.

"You were never in danger." Her mother mopped up the blood. "I sang songs to appease the spirits and gave them meat." She hunched at Lilian's feet, holding a bowl of warm water. "We buried your *kintir* so no harm would come to you."

She dribbled the liquid over Lilian's wound and Lilian raked the ground with her fingers. "I want to see Taata."

"*Wonsetibik* is women's business."

"But he knows?" Lilian said, grabbing her mother's arm. "He knows I was cut?"

Her mother shook her off.

"He doesn't know?" Lilian gaped at her mother. "If he doesn't know about me, he didn't know about Goodness or why Nakato left." Her mother didn't answer. "How *could* you?" Lilian whispered, shrinking from her mother.

"Her leaving broke him. Do you know what people said after your sister ran away?" She looked down at her lap. "They said she brought shame on your father's name. I heard them. They called him the father of the spoiled runaway. It is a shameful thing for him to carry the rest of his life."

Lilian closed her eyes and tried to pray but the words felt hollow. She wished her father were here to help fill the emptiness. She wished Nakato was with her, telling her everything would be okay.

"Come, you must go to the toilet. It will help the wound heal." Her mother offered Lilian her arm, but Lilian refused it, rising from the soggy mattress on her own to crouch over the dirt.

Her mother crept into the hut the next morning to spoon milk into Lilian's mouth. At dusk she returned with a bowl of warm soup. Lilian could smell the groundnuts on her mother's breath and see the orange papaya stains on her fingers, but when she asked for food her mother refused.

"It hurts to pee," she said. "Going to the pit is worse. It is better if you don't eat hard foods." She fed a rag into Lilian's mouth so the spirits wouldn't hear Lilian curse and dabbed a purple liquid onto her torn skin. Lilian thrashed her legs and clawed the dirt. It felt like her mother was rubbing salt into the wound.

"If you can stand *this*, you can meet any challenge," her mother said, feeding Lilian's feet into underwear. Lilian spat out the rag.

She knew her mother's voice well enough to know it harboured a smile. Her mother was proud of her, maybe for the first time.

"*Fuluma*! Get out!" Lilian said in a voice that deserved a slap.

Lilian's mother stayed away for two days to allow Lilian's anger to simmer but it continued to boil, fuelled by lack of sleep. On the third day her mother left her a meal and on the fourth she returned to bathe Lilian and shave her head. Lilian didn't put up a fight. She watched her black hair burn in the fire, listening to her mother talk of her own initiation, of the gifts showered upon her and the dancing and drums. The cutter had dunked her in the freezing waters of the River Kapchwaut with her age mates, and they'd waited, their legs splayed for the cutter's knife. Lilian dreamed of knives. Hunting knives and paring knives and rusted blades grown blunt with use. Sometimes the cutter would use them on her and sometimes her mother. They came for fingers and ears and lips.

A week later the cutter took Lilian deep into the bush. She followed the old lady, silent and numb. Nothing was as sweet or pretty as it was before, not the sugar cane her mother brought her or the pink sky. Lilian had felt the seeping wound between her legs and knew that she was hideous.

"There's one last ritual before you go home to heal." The cutter flung a hunk of raw meat on the ground in front of a tent that had been set up in a clearing.

"She's inviting the leopard in," her mother whispered, helping Lilian to the tent. She slid her shawl from her shoulders and balled it into a cushion for Lilian to sit on.

"Turn your right hand over." The cutter showed Lilian the back of her own wrinkled hand, puckered with thin scars.

"It is the last cut," her mother said, "to mark you as Sabiny." She held out the hand Lilian had stroked as a child. *A leopard scratch*, her mother had said, when Lilian had asked about the darkened ridges on the back of her mother's hand. Lilian had stared at her mother in wonder, this brave, strong woman who fought off leopards and had built their mud hut. *She's not brave*, Lilian realised, looking at the stranger who was supposed to be her mother. *She's afraid*. Not of snakes or hard work, but almost everything else: *mzungu*, albinos, her ancestors' spirits, Sunrise's grave and her daughter's reputations. She was scared of books and Lilian's rags drying on the line.

I'm scared too, Lilian wanted to shout. *I'm scared you won't keep your promise and will make me marry an old man*. Lilian swallowed her fear and held out her hand.

"If I do this, we go home and I go back to school."

Chapter 30

Lilian lay on her back and spread her legs.

"You are healing well," her mother said, her voice washed with relief. "I will come to take you home tomorrow and we will not speak of this again." She took a bundle of paper and a stubby pencil from her apron pocket.

"You need to bury your pain." She rested the gift on Lilian's chest.

Lilian unfurled the paper as the door creaked shut. She took a deep breath and tried to let go of her rage. The cutter had marked her, but it was only skin deep. She rolled onto her belly and snatched up the pencil, pain rippling through her. *I am still me, Lilian Chelangat. The cutter has stolen my skin but I still dream the same dreams.*

Lilian wrote through the night – through her rage and fear and pain and sorrow. By the time the pencil was no more than a stub and the candle her mother had left her, a wide wax pool, she was able to write the words *I will try not to hate her*. Lilian wanted to understand why her mother had cut her. Understanding wasn't the same as forgiveness. Lilian didn't know if she'd ever forgive her mother. All she knew was that the hating hurt.

Lilian had hoped her father would be waiting for her when she returned. She was sure he'd know right away that something had shifted. Her face hadn't altered, but there were brackets of worry around her eyes and a hardness to her mouth she was sure he would notice.

"Your taata is in Mukono," her mother said, shaking the dust from her skirt. "Wekesa is inside."

"I thought you were lost." Wekesa threw Lilian a grin.

"Not lost," Lilian said. "Just changed." Wekesa rose from his mat to restring the curtain between their beds. He didn't ask where she'd been.

Lilian picked up her pen and shifted the page so the moon hit the paper. *Once upon a dark time*, she wrote, *a girl lost her voice*. She put down the pen, the months ahead stretched out in front of her, unknowable and empty. *Bury the pain,* her mother had said but she didn't want to bury it. She needed the memory as a reminder. She picked up the pen and let the words draw her back, and in the hours of sitting and writing and trying to make sense of her story, in the failing and trying again, and the tangling and untangling, she began the job of writing herself back together.

Her father returned home two days later. Lilian was sitting in the yard on a carpet of dirt, a book in her lap, a mud doll baking beside her. Wekesa was at school.

"Tiny Mosquito," he called, shuffling into the yard. "Why aren't you in school?"

Lilian's book slid from her lap. She rose from the dirt to run to her father, but slowed to a walk, her scar throbbing, every step like hot chilli being rubbed into the wound. She flung her arms around his neck and tried not to cry. *Do not speak of this to anyone*, her mother had said. Lilian remembered her father in the grain store leafing through Nakato's school books looking for clues. *She didn't say goodbye*, he'd said, burying his face in his hands.

Lilian had never lied to her father.

"The cutter came," she began and her father looked confused.

"She held me down." His mouth fell open.

"I didn't want–" Lilian fell against him, sobbing.

"You were cut?" She could feel his sharp intake of breath. "Your mother was responsible?" He took Lilian by the shoulders and she nodded.

"We're Sabiny." Lilian shrugged. "She said if I didn't ..." She buried her face in his shirt and neither of them spoke for a long time.

"You *are* Sabiny," her father finally said, peeling her off him. "And many moons ago, our chiefs believed we should purify our daughters. *Wonsetibik* became part of our culture but that is no excuse to take a knife to a girl." His face darkened. "Cultures change." He caught sight of Lilian's mother in the garden pulling corn. "If your maama had given birth to the twins thirty years ago, I would have had to run through the village naked. That tradition has thankfully died." He tried to smile. "We break traditions that don't please us and invent new ones to draw us close." He took Lilian's scarred hand in his. "People invent traditions and people discard them. People make a culture. The culture doesn't make us."

Lilian crept to the garden after her father but stopped at the gate. She saw him tear the hoe from her mother's hand, his face like thunder.

"Why?" she heard him say. Her mother whispered a reply.

Lilian crept closer.

"Protect her?" her father growled. "From what?"

Her mother mumbled. Lilian heard the word *kintir* and *another man's bed*.

"In our grandparents' day they extracted teeth." Lilian heard her father say. "Practices die out. We're in Walumira now. You've got to let go. We will still be Sabiny. We will *always* be Sabiny." Her father's anger drained of heat. "It is against the law." He sat down on a log. "It is against nature." He lifted his hand and pulled his wife down to sit beside him.

Lilian had to sneak into the garden to hear what he said next.

"A wife is supposed to find pleasure in her husband's bed."

"Nakato got away before she was cut. I'm glad," Lilian's father said, when they were alone in the grain store. She waited for him to say everything would be okay. *However long the night, the dawn will break*, he'd said after Sunrise died. But he said nothing; just drew her close. After the cutter had sliced Lilian open like a watermelon, her mother had told her she would be okay. The words came too easily and Lilian had wanted to claw at her mother. Her father understood that it *wasn't* okay.

"You and I, we grew up here, far from Mount Elgon. Your mother grew up with the Sabiny and learned how to care for you from them. She carried you on her back and fed you. She kept you safe." He cupped Lilian's chin. "I know you can't forgive her," he said, echoing Lilian's thoughts, "but I hope you are big enough to at least try to understand. She did it because she was scared not to."

"But she watched," Lilian said, "dry-eyed."

"She loves you." Her father stroked her cheek. "She held back her tears to make room for yours."

Lilian pulled away from him. She wasn't ready to forgive her mother and didn't want him to either.

"Life was dangerous for the Sabiny," her father said, sounding tired. "Wild animals prowled the bush and the Karamajong stalked her family. They had to be fearless to survive. To cry was to be weak."

"I saw her." Lilian cut her father off. "I saw Nakato."

Hope sparked in her father's face. "Where? How?"

Lilian didn't have the heart to tell her father where she'd found Nakato or what she did to earn coin.

"I saw her in Kampala." She looped her arm through her father's. "You have another grandson, Taata. And he looks just like you."

Chapter 31

Lilian Chelangat Kwehangana. Lilian put down her pen and stared at the school book which bore her new name. *After a child is circumcised and becomes an adult*, her father had said before he left for Mukono, *their parents are supposed to give them a new name. Kwehangana*, he'd said. *It means to endure. You will*. His face was suddenly serious. *You've always been a fighter. You don't need your grandfather's spear. Your strength is hidden here*. He'd touched her forehead. *You have a good mind*. He reached into his pocket and pulled out a pen, a sleek silver pen, which he handed to her. *Your best weapons are words*.

Lilian slipped the pen into her schoolbag and hurried through the front gate. She'd missed ten days of school but she was going back. *Your father has it in his head that you will go to school*, her mother had grumbled. *I don't know where he will dig up the money*.

Lilian was too sore to ride, so she walked, glad Wekesa hadn't waited for her; it gave her the chance to stop at Madam Kiyonga's shop to post Amara's letter. She used the last of her savings to buy an envelope and stamp, hoping that when she returned to school, she still had a job. She slipped her note to Nakato between the folded pages, addressing the envelope to Amara Bukulu care of Beneh Bukulu, with the words *Feminine Hygiene Products* scrawled across the top. She hoped Amara hadn't given up the search for Nakato.

Taata knows why you left, Lilian wrote to Nakato, *and he's glad you did. He didn't want us to be cut.* Lilian didn't tell Nakato that their father thought she was a dressmaker. *I told him about Joseph and he said you should come live with us.* Lilian's father had said he wouldn't look for his daughter if she didn't want to be found, but if she ever came home, they would make room for her and her boy. *Joseph*, he'd whispered. *That was your great grandfather's name.*

Lilian walked through the school gates, sure everyone could see the truth through her uniform, but when Jemimah asked why she'd been absent, none of the girls blinked when Lilian said *malaria*. Masani ran a hand over Lilian's spikes. "What have you done to your hair?"

Madam Namusisi appeared behind them, holding a broom. "A talkative bird will not build a nest." She stepped between the girls. "It is good to see you back, Lilian." She passed her the broom.

"Do you think she'd have work for me?" Masani asked, following Lilian through the yard to Madam Namusisi's room.

"What? The boys aren't paying?"

"My father is back." Masani's voice was brittle. "So money is tight."

"Your father?" Masani had only ever talked about her mother.

"He's a policeman up north. Comes home twice a year, sells our crop and disappears again."

Lilian bent to scoop a plastic bag from the dirt.

"A friend of mine in Kampala used to make plastic flowers out of these. She stuck them on hairpins. She made good money." She passed Masani the bag and stalked towards Thomas who was slouched against a wall, a pigtailed girl smiling up at him. He had something shiny in his hand and was offering it to her. Lilian stepped between them. "She doesn't want your money," she said, her black eyes fixed on the girl, "because she knows if she takes it, you'll expect something in return."

Lilian spent lunchtime in the library catching up on schoolwork, the words and numbers making so much noise in her head, there wasn't space for her sadness, or the memory of the old woman's cold fingers on her skin.

"Meet at the usual spot after school?" Amal whispered, catching up to her on the oval. He didn't mention Lilian's absence or her shorn head. He didn't ask where she'd been or how she was. *Maybe he knows?* Lilian's heart thudded. No. She could read his face like a book. There was nothing beneath the smile.

Amal tugged on his soccer boots and waited for the ball he knew Mr Chebet would throw him. "Amal will choose first," Mr Chebet announced to no one's surprise. "Thomas, you're captain of the other team."

Amal made his first pick, Ejau, a meaty boy on the school

soccer team. Thomas chose predictably, then Amal chose Benjamin, who wasn't as muscled as Ejau, but fast. Lilian waited while Amal filled his team, each boy smaller and slower and more clumsy than the last, until there were only four students left, Jemimah, Masani, Lilian and Mukisa, who took a puff of his Ventolin and asked, between wheezes, if he had to play. Lilian didn't want to play – running still hurt – but she wanted Amal to choose her, to prove he knew her worth.

He chose Mukisa.

The school gong clanged to mark the end of another day.

"Hey!" Amal jumped on his bike and chased after Lilian. "Wait for me."

Lilian slowed but she didn't stop.

"Don't you want my notes?" He climbed off his bike to walk beside her. "I can tell you what you missed."

"I asked the teacher," Lilian said, "and by the way I'm pretty good at soccer."

"And I bet you'd make a great head girl." He lifted a branch and ducked behind the trees that lined the path. "The announcement is tomorrow."

Head girl. Lilian followed Amal into the bush, whispering the words to the spangled leaves. She imagined stepping onto the podium to shake the principal's hand. She'd been cut and would never be the same, but maybe good things could still happen for her, things to make her forget. "Think I'll win?" she called, forgetting her anger.

"I *know* you will." Amal flashed her a white smile. "I'll be head boy of Senior Two and you'll be head girl. So you want me to catch you up in maths?" Lilian sat cross-legged next to him, the backs of her knees sweaty. She set an exercise book on her lap and flipped it open to an empty page. "Your hands are so small," he said, flattening her hand on the page to trace the outline of her fingers. He rested his hand over hers, his long fingers making hers looks squat, and she wondered whether he could feel the tight ridges of skin beneath his palm.

"We should go," Lilian said, feeling claustrophobic, wishing he'd look up from her legs to her face to look at her, really look at her, and see how much she had changed.

"Of course." He reddened. "You're right. We shouldn't be hiding here like we're doing something wrong. I'll visit when your mother is home. I'll ask her permission."

Permission? Lilian bristled. "I don't need her permission. I can spend time with whoever I want." She grabbed Amal's arm and pulled him close, pressed her lips against his and felt his tongue against her teeth and his hand on her thigh. It was *her* body and she'd decide what to do with it.

Lilian lay on her mat in the dark, Amal's earthy smell on her skin, a ribbon of sweat at her neck. She lifted her skirt and peeled down her knickers. She hadn't let Amal touch her. She'd pulled away after the kiss. She wasn't ready to be touched. She hadn't touched herself. *Amal thinks I'm beautiful*, she reminded herself, forcing her fingers to find her puckered, healing skin. She rubbed softly, slowly, willing her tender skin to grow warm and her breath to quicken. She needed to know that she was still whole, that she could still feel pleasure.

She felt nothing.

Amal stood in the dripping March rain at the entrance to their secret clearing.

"Congratulations!" he said, lifting a wet palm frond to let Lilian through. "I knew you'd do it! You're head girl of Senior Two. Told you." Lilian let his fingers fumble with her buttons and his mouth trail down her neck. He was head boy and she was head girl and she wanted to enjoy it, wanted to feel normal.

"You too," she said, sheltering from the downpour under a fat oak. "Congratulations." She wanted to dissect the election and replay the moment Mr Lubega pinned the gold badge to her collar, but Amal was kissing her mouth and his hands had found her skirt. Lilian closed her eyes and tried to open herself up to him. The cutter's knife had made her numb but she wouldn't be tamed.

"Slow down," Lilian whispered, when his fingers lifted her skirt.

"But I love you," Amal said, his face scraped with longing. "Lala," he whispered, her name intimate in his mouth, "it's okay." She felt his fingers at the elastic of her underpants. "It's okay," he said again, his breath warm on her skin.

But it wasn't. It wasn't okay for Trinah to sit on her teacher's lap. It wasn't okay to force Dimple to undress and it wasn't okay to stuff a rag into Lilian's mouth and force her legs open.

"Amal!" Anger crept into Lilian's voice – anger and fear.

"I'll speak to your father." He reached for his zip. "It's not wrong if we're going to be together forever." He tugged down her underpants and forced her legs apart.

Forever, Lilian faltered. *Forever meant not having to marry a man she didn't know. It meant going to university in Kampala and writing novels while Amal saved lives.*

She didn't fight him. She lay immobile as he struggled out of his pants, his mouth on hers, his tongue insistent. "We'll marry," he said: *said* and not *asked*. And then he was on top of her, heavy as death, and everything turned black and Lilian couldn't breathe or cry out because the cutter was forcing a rag into her mouth.

"No!" Lilian shouted, forcing herself back to the clearing, back to Amal. "No!" She dug her fingers into his arms. "Not like this." She clamped her legs shut and waited for him to roll off her. She hadn't meant to wound him. She just wanted him to slow down. "I'm not ready," she said, as he turned away. "I'm sorry." She reached out to touch him. "I'm just scared."

She waited for him to ask her what she was scared of. *Being touched down there*, she'd say, telling him about the cutter. *Getting pregnant*, she'd whisper, *and dropping out of school. Having babies instead of writing. Becoming your shadow.*

She would have told him everything. If he'd asked.

Chapter 32

Lilian flung herself into her schoolwork. Amal hadn't talked to her for two days. He avoided her in class and rode home with Wekesa when the final bell rang. She caught him staring at her at assembly once, but she couldn't read his face, didn't know whether it was anger or hurt that sat just under his skin. And why shouldn't he be angry? He'd told her he loved her. He said he'd marry her as soon as he finished school. *Said* and not *asked* because he knew her answer would be yes. *Said* and not *asked* because he grabbed what he wanted, and he wanted *her*. And wasn't that what she loved about him? That he didn't wait for good fortune, but went out and found it? Wasn't that what she wanted for herself, to shape her own future and take what was owed to her? To believe in herself as much as *he* believed in her?

Lilian closed her maths book and scanned the library shelves for another book on the human body. She found one she hadn't read – *Diseases in Childhood* – and lifted it from the shelf, her mind still on Amal. So, he hadn't asked why she'd been away. He was smart. He knew she was Sabiny. Maybe he knew what had kept her from school. And if he didn't, why tell him? He didn't need to know she'd been cut to know what type of woman she was. He didn't need a list of her fears to promise he'd protect her from them.

Lilian flipped the book open and sank deep into her seat. She felt safe huddled among the sagging shelves of books, and closer to Sunrise, whose spirit brushed against her every time she turned a page. Lilian started at A – Aids, scanning the diseases that might have killed her sister, searching for one that matched her symptoms. She stopped at *P*.

"Can we ride home and talk?" Amal asked at the end of the day. They pedalled in silence, under the colourless sky, skidding in the slippery mud from yesterday's rain. Lilian was glad the mud slowed them. She was still tender and every pothole made her wince with pain.

"I'm sorry," he said, dumping his bike to stand beside her. He watched her for a moment, and it felt good to be watched, to have his eyes on her again, to be in their secret place. He threaded his fingers through hers. "You were right," he said. "I shouldn't have pushed. It's just when I'm with you. I want to *be* with you. I know you trust me," he said, leaving no space for an answer. "You just want to do this right. And I want that too. I respect you too much to ..." he searched for the right words "to make you do something you're not ready for."

"I'm ready," Lilian shot back. If *he* was ready, then so was she. "It's just ..."

"It's okay," he said, his smile undoing her. "We can take it slow."

The bush was silent, save for the whisper of insects and the squelch of his shoes as he stepped towards her. Lilian wanted to kiss him, wanted to prove she wasn't a child, that she could take what she wanted without being scared. She touched her hand to his shirt and felt his heart pounding.

"Slow," he whispered, his hand disappearing under her sleeve to toy with a bra strap. He waited a beat, then tugged the strap down. "We'll be careful."

Lilian found a fallen log and sat down. She couldn't think straight with his hands on her skin. "I don't want to get pregnant."

"Neither do I."

She thought of his baby growing inside her.

"Accidents happen."

They were both silent for a moment.

"I won't leave you with a baby if that's what you're worried about." Amal squatted beside her. "I told you this is forever. Whatever happens I'll take care of you." He grabbed her hand. "There's a hut at the back of my parents' plot. It will be mine one day. You could stay there. It'll be tough for a few years but once I'm a doctor ..." His face grew serious. "I'll take care of you." Lilian knew that he meant it, and it broke her heart into a thousand small pieces.

"I don't want to have a baby. I want to finish school." Sadness lodged between her ribs. *Please tell me you know that.* "I want to be a–"

"I know," he said, brushing a mosquito away. "You want to be a teacher."

"A writer," Lilian said, but he didn't hear her. *I want to be a writer.* She was sure she'd told him.

"My mum's a teacher's aide. As soon as my sister started senior school, she got a job at Walumira Primary."

"So, I finish school and have babies?" Lilian felt winded. "And after we're done having babies I get a job as a teacher's aide?"

"Only if you want to," Amal rushed to reassure her. "I'll be making lots of money, you won't have to–"

"Work?" A terrible understanding unfurled inside her.

"Yeah." His face creased in confusion. "What's wrong?" There was an edge to his voice, a creeping impatience.

"So *you're* going to be a doctor," Lilian took a deep breath, "and I'll *marry* a doctor."

"Isn't that what you want?" Amal looked wounded.

"I want the same things *you* want." Lilian found her voice. "I want to finish top of the class. I want to be head student in Senior Six. I want *you*," Lilian said, touching his arm, "but I also want to go to university."

"Why?" The question hung in the air. "I know you're smart. You're head girl," he said, as if that were enough. "I like that you're smart. That's why I chose you and not one of those empty-headed girls. I can talk to you." He urged her on to her back. "But can we stop talking now?" He didn't tell her he loved her.

He pushed her dress up and pressed his hips against hers. His eyes were glazed, looking through her, or past her, at this thing they were doing. She saw it too, as if crouched high in a tree: Amal mashed against her, reaching for his zip.

She shoved him away with the heel of her hand.

"What's wrong?" Amal stared at her, uncomprehending. "I told you I loved you."

"You say you love me but you don't *know* me."

"I know you," he said, "and I know what you want. It's not going to happen." The pity in his voice was terrible. "How many girls from around here go to university, Lala?" He didn't wait for her answer. "I am not trying to hurt you but you have to be real. You'd be competing to get into Makerere with boys from all over Uganda. And even if I helped you and you got in, your taata can't afford to send you to university. They'll want you to work." He looked at her, unblinking. "Then they'll marry you off to some rich old man. I'm offering you a way out."

Lilian stared at him, her eyes huge in the dim light. He'd never lied to her, never pretended he was anything but this: a boy who wanted a girl to stand *behind* him. Someone smart enough to recognise his brilliance but not too smart. Someone he could teach. Someone sweet and compliant. She just hadn't let herself see it. All she'd seen was her Prince Charming, a brilliant boy who would build her a house full of books. She'd written the part for him – and he'd played it well – but she didn't *want* to be saved. She didn't want his idea of a happily ever after.

"I just want–" she struggled for the right words. She wanted to talk and have him listen. She wanted him to *see* her.

"We'd be happy," Amal said. "Living in the city and eating meat every day. You know I'd be good to you."

"And I'd be expected to be a good wife. What if I don't want to be a good wife?" Lilian felt a swell of anger. "What if I don't like washing dishes?"

Amal threw his head back and laughed.

"And you still haven't asked–"

"Asked what?" Amal looked hopeless and that made it worse. "Is this about that club you're in? No, it's about that soccer game. You're still angry I didn't choose you."

"Yes," she said, knowing it sounded silly and small. "But it's more than that. It's the fact you never ask for help with English and assume I want your help with maths. It's every conversation we have and all the ones we don't. I'm sorry," she said, getting to her feet. "I can't be who you want me to be."

"I don't want you to be anyone, except who you are right now."

"I know," Lilian said, "but I want to be *more*."

A lizard clung to the wall of Lilian's bedroom, its black eyes glued to her, its grey tail flicking from side to side like a teacher's wagging finger. *This is bullshit!* Lilian could still hear Amal's voice, blistering with anger. *Are you breaking up with me? You don't get to break up with me. You don't get to lead me on and then walk away.* Lilian had watched him grab his bike and drag it from the clearing. *You don't get to dump me, Lala,* he'd yelled over his shoulder. *I dump you.*

"You are home late." Lilian's mother dragged the curtain aside.

"Sorry. I stayed late at school." Lilian wiped her eyes with the back of her hand. "I wanted to do some reading." She took a deep breath. "I've been trying to work out why Sunrise died."

"Don't." Her mother stiffened.

"Maama, I know–" Lilian wanted to say *that you blame yourself*, but her mother reared at her.

"What do you know? Say it." Spit gathered at the corners of her mouth. "Go on, say it. It was all my fault. My fault," she whispered, her chest heaving, her fingers finding the worn leather pouch under her apron.

"But it *wasn't* your fault," Lilian said, pressing a sheet of paper into her mother's hand.

When Lilian emerged from the hut, the sky was darkening. She stood watching the fire sizzle, wondering whether her mother had fed her words to the flames. Lilian had only gotten through a few words – *I think it might have been pneumonia* – when her mother stormed out.

When the sky turned black Lilian's mother joined her, standing back from the fire, a black shape in the dark. A huge moon came up and they stood under it, neither of them speaking, the only sound the quiet bleat of a goat and the wind singing in the shadows.

"Lilian," her mother said, in a voice she didn't recognise. "I can't ..." She held out the page, trying to make out the muddle of letters in the moon's slanting light.

Lilian stood beside her and peered down at the page. "Pneumonia," Lilian cleared her throat, "is an inflammatory condition. That means swelling." She couldn't meet her mother's eye. Lilian scanned the page, saw the hulking four syllable words and thought of Sunrise buried underground, waiting for her mother's footsteps. "It says," Lilian slid her fingers over the words and pretended to read, " it is caused by a virus and hurts millions of people, especially in Africa, and especially children." She didn't tell her mother you could get a vaccine to prevent it. She didn't tell her if it was bad, you went to hospital where the doctors made you better, because they didn't have money for needles or doctors. All they had was God, the witchdoctors and their ancestral spirits.

Lilian remembered her mother offering the spirits food in exchange for her dead daughter and her desperate attempts to wake Sunrise up. "It says," she reached for her mother's hand, "that pneumonia is a medical illness and *not* a curse."

Chapter 33

Lilian didn't sleep that night. She lay in the dark worrying what Amal would say when he saw her at school, what he would do, who he would tell. She needn't have worried. He didn't look at her or talk to her and Masani had heard nothing about what had transpired between them. *And if I haven't heard about it,* Masani reassured her, *then no one knows.*

Lilian and Amal spent lunchtime in the library, bent over their desks, the air crackling between them, in a race to top their class. Lilian needed to be the top student, now more than ever, not just to beat Amal, but to prove to her parents that she was deserving of an education. She watched the Senior Six girls move down the library's aisles in their long sleeves and long socks and itched to carry a bag as heavy as theirs.

The days snaked past, one after the other, dragging her sadness away with them, so that after a time Lilian could look at Amal without feeling something had been stolen from her. Loving a boy was too dangerous: you had to give away too much and she was tired of giving. Tired of giving her brother the biggest helping of dinner and washing his uniform, tired of crawling out of bed to plant cassava while he slept. The pink-gold sky – and time with her mother – made it worthwhile. Her mother never mentioned Lilian's note or the pneumonia. She didn't ask about school or mention what had happened in Jjaja Wange Olufeni's hut, but Lilian felt a shift in her mother, a black sadness lifting. She saw her handwritten note poking from under her mother's sleeping mat and once, when she visited Sunrise, found a bunch of wildflowers on her sister's grave. Two days later, when they stood fanning the flames of the fire Lilian saw her mother's pouch – the one she believed had killed her daughter – stuffed under a burning log. Neither of them said anything as they watched it blacken to ash, but that evening Lilian's mother let the lantern burn late into the night so Lilian could read.

She let her cradle a book in her lap while she fed twigs to the flames and take her schoolbag with her when she set off to milk the cow.

Read books that will inspire you, Madam Namusisi had said, handing Lilian a library bag. *And bring what you learn to Empowerment Club.* So she read NoViolet Bulawayo and Mariama Bâ, marking the best pages to read to the younger girls. She pulled the ragged paperbacks from her library bag and the girls clustered around her, heads tilted, eyes wide. They were like the sponges from the laffa trees that grew wild in the forest, absorbing new words and mopping up sentences.

Lilian filled them with stories, filled herself up too, the printed words staying with her long after she closed the books.

When you are ready, Madam Namusisi had said, pointing to a shelf in the library piled high with newspapers, *read these*. Lilian read the articles, her heart knocking against her chest. Forcing a child to marry was against the law. Teachers weren't allowed to touch students and women had a right to share their husband's wealth. Education was a right, for girls as much as boys, and cutting was illegal – and punishable by law.

Lilian had heard Madam Namusisi say these things, but seeing the words in print, in a national paper, seeing it typed in black-and-white made Lilian want to do something – write something – important, something from a place deep inside, where the darkest words hid. She didn't keep her writing hidden. If her mother had asked, she would have read the pages to her. *They're not make-believe*, she would have told her mother *I'm just writing what I see*. She saw drunken fathers and daughters with black eyes and teenagers forced to marry. She saw girls carrying babies on their backs instead of schoolbags, but she also saw women wearing soccer boots. She saw girls writing speeches and women delivering laundry and her mother, who had lost everything, get up and start again.

"If you don't want me talking to other girls, just say so." Thomas slunk up to Lilian as she yanked her bag from its hook. "You don't have to worry. I'm still interested in you." He held out a small white box.

Lilian lifted her eyes from the gift. "*You* might be interested," she said. "I'm not."

"So you keep saying, and then you get angry when I flirt with other girls. What's that about?" He opened her bag and dropped the box into it.

"The girl with the pigtails?" Lilian sneered. "I felt sorry for her. The thought of you kissing anyone makes me feel ..." She tried to twist away but Thomas pinned her to the wall.

"You think about me kissing other girls? Or kissing you?" He pressed against her, his face dangerously close.

"Get your hands off my friend!" Masani's voice cut through the yard. She charged towards them, aiming a book at Thomas's head.

"I was just leaving." He stepped away, his voice dripping with contempt. "She's not my type. Anyway, everyone knows she's spoiled goods. What?" he scowled at Lilian. "You think Amal was in love with you?"

Lilian flinched.

"He was just practising. Same as me."

Practising? Lilian felt as though she'd been punched in the heart. She watched Thomas walk towards a group of sniggering boys, heard the word *spoiled* and saw a boy high-five him. *Spoiled*. Nakato was spoiled. What did that even mean? Nakato did what she had to, to feed her boy. Was Amara spoiled? She was married to a rich man, but she was just as broken.

"Let's go home." Masani took Lilian's arm. "We can go the back way."

"I'm not spoiled," Lilian whispered. She'd kissed Amal, but she wasn't spoiled. He didn't have that power; she'd *chosen* to kiss him. And even if she hadn't, even if he *had* stolen her first kiss, he couldn't ruin her. The cutter had stolen her skin, but she was still whole. Every touch, every insult, every mark on her body, made her stronger.

"So ... home?" Masani asked.

"No," Lilian said, making her voice hard. "I'm not going to hide. I've done nothing wrong." She grabbed Thomas's gift and stalked to the gate, vibrating with anger.

"Hey, Tom," she called, "I don't accept gifts." Ten razored heads swivelled towards her as she crossed the yard to drop the box at his feet. "If you want me to tutor you in maths," she spoke loud enough for everyone to hear, "I want cash."

Lilian rode home from school slowly. She was still tender, but she felt strong. Thomas wouldn't bother her again and she was done with Amal.

"Taata!" Lilian leaped off her bike as she rounded the path and caught sight of home. "Taata, you're back!" She ran towards the fire, ignoring their guest and the smell of roasting chicken.

"Let me take your bag," her father said, ducking a hug. "It looks heavy."

"That's because it's full of books. I've been reading, Taata. Books by African authors." She glanced back at the stranger who'd stopped talking to watch her. "*The Daily Monitor* too."

"Lilian," her mother frowned, "we have a visitor."

Lilian dropped to her knees, as she'd been taught and introduced herself. "*Ono ye Muwala wange*, Lilian."

The man slid the last of the meat into his mouth and sucked his fingers. He had thick glasses and thinning hair. He looked bookish, Lilian thought. A professor from the university? Her heart drummed fast. She'd heard stories of boys given scholarships to university, had their housing paid for, even their meals.

"I'm head girl of Senior Two and class–"

"If I could just have a minute?" Lilian's father took her by the arm. "I should have said something," he whispered, hurrying her to the fence.

"It's okay, Taata, I don't need to prepare. I can show him my reports and answer his questions."

"His questions?"

"He'll want to know if I'm up to the university's standards." Lilian's voice faltered. "Unless he's not from Makerere?" She held onto her smile. "Where's he from then? A boarding school?"

Her father's face fell. "He's been paying for your education." His voice was flat. "When you came back from Kampala your mother wanted to keep you home, but I couldn't let you stop school, you were doing so well."

"I still am."

Her father studied the dead watch on his wrist. "I didn't have any money. He's a friend of Uncle Lwanga's, a carpenter from Mukono. He agreed to pay for school."

Lilian stared at her mother. She was talking to their guest

but her smile was tight. *There will be boys who want to help you and give you things. Nothing is free*, her mother had told her. Lilian shivered.

"I have to thank him," she said, but she didn't move.

"He paid," her father said, sounding old and tired, "on condition that you marry."

Lilian felt a door slam shut. "You said you'd fix things." She flinched at her father's touch. "You said you wanted me to go to university. I thought you meant it." She shook him off. The man was staring at her, but she didn't care.

"I did," her father silenced her, "things have changed." His mouth sagged. "I'm sorry, Tiny Mosquito. I wanted better for you. I wanted more."

"How is marrying an old man *more*?" Lilian saw her father's eyes grow damp but she couldn't stop. She'd never felt so alone. "How is forcing me to—"

"It was meant to be a loan. I was going to pay him back ..."

"So, let's pay him!" Lilian grabbed her father's hand. "You must have saved something?" She tugged at his pocket.

"Tiny Mosquito." Her father turned his pockets out.

Lilian stared at his empty palms.

"You still have your job." She held back the tears. "I've got one too. I'll get a second one."

Her father shook his head. "He's tired of waiting."

The man left a bag for her, a small black suitcase with metal clips, and money for a dress.

Can she at least finish the year? her father had asked. She hated to see him beg but she had no space for pity. Her father had betrayed her.

I'll be back in a week, the man had said. *No point putting it off. I'm not getting any younger.*

Chapter 34

"Who was that?" Wekesa drew aside the sheet. Lilian lay on her mat, her knees pulled to her chest, her eyes shut tight. Her breath came in sobs. "He's–" She blotted the tears from her face with her sleeve and tried again. "He's going to be my–" Her mouth wouldn't form the words.

"Oh," he said, his mouth tightening. "When?"

He backed away from her, steeling himself. *For another goodbye?* Lilian wondered. She'd never thought losing his sisters may have scarred Wekesa in some way, but she could see now, it had. That he'd pulled away from her when she'd grown curves to protect himself from the pain of another sister lost. A memory unfolded: Wekesa up a tree, his legs wound around a branch, his eyes narrowed, searching for Nakato. And then another that made Lilian flinch: her brother wrenching his hand from hers at Sunrise's burial and running towards the open grave.

"Out! I need to talk to Lilian." Her mother swept Wekesa from the room. Lilian had nothing to say to her. She had cried and begged and threatened to run away, but her mother had been unmoved. *He's a stranger*, Lilian had finally said. *I don't love him. I don't know him.*

Love? Her mother had looked at her with something close to pity. *What does love have to do with it?*

"Marry him," Lilian's mother said, looking at Lilian, not through her, or past her but into her eyes. "Don't run away. Sunrise's death tore your father apart and then when," she swallowed, "Nakato left ..." The name sounded strange in her mother's mouth. "He won't survive losing you ... losing this ..." Her eyes travelled from the mud brick walls to the thatch shot through with starlight. "It is all we have."

"It's all we'll *ever* have if I marry that man."

"What's done is done." Her mother squared her shoulders. "You're sixteen, boys will be sniffing around. Now you'll be safe."

"Safe?" Lilian's voice splintered. "He could take another wife." She pictured Amara alone in Beneh's house. "I don't want to wait for handouts from a husband. I want to be able to buy my own things and if he beats me," she said, hoping to spark some regret in her mother, "I want to be able to leave."

Her mother was quiet. "He is rich," she finally said. "If you are good to him and do as he says, after you have his babies, he might give you money for school."

"I'm not for sale," Lilian said, looking straight at her mother. "Things are changing, Maama. This is *my* time. *You* did something big. You escaped the Karamajong and came here and built a life. Let *me* do something big. You taught me to be brave. Let me be the first girl in this village to finish school." Lillian thought she saw her mother nod. "Let me be the first girl in Walumira to go to university."

Lilian gazed down at her hand, surprised to see her fingers entwined with her mother's. "Remember the first time I had to go to the well by myself? It was after Goodness left?"

Her mother listened through half-closed eyes.

"You told me that to get lost is to learn the way. Let me learn the way, Maama, by myself."

"I'm sorry," her mother said, pulling her hand from Lilian's. "There's no undoing it."

She lifted the curtain.

"You can't do this, Maama. *He* can't do this. Marrying a sixteen-year-old is against the law. We'll pay him back when we can. There's nothing he can do."

"But he can." Her mother said. "He can sell the land. Your father had to sign some papers before he got the school fees."

"And if I don't?"

There was no light in her mother's eyes, and no fight. "It will all be his ... the land, the huts. There will be no more school for you or your brother. We will have to leave Sunrise and move to the slums."

Lilian walked to her aunt's hut, the sky grubby with clouds, the stars above hard and bright. She'd always been able to puzzle out the answer to the most difficult problems, but this ... Lilian felt a pit crack open under her feet. There was no way out. If she refused to marry, her family would be homeless and her brother chased from school. *He's not a bad man*, her mother had said. Was that the best Lilian could hope for? A man who wasn't bad? A man who *might* not beat her? *Go to Afia*, her mother had said, dabbing at Lilian's eyes with her apron. *The introduction is in a week. There is a lot for you to learn.* Lilian didn't want to learn how to please a husband. She didn't *want* a husband, but she did as her mother asked because, what choice did she have?

Uncle Lwanga answered the door and threw his arms around Lilian. He seemed to think it was a *good* piece of news. "So there's to be a wedding in the family. My friend and my niece. Two of my favourite people."

Ajani waved his congratulations and Mirembe slipped a ring from a can of Coke onto Lilian's finger.

"Will there be a party?" MoreBlessing asked. "Can I get a new dress?"

"We'll see," Afia said, shepherding the children to bed.

"I know you don't want this." She poured them each a cup of ginger tea. "He is a little older than you would have chosen but he's a *Mubazzi*. Carpenters make good coin and you'll be his first wife."

"We need to postpone the wedding," Lilian interrupted. "If I finish school, I'll have some power over him. He wouldn't beat a woman who brings in money." She kneeled beside her aunt. "Please, Aunty. Lwanga knows him. He could ask him to wait."

Afia drained her cup and set it on the table. "I'm sorry, Lilian, your father already asked Lwanga and he tried. Bukenya won't go for it."

Bukenya. Lilian swallowed the scalding tea. She hadn't wanted to give a name to the man who would shackle her. *A man of thirty or forty,* her mother had told her, *with strong bones and good teeth, well fed on milk and meat.*

"A carpenter can build you a solid home," Afia continued. "Better than a barman who smells of booze or a mechanic whose clothes are filthy. Too much laundry." Afia's smile faded when she saw Lilian's wet cheeks. "He won't cause you trouble if you keep him happy. Men are simple creatures. Feed them, give them babies and they'll do what you want."

"Bukenya's here." Lilian's mother told her the next day when she found her in the shadow cast by the mvule's gnarled trunk. "He's talking to Taata." Lilian felt as if she'd been emptied of air. As if she were a ghost. She would soon be split in half by a man she didn't know. *Bukenya will open your legs,* Afia's voice returned to haunt her, *and push himself inside you. You'll bleed. Don't wash the sheets.*

"I wanted to give you this," her mother said, handing her a small package wrapped in newspaper.

A wedding gift. Lilian turned it over. *The first present her mother had ever given her.* Lilian wished it was for Christmas or because she'd done well at school. A celebration of something, instead of a consolation prize.

"Open it."

Lilian peeled away the wrapping and lifted a pen from a mountain of paper, unsure what to say.

"We should join the men," her mother said, looking deflated. She handed Lilian a dress without holes. "Put this on. And no sad face. In a few days Bukenya's family will come. Afia will be there and all your cousins."

Lilian slipped the yellow dress over her head.

"I only had Amara at my *Kwanjula*. Maama was dead. So was Baako."

"What about your taata?" Lilian fastened her buttons. "Did he come for the wedding?"

Her mother stuffed Lilian's work dress into a bag. "He was killed three days after we left Mount Elgon." She knotted the bag and dumped it by the tree. "Bukenya can feed you and look after your children. You're luckier than most."

Marrying at sixteen and having a stranger claim you like a prize wasn't luck but Lilian would do as her mother asked because it was her mother who had planted the garden, made sure they had clean water and kept the thatch from falling in. Her father had sent Lilian to school but her mother had raised her, the best she knew how. *I owe her.* Lilian stood up. *She fed me and bathed me and taught me to walk.*

They walked to the yard together and there was some comfort in that. Rounding the hut, Lilian glimpsed her father hunched by the flames. She had seen him in the dark days after

Nakato disappeared, had seen him slumped by the fire, not talking or eating. *I've lost one daughter,* she'd heard him rail at the sky, *why must you take another?*

She wouldn't make him lose a third child. *If I run,* she forced herself to bow to Bukenya, *Taata will have* two *daughters to search for.* She wiped her eyes with the back of her hand. She had no choice. If she didn't go with Bukenya, her family would lose everything: the cassava, the bananas, their home and Jjaja's hut. Lilian looked at the bags of sugar and boxes of soap Bukenya had brought to seal their bloodline. He'd already paid for her with a year of schooling.

"This makes it official," her mother whispered, encouraging Lilian to take her father's place by the fire.

"Would you like tea?" Lilian offered, when her parents left them to talk. She wished she hadn't put on the yellow dress. It looked like she cared, like she'd dressed up for him.

Lilian stared at the flames. *Who would she become once she had a new name? Would Bukenya let her read? Would he let her visit Dimple? What if Nakato came back?* Fear jagged through her.

"It is good," Bukenya said, in rusty English, "that you know what I want." Lilian looked up from the fire. "I live in Mukono, but I don't want a modern girl. I don't want a *Mukyala* who puts on make-up and goes dancing. I want someone to bring up my boys." He spoke without feeling. "I make good coin. You won't need to work." He picked up a branch and poked the fire. He didn't stare at her legs, like Thomas, or sidle up close to her, like Amal. This was business.

"Do you read?" Lilian asked.

"I read ... things," he said, but he didn't say what.

Lilian dragged her eyes from his balding head. There was nothing to fall in love with here, no conversation, no love of literature, no hair.

"*Osiibye otya nno?*"

Lilian turned at the sound of her uncle's voice.

"I heard you were here." Lwanga shook Bukenya's hand. "Thought I'd come say hello. Well, look at *you!*" Lwanga stuck two fingers between his lips and whistled at Lilian. "I told you she was beautiful." He slapped his friend on the back.

"They are all beautiful," Bukenya sneered, "until they open their mouths to speak."

Five days later, a letter arrived. Lilian held the envelope in her trembling hands. It was postmarked Kampala.

Maybe it's money. A wedding gift from Beneh, Lilian's mother said, waiting for her to tear it open. But it wasn't from Beneh. Lilian knew his brash script and it wasn't from Kamali. Lilian knew her handwriting too. *I have to go pee*, Lilian lied, escaping to the latrine. She hid behind the mud hut and, listening for footsteps, tore the envelope open, her heart beating hard as though she'd been running.

I heard about the wedding. Your mother called from Madam Kiyonga's shop, the note began. It was from Amara. Lilian had hoped it would be from Nakato. *You don't have to do it*. Lilian read the sentence twice, wanting to believe it, willing it to be true.

"But I do," she whispered, sagging against the wall.

You don't, she imagined Amara's reply. *When Nakato left your parents survived.*

"Yes," Lilian said to the sky and the trees. "When Nakato left, she stole Taata's sleep. If *I* run away, he'll lose everything."

You can stay here, Lilian returned to her aunt's letter. *You can stay with me until you work out what to do. Beneh hasn't been here in weeks. He won't know.* Lilian turned the page over. *I'm still washing laundry. I have two girls working for me and have enough to feed both of us. You could try for a scholarship and finish school.* Lilian's grip on the paper tightened. The only children she knew on scholarships were children who had lost both parents or were battling Aids. Children worse off than her.

I made a mistake. Lilian traced Amara's words, imagining her aunt, leaking miserable tears. *I convinced myself I'd grow to love Beneh, and that I'd be happy if I had a house with windows and a cupboard full of shoes. It wasn't enough. Stay in school*, she wrote in a trembling script. *I'll do whatever I can to help. Don't marry him.* She signed it, *With love, Amara.* And there was a postscript.

PS: I gave Nakato your letter. I saw her last month. She came to the house. She was thin and looked tired but she is doing better. She's not working there anymore. Amara didn't say where *there* was, but Lilian knew. *She wouldn't take any money. She lives with Joseph at the back of a dress shop. She does the alterations. She wanted you to know she is doing okay.*

Chapter 35

Lilian sat cross-legged on her mat, the suitcase open on the ground beside her. The smell of roasting meat filled the hut, but Lilian wasn't hungry. She picked up a dress furred with dust, dropped it into the empty case, and took another from the shopping bag that served as her cupboard. She wondered if Goodness had felt this low in the long days and nights before her marriage. She'd never thought to ask.

Her father poked his head into the room. "Do you have anything for the car?" He looked apologetic.

She pointed to her schoolbag. "You can take that. And those." She nodded towards the stack of books and papers she'd piled on the floor: battered exercise books filled with tumbling paragraphs, a bruised dictionary that she'd salvaged from a bin and the stories she had written to knit herself back together after she'd been cut.

She lifted the stack from the floor and dumped it in her father's arms. Her cheeks were wet, but she didn't dry them. She wanted him to see how broken she was.

"I don't know how to stop dreaming for things, Taata. I'm trying but I don't know how to stop wanting."

Lilian waited for her father's advice. She knew it would come, as it always did, wrapped in a riddle or cloaked in a story but he didn't say anything. He'd run out of words.

The last thing Lilian put in her suitcase was a banana fibre doll. She knew it would be crushed inside the case, its stone eyes lost in the folds of her skirt, its painted mouth smeared. If she could have grabbed a handful of red dirt and tossed a bit of Walumira into the suitcase, she would have. She closed the lid and snapped the metal clasps shut. It would be a comfort to open her suitcase in Bukenya's home and find her clothes smelling of wet soil and banana. She'd sit at Bukenya's table with the doll's lipstick smeared on her shirt and its pebble eyes in her pockets, the smell of home clinging to her skin.

"Are you alone?" Wekesa lifted the sheet strung between their mats.

"For now," Lilian said, "Bukenya's outside."

"Madam Namusisi keeps asking why you are away." Wekesa tugged the sheet from the twine that cut a swathe through their room and handed it to her. "She wants to know when you'll be back."

Lilian had made her brother promise he wouldn't tell. There was nothing Madam Namusisi could do, except cause trouble. "She said the Easter assembly is in a few weeks and as head girl of Senior Two you'll be expected to speak."

Lilian grabbed his shirt. "Speak? About what?"

Her brother shrugged. "She said you and Amal both get three minutes to address the school. Should I tell her you can't?"

Lilian opened the suitcase and smoothed the sheet over the crumbling doll. There wouldn't be any more speeches. She was about to leave home to start a life she didn't want with a man she didn't know. She closed the lid. "Don't say anything."

"The guests will be here soon." Lilian's mother stopped Lilian as she dragged her case through the yard. Her work dress was streaked with dust and her feet were bare. "It's time you got dressed," she spoke softly, handing Lilian a package wrapped in brown paper. Her mother had asked if she wanted to go to town to buy a *gomesi*.

I didn't choose the husband, Lilian had grumbled, *so why choose the wedding dress?*

Lilian ripped open the package and saw the stiff red *gomesi*, her mother had bought with their best laying hens.

"Lilian!" Afia swept into the yard, wearing a dress the colour of the sun and a head wrap to match. Lwanga walked beside her, a tangle of children between them.

"*Lunaku lukuulu*." Lwanga trumpeted his congratulations. He delivered Dembe from his shoulders and shook the dust from the white *kanzu* he wore over his pants. "Are we the only ones to put on church clothes?" He looked Lilian up and down.

"She will dress after she bathes." Afia grabbed Lilian's dress and led her to the bathroom. "It is my job, as your *Ssenga*, to prepare you, just as I did your sister," she said, undressing Lilian and lifting a bucket over her head.

Lilian stood with her back to her aunt, so Afia wouldn't see her tears. When she'd been scrubbed of her childhood – and the smells of home – she followed Afia to the small fire Lwanga had lit behind the latrine. She stood there naked, her hands splayed across her groin, while Afia emptied a goatskin pouch over the blaze.

The herbs crackled and spat. "For a happy union and fertility," Afia whispered, guiding Lilian to stand naked over the blistering wood. "Let the smoke rise up into you."

Lilian returned to the yard, smelling of ash.

"I asked you to be quick. The boy and his family are here soon. Put on your dress," her mother scolded, squeezing her swollen feet into blue high heels. Lilian couldn't remember the last time she'd seen her mother dressed in a *gomesi* that skimmed the ground. She would have been pretty in the floral dress if her face wasn't warped by worry.

Lilian let Afia put make-up on her face.

"Blush," Afia called, palm up, and Lilian rummaged in her aunt's bag for what she thought might be blush. Mascara, eyeliner, lipliner, setting powder. Lilian handed them over, one by one, holding her face up to the light so Afia could see how best to mask her sorrow and conceal her fear.

"Bukenya is a lucky man." Afia held up a mirror when her work was done. Lilian waved it away. Her reflection, had she dared to look, would have been the woman Bukenya would marry: a blank canvas slathered with tinted creams and powders. A picture painted to please a man.

Finally, when she could put it off no longer, Lilian climbed into the stiff red dress, holding out her arms so Afia could feed them into sleeves. "Come on, now," Afia said gently, dabbing at Lilian's eyes. "Your mascara will run and I'll have to do your face again. You will be fine," she said, stuffing her handkerchief back into her bra. "I taught you how to handle a man in bed, and if you do anything wrong, I will be there to guide you." Lilian knew she wouldn't be left alone with Bukenya on her wedding night. Afia had told her that she would accompany Lilian and her husband to their new home. *I will sit in the corner and only speak if you are not pleasing him. What?* Afia had asked, seeing the horror on Lilian's face. *You don't want him to return you.*

"It's not that." Lilian slid her feet into shoes. "It is just ... I don't—"

"Love him?" Afia straightened her sash. "I didn't love Lwanga. I worked on loving him." She walked to the door. "It takes time, Lilian. Come, your man's family is arriving."

Lilian could hear laughter and someone playing a drum. There would be a wedding today. Lilian would marry Bukenya and after the *Kwanjula* would receive God's blessing in her husband's church. His *blessing*. She tried to make her mind go blank, tried biting her lip so that pain blunted thought. She couldn't step into the celebration bleary-eyed. Her mother was already nervous; her father hadn't smiled in days. If she stood next to Bukenya in tears, it would only make things worse.

She followed Afia to the doorway.

Three cars and an open-air truck had parked by the fence and Lilian watched as Bukenya's family poured into the yard, the women dressed in a rainbow of colours and the men in white *kanzus* worn over long, black pants. Afia fled the tent to lift a papyrus basket from a young girl's head, but Lilian hovered at the door, listening to the sounds of a wedding: jangling bangles, the scrape of chairs and the drums that would tell the story of her wedding day. A boy lugging a tent waved at her. She didn't wave back. Someone had carried a faded green armchair into the middle of the yard and Lilian's father sat in it, his lips pressed into a hard line. Lilian looked for her cousins and found Mirembe and MoreBlessing weaving between the guests, clipping knotted ribbons to shirts. And then there was Bukenya, sitting at the back of a large tent, bent over his laces, his thinning, damp hair stuck to his head. Lilian's stomach knotted tight.

"It is a shame Goodness couldn't come," Afia said, shepherding Lilian and her mother into the yard, "she is due any day and probably big as a drum." She plucked a basket from the ground and inspected the contents. "Bread, salt, sugar, paraffin." She shuffled the gifts around. "And soap." She lifted a bar furred with red dirt from its basket.

Lilian stepped into the sunshine and scanned the yard. Girls with hair in bright wrappers stood in the muggy heat, busy with talk. Dimple wasn't among them. Lilian wished she hadn't kept the wedding a secret. She'd tried to tell Dimple, but the words wouldn't come. Pinning a date to the ceremony would have made it real, and there was a part of Lilian that, even now, hoped for a twist to the story – a happily ever after instead of a night in a dark hut.

A man with a head smooth as polished stone shook Wekesa's hand and gave him a chicken, and then a boda boda puttered to a stop outside the thorn fence. "I thought she would stay home," Lilian heard her mother whisper as Afia waved Amara over.

They watched her walk towards them. She wore flat shoes and a simple black dress – the kind women wore to funerals. Her hair had been cut short.

"I know Beneh gave our apologies," Amara said, kissing Lilian's mother on the cheek, "but I *had* to come." She wrapped Lilian in a hug. "We have to talk," she whispered. Lilian couldn't hear what she said next. Isaac Mwanga's fists were pounding the drums and Lilian's neighbours had leaped from their chairs.

A line formed, Afia at its head and Patience Ssegobe at the tail, the stomp of dancing feet swallowing Amara's words. Lilian watched it snake its way to the guests' tent, the women rolling their hips and waving their arms in time to the beat.

"Go inside," Lilian's mother shouted, over the whooping and clapping. "After the women greet our guests, Afia will come get you."

"I'll go with her," Amara said, taking Lilian's hand.

"Coming through!" Lwanga sang out, pushing past them into the hut. He grabbed the edge of Lilian's sleeping mat and whipped it from the floor. A pile of coins and notes lay scattered in the dust. Lilian dropped to her knees to scoop them up. She had saved ten thousand shillings working for Madam Namusisi but it wasn't enough to buy her life back, not even with Amara's ring, which she'd buried in the ground the day she got home.

"Don't take it, Uncle." Lilian reached for the mat. What if I come back? I might visit."

"It has to be burned." Lwanga eased the mat from her. "It is part of the *Kwanjula*."

Lilian stared at the knotted fibres. Had she remembered wrong? She closed her eyes and saw the fire licking the corners of Nakato's mat. Maybe it hadn't burned the night Nakato fled. Maybe what Lilian had witnessed all those years ago was Goodness's mat going up in flames the night she was to be wed? Lilian loosened her grip. Maybe her mother hadn't been incensed by Nakato's disappearance, just wounded.

"You'll have a new home and a new bed." He tucked the mat under his arm. "If you still had a resting place in your parents' home, you'd fly back at the first sign of trouble."

"Trouble?" Lilian's eyes grew wide.

"Well, not *trouble*." Lwanga waved away her concern. "Bukenya can be a bit pig-headed sometimes. He likes to have the last word." Lwanga lifted the curtain to leave. "His bark is worse than his bite."

His bite. Lilian could feel her eyes welling. Amara held her arms out and Lilian fell into them, her body heaving under her silk wedding dress.

"Shhh," Amara whispered, taking her gently by the shoulders. "It will be okay."

"No," Lilian said, her sadness spilling out of her. "You don't understand. He's been paying for school. If I don't marry him, we lose everything."

"I know," Amara said, pulling Lilian onto the floor to sit

beside her. "Your mother told me. How much do you owe him?"

Lilian whispered the obscene number in Amara's ear. "He'll throw my parents on the street," she said again. "I don't have a choice."

Amara's eyes gleamed like burning coals. "I won't let your parents hand you over like a bundle of washing." She opened her handbag and fished out an envelope.

"You don't have enough." Lilian swatted the envelope away. Amara could feed herself. She had a business, but she wasn't rich. "I'm sorry aunty. It's not your fault." *It's no one's fault*, Lilian realised. *Not her father's or her mother's.* Lilian's mother was a daughter of the *Kapchemweny* clan. A girl taught to build thorn fences and raise strong sons. A girl who was cut and would cut her daughters to protect them. A girl who married a man she didn't love and would watch her daughter do the same.

"But I *do* have enough," Amara said. "After Beneh moved in with Joyce he used to visit me. He never stayed the night," she said without emotion, "but he always left an envelope." Lilian remembered the envelopes swollen with cash. She'd picked one up once, just to feel its weight.

"In the beginning I thought if I just tried harder, if I was the wife he wanted, I could make him love me, but part of me knew that was never going to happen. I needed something to fall back on if he threw me out." Her eyes grew steely. "I tucked away half of what he gave me every week in case I needed it. And then *you* came." She took a breath. "And I realised he wasn't going to throw me out. *I* was going to leave *him*." She closed her eyes and when she opened them again, her face was lit like a warrior.

"I started planning my escape. *You* did that," she said, dropping the envelope onto Lilian's lap. "There's enough in there to settle the debt. Take it."

Lilian opened the envelope and stared at the thick wad of notes. She had held a one hundred shilling note, never a twenty thousand. She counted the notes twice then ran to the door. She wanted to run outside and fling the money at Bukenya. She wanted to pull her books from his backseat and slam the car door. But then she thought about her aunt returning to Beneh's home. He'd be back, knocking at her bedroom door, soon as he grew bored of his second wife. Lilian remembered her first night in the house, watching her aunt's smile disappear as Beneh slid his hand up her top.

"I can't," Lilian said, holding out the money. "I can't go back to school knowing you're in that house. It'll take you another ten years to save enough to—"

"Leave? I didn't need three hundred thousand shillings to end my marriage. I could have looked for a job; we don't have children. I didn't have the guts." Amara shrugged. "Not until *you* came to stay. I saw the light coming from under your door when you were studying. I saw the plastic you brought home from the dump and the dolls you made. I saw this skinny barefoot girl in a second hand uniform building a future and it made me think, maybe I could too." She fed her fingers through Lilian's. "It was because of you and the flyers you brought home from Empowerment Club and the stories you wrote that I started washing the neighbours' clothes, and now I have a business." She pressed the envelope into Lilian's hand. "I don't want to use

Beneh's money to fund my freedom. I want to pay my own way. But I worked hard for that money and I'm not going to give it back to him."

Amara stood up. "I want you to use it, Lilian. I need to know all those years weren't for nothing." She nudged Lilian towards the door. "Please. I *owe* you."

"What if he comes back?"

"If he comes back, I'll leave. That story you left on my bed, the one about the bird with the golden beak who pecked the lock open? That was *me*." Amara squeezed Lilian's hand. "I make good money. I can afford to pay rent." She ducked through the doorway and stepped into the sun. "Now go buy your future back."

Chapter 36

"Here she is!" Afia grabbed Lilian's hand and pointed her in the direction of an open-air tent. "Go sit with your maama," she shouted over the whistling and clapping. "I'll get the groom." Lilian tried to protest but Afia was wriggling her hips and waving her arms in the air, making a big show of searching for the groom. When she reached Bukenya and pulled him from his chair, the cheering grew louder. Afia escorted him to a white wicker chair festooned with a gold bow. The drumming stopped when she held up her hand. "This is the man who has gathered us together." The stomping started up again and a set of hands grabbed Lilian's waist and she found herself in a conga line snaking its way towards Bukenya.

She dug her heels into the soil but the slithering line pushed her forwards. The more Lilian squirmed, the tighter Angel Chelangat gripped her, until finally, the line stopped at the empty chair next to Bukenya's.

Lilian didn't sit down. "Taata?" she called, loud enough for the women at the back of the line to hear, loud enough that her mother looked up from her lap and her father shot up out of his chair. "Taata, we have to talk."

Isaac Mwanga stopped drumming and the children stood still, all eyes on Lilian's father as he walked towards her. Lilian handed her father the envelope.

"It's all there," she whispered. "You can pay off the debt."

Her father opened the envelope and riffled through the notes. "Is this Beneh's?" he asked, anger creeping into his voice. "I won't take his money."

"It's mine. I earned it." Lilian scanned the swarm of guests and found Amara standing beside her mother, whispering in her ear.

"It doesn't matter." Her father's mouth sloped downwards. "I won't take Beneh's money and I can't accept yours. Bukenya paid the bride price. I'm sorry, Tiny Mosquito." He pushed the envelope towards her. "I have to honour my promise. I gave him my word."

"And what about the promise you made *me*?" Lilian insisted. "You told me you'd fix things. You told me my life would be better than this." She glanced across at the angry stranger she was meant to marry, a balding man who didn't read books.

"I *did* say that." Lilian's father dipped his head. "I gave you my word." His voice faltered. "I promised to do everything I could to put you through school." Lilian had to lean close to hear what he said next. "I promised *you* first."

"What's going on?" Bukenya rose from his chair. His face was flushed, his mouth a thin line.

Lilian's father pocketed the envelope and turned to their guests.

"Thank you for your patience. I know you are hungry and expecting a wedding. We will eat and drink soon, if I could just have your ears for a moment longer." Lilian saw her mother nod, the ghost of a smile on her lips. "A long time ago," her father continued in the voice he reserved for fireside stories, "I made a promise to my daughter. I promised I would do everything in my power to put Lilian through school. When our cassava crop failed I borrowed money from Bukenya Jjoloba to pay Lilian's fees and I signed a paper to say he could marry her if I didn't pay him back. I tried." His voice was strained. "But there is not much work for an old man like me." He waited for the bobbing heads to grow still. "So I asked for his patience." He shrugged. "He is not a patient man. He grew tired of waiting. He wants a wife." Lilian's father turned to Bukenya and shook his head. "It won't be Lilian."

The whispering grew to a loud hum.

"I am a man of my word and I pay my debts." Lilian's father held up the envelope. "I promised to pay Mr Jjoloba back, and," he pressed the envelope into Bukenya's hand, "now I have. The debt is settled. It is all there. Every shilling you spent."

Bukenya's eyes bulged. He opened his mouth as if he might swallow Lilian's father whole.

"You think you are so smart with all your big talk? Enough words. My family came to see me joined with yours. Let's not make trouble."

Lilian's father didn't raise his voice. He pulled himself up to his full height and pressed the crumpled envelope to Bukenya's chest. "It is all there. Take what you brought, the baskets, the goat, take everything that's yours." His voice was icy. "Our business is settled."

"Business?" Bukenya swung around to face the crowd, to shame Lilian's father. "This is not business." He picked up a basket bloated with food. He pointed to the tents jammed with guests and the chairs strewn with ribbons where his parents sat in their Sunday clothes. "This is not business," he scowled. "This is a wedding!"

"Not anymore," Lilian's father said.

Chapter 37

Lilian sat at Wekesa's desk under the slanting moon. Her brother had dragged the desk into the yard for her after Bukenya had stormed out. *Next time I spend money*, Bukenya had said, grabbing a rooster by the throat and heading for the gate, *I'll spend it on something worthwhile.* His family had trailed after him, cursing and carrying away the baskets of fruit and the faded green armchair.

Lilian looked at the fire, still flickering in the yard, and the empty beer barrel and the unwashed plates. *Let's eat*, her father had said as the truck disappeared in a cloud of red dust. *Lilian will need an early night. She has school tomorrow.* Lilian's mother had passed around a plate of Madam Tumeetu's sweet pineapple and told Lilian to get changed. *You don't want the juice to stain the silk*, she'd said, pointing at the *gomesi*. *They said we can get our money back if you don't wear it.*

Lilian had pulled off the dress and flung her arms around her mother. She hadn't forgiven her, but she was beginning to understand her, and that was a start.

The moon lit the envelope Wekesa had left on the desk. He had apologised for not giving Madam Namusisi's letter to Lilian sooner, but with all the preparations for the *Kwanjula*, he'd forgot. Lilian tore the letter from the envelope.

Dear Lilian, Madam Namusisi wrote in response to Lilian's note. *I was so glad to hear from you last week. When you didn't show up at school I was worried, but Wekesa explained you have a fever and will soon return. I'm glad. We miss you at Empowerment Club and are looking forward to hearing you speak at assembly. About your request ...*

Lilian tried to remember what she'd written in the note Wekesa had carried to school. *I have a friend*, she'd written, filling the note with details about the chapatti seller and his threat to leave Dimple in the bush if she didn't give him sex. *We could demand money from him*, Lilian had ended her note, *but making him pay a few shillings for what he did isn't enough. He will do it again. We have to stop him. You said that silence keeps us small. Can you help Dimple make some noise?*

Lilian held Madam Namusisi's letter up to the moon's gleaming light so she could make out the next line. *You might remember I mentioned an organisation that help girls like Dimple? They call themselves Girls Fight Back*, Madam Namusisi wrote, *and I've taken Dimple to see them. They are going to help her press charges. By the time you read this letter, Mr Musoke could be in jail. Don't worry about his wife. She will take over the business and earn her own money.* Madam Namusisi finished her letter with a PS. *We will ask the judge to order Mr Musoke pay for Dimple's education. If we're lucky, she will be back at school in time for your speech.*

Her speech. Lilian looked down at the blank page on her desk. She wouldn't need the lantern to write tonight; the sky was full of stars. She sat in the quiet yard and breathed in her freedom. *You have three minutes to address the school*, Wekesa had said. She was going to make them count.

Principal, teachers, fellow students of Walumira Secondary ... Lilian gnawed on her pen. She had escaped a marriage and set herself free. She could slip back into the classroom quietly and pretend none of this had happened. Just focus on school. She could thank Mr Lubega for the opportunity to address the school and sit down.

She stared at the blank page. She'd survived the despair of the last few years by writing stories and reading books. Soon as she touched pen to paper or read the opening line of a book, her pain disappeared. It was a vanishing act. But she couldn't hide between the paragraphs forever. She had to emerge from behind her books and put down her pen. *If you want to be a leader*, Madam Namusisi had told her, *you have to open your mouth.*

Lilian thought about her mother, unschooled and illiterate, watching her baby die of an illness that could have been cured. She thought about the night her legs were spread for the cutter's knife and the baby Mr Musoke had put inside Dimple. She thought about Trinah sitting on Mr Igbe's lap and Thomas's greasy smile. She thought about the man with the caterpillar eyebrows and how narrowly she had escaped the same fate. Nakato had escaped too – she was sewing again – and Amara had a business that could pay her rent. *I escaped because of you*, Amara had said. *Because of your stories.*

Lilian pictured the rows of girls sitting cross-legged at assembly, waiting for her to speak.

If you want to move mountains, her father had once said, *you must start by lifting stones.* She touched her pen to the page.

It was time to make some noise.

This is for all the girls who have been whistled at on the street or groped behind classrooms, she wrote in black ink. *For anyone who's hidden bruises or been visited by the cutter or been asked to stay back late after class. For girls who said "No" to boys who heard "Yes", and for all of us who've been told not to dream big.*

Lilian turned the page over.

When I was small I was expected to ask questions and be curious. I was encouraged to learn and find the right words to describe what I saw. And then I grew up and everything changed. I was told to be quiet. I was "only a girl". I belonged in the kitchen. I had to do as I was told, do what was expected of a teenage girl. A girl with curves wasn't supposed to sit at a desk.

Lilian's eyes slid from the page, looking for words in the dirt. Her mother wanted her to keep the cutting a secret but she didn't want to keep quiet. She didn't want to pretend that what happened didn't hurt, that she hadn't lost a piece of herself the day the cutter came. It had taken her weeks to tell Dimple about the cutting, but it was easier than she'd thought, and the telling helped. The small door she'd invited Dimple through, opened Dimple up to her and they'd wiped each other's tears and mourned their losses together.

A teenage girl wasn't supposed to read books, but I was rebellious. I read and I learned. I learned that what I went through last month is called female genital mutilation. Lilian hoped she could say the words out loud. *I learned that it is against the law in Uganda and nearly everywhere else. I learned that I didn't have to trade a part of my body to go to school. I have a right to be here. And the right to decide who to marry, and when.*

I'm telling you my story, Lilian wrote, *so you can tell others. I'm sharing my story with you in the hope you will pick up a pen and write your own. Being a girl doesn't mean we are weak. Being female is our strength. We can build fences, do maths and feed our families. We can have businesses and babies. We are not stupid or dirty or lazy or weak. Armed with books and pens we can do anything.* Lilian remembered her father's whispered words after he'd learned of the cutting: Many moons ago, our chiefs believed we should purify our daughters and *Wonsetibik* became part of our culture. But that is no excuse to take a knife to a girl. People invent traditions and people discard them. People make a culture. The culture doesn't make us.

I love Walumira, Lilian wrote. *I love the sounds of the bush and my father's stories of clan. I love hearing my family's voices raised in song and playing sonko with my cousins. I am daughter of the Kapchebasa clan and the traditions I was brought up with make me who I am. But I am also a girl who likes copying words off a blackboard. I like reading and writing and dancing and maths. Traditions are important, but traditions can change. Things have changed in the city. In Kampala girls can be head prefect. Women run businesses and choose who to marry. Things have changed in Kampala and the change is coming here.*

It is up to us to convince our parents that we can do anything boys can do. Tell your mother you matter. Tell your father you want to stay in school. And for those of us whose parents don't want to listen – or can't listen because they are still tethered to the past – we must be the change we seek. Don't wait for the world to bend to suit you. Grab your future with both hands and hammer it to fit your dreams.

Don't let them tell you things can't change. Be the change.

Lilian put down her pen.

"Don't tell me who I should be or what my life should look like," she said out loud, her words spiralling up, like the smoke from the fire.

"I am Lilian," she thundered. "And I am change."

The End

Author's Note

In 2014, more than 200 school girls were abducted from their boarding school in Nigeria by armed militants of Boko Haram, a terrorist organisation with a history of targeting schools. The attackers stormed the school, set it on fire, herded the girls into trucks and disappeared.

The kidnapping haunted me. I wondered what I could do. Not just for the 200 terrified girls held at gunpoint but for the 200 million girls scattered around the globe who were being denied an education. Girls kept home from school to cook and clean while their brothers sat at desks; girls forced to stay home because they couldn't afford sanitary pads; girls sold into prostitution and girls sold into marriage to men twice their age for a cow or a goat.

And then, by chance, I met Nakamya Lilian, a 29-year-old Ugandan girl visiting Australia. We spent an afternoon together and as soon as she told me her story about growing up in a small impoverished village, desperate for an education, I knew my next novel would lay bare a story that was being played out across the globe, hurting the most vulnerable among us: girls, who with our help, could soar, transforming their lives and the lives of those around them. As Nicholas J Kristof says in his brilliant book, *Half the Sky*: "It's hard to escape abuse if you can't read or write."

But Lilian's story was only one story, one voice. I needed to learn more so I flew to Uganda. I didn't know what it felt like to be a poor African girl without shoes or schoolbooks, so I spoke to young Ugandan girls. Thirty of them. I went to their villages, visited their huts, walked to the wells where they gathered water and visited the dusty schools where they learned to speak English until one by one they were forced to drop out. They told me about forgoing meals to pay for textbooks and trading their bodies for school fees. They told me about the lessons their aunts taught them about their bodies and about men.

None of the girls I interviewed had both their parents. Many were orphans, their mothers dying of diseases the witchdoctors couldn't cure and their fathers abandoning them for second and third wives. They lived without running water or electricity. A lucky few were in secondary school, on scholarships, the only girls in their class. They lived in concrete boxes in the city's slums, walking an hour to school on an empty stomach and they considered themselves blessed. They were lucky to be learning, they told me, their faces lit by smiles. "If you can read and write you can get a good job and you won't be hungry."

I gave them sugar, flour, soap and pencils, but it wasn't enough. I left Uganda with their secrets and dreams in my notebook and a pressing need to give them a voice. *I Am Change* is their story, their pain and joy and fear and bravery. I am privileged to have written it and know that with that privilege comes a deep and profound responsibility to get the details right. Namukasa Sarah's foreword gives me hope that I might have.

Suzy Zail
October 2018

Acknowledgements

I couldn't have written this book without the thirty brave Ugandan girls who shared their stories with me. Every page is embroidered with their experience. It couldn't have been easy letting me into their lives. I asked hard questions and mined their most private and intimate moments and they forgave my ignorance and shared their heartbreak with such warmth and generosity. I hope I have told their truth.

Special thanks to Michelle Dubrowin and Kazia and Tomasz Zurek for getting the ball rolling with an introduction to Nakamya Lilian. As soon as I heard her story, this book was born. Thank you Nakamya for offering up your story, and your nickname, and for being such a warm and enthusiastic tour guide through Uganda's villages and slums.

To Namukasa Nusula Sarah for answering my endless questions while you juggled work and university so I could tell an authentic story. You helped shape Lilian, and in turn shape me – as a writer and a person. Your courage and generosity blow me away. Thanks also for your careful, close reading of my manuscript and the wisdom you imparted. Your advice on voice, language, custom and the intricacies of daily life in Uganda were invaluable.

And to all the women and men on the frontlines, fighting to keep young girls unmarried, off the streets and in school, thank you for introducing me to the girls who informed this story. Your passion and dedication to gender equity buoyed my belief that things have and will continue to change for girls both in Uganda, and globally. Richard Kafuma and Farai Mazvimbakupa at AFFCAD – Action For Fundamental Change And Development, Nakazibwe Hadija, Head teacher at Excel Education Centre, Bwaise, Memory Bandera, Tracy Kobukindo and Christine Adero at Girl Child Network, Uganda, the helpful staff at Girls Not Brides, Mukisa Davis and Joan Amanda Banura at Youth Alliance for Family Planning and Adolescents Health, Uganda (UYAFPAH), and Margaret Kasozi and Stephen Kasule Sewava at Concern for the Girl Child, Uganda. I hope, in some small way, this story contributes to your cause.

I am also indebted to Chekwech Allan, editor at the *Daily Monitor* in Uganda and Neumbe Adreen Brendah for their generous advice on Sabiny culture and to Joan Amanda Banura, Country Coordinator – UYAFPAH Uganda, who gave me my first lesson in Baganda customs and language.

Huge thanks to Walker Books Australia for allowing me to chase stories I care deeply about, and to Maryann Ballantyne for always championing me. Thank you for trusting me to tell this story respectfully and for steering me in the right direction. I am also indebted to Nicola Santilli for her excellent advice, Sue Whiting for her masterful copyedit, and Gayna Murphy who dreamed up the book's wonderful cover.

Thanks also to Bayside City Council's Artists in Residence program for the generous gift of a quiet room in which to hide away and write. And to my writing family who feed me in so many ways. Thanks Ilka Tampke, Michelle Deans, Carla Fedi,

Richard Holt, Brooke Maggs, Melinda Dundas and Danielle Binks for always telling me the truth and for your generous advice and friendship.

To my parents, whose education was cut short by war, thank you for teaching me to dream big and study hard. And finally, to my husband Shaun and our three children, Josh, Tanya and Remy, I couldn't do what I do without your constant encouragement and enthusiasm. Thank you.

The quote on page 10 is from *I Am Malala: The Story of the Girl Who Stood Up for Education and Was Shot by the Taliban* by Malala Yousafzai. Reproduced with kind permission from the publishers, Orion Publishing Group.

How to Help

Lilian and the characters who people her world are fictional, but their circumstances are real. The long, dangerous walk girls make to school, the leaves crammed into underwear to soak up their blood, the fathers who leave for second and third wives, the mothers lost to disease, the bad touches from teachers, the lack of money for schoolbooks, the forced marriages and unmet dreams ...

Every one of the thirty girls I interviewed had experienced a number – sometimes all – of these hurdles before they turned sixteen. And they were the lucky ones, the ones I met through aid organisations that were now helping them achieve their dreams. Organisations like Girl Child Network, Uganda, who run empowerment clubs for girls; AAFCAD, who improve the lives of the people who live in Kampala's poorest slum; Girls Not Brides, a global partnership committed to ending child marriage and enabling girls to fulfil their potential; Concern for the Girl Child, who empower vulnerable girls through sponsored education and The Uganda Youth Alliance for Family Planning and Adolescent Health, who educate young people about the dangers of early sexual activity to enable them to stay in school longer.

I saw the difference these organisations made, how they'd saved these girls from unwanted pregnancies and marriages to older men, fed them when they were hungry and sat them at desks. Girls who'd been forced to sell their bodies on the street were now able to read. Women who'd grown used to being beaten now lived independently and ran their own businesses.

I couldn't leave Uganda having picked through their sorrows and done nothing to improve their lives, so on my return to Australia, I established Help Girls Learn, Uganda, an initiative to get girls into schools and keep them there. If you want to help better girls' lives, you can donate via the link below. Money received by Help Girls Learn, Uganda, will go to the five incredible organisations I worked with and will be used to empower and protect vulnerable girls in Uganda. Anything you can offer will be deeply appreciated.

To donate to Help Girls Learn, Uganda:
mycause.com.au/page/106767

To read more about the five charities you will be supporting:

Girl Child Network, Uganda
www.gcnuganda.org

AAFCAD
www.affcad.org

Girls Not Brides
www.girlsnotbrides.org/take-action/

Concern for the Girl Child
www.concernforgirlchild.or.ug

The Uganda Youth Alliance for Family Planning and Adolescent Health
www.uyafpah.org

While writing this book, I met another awesome organisation who do important work in Uganda. One Girl (onegirl.org.au) harness the power of education to drive change for girls and their communities through a range of education-focused projects in Sierra Leone and Uganda. Their Business Brains program not only provides girls with vocational skills, personal and career development and financial literacy, it also teaches them about sexual and reproductive health and rights and menstrual hygiene management.

To Donate to One Girl: donate.onegirl.org.au

Organisations in the UK who work to help support women and girls in Uganda:

ActionAid
www.actionaid.org.uk

Amnesty International
www.amnesty.org.uk

Womankind
www.womankind.org.uk

About the Author

Suzy Zail started her working life as a solicitor but left the law to write *The Tattooed Flower*, an account of how her father survived the Holocaust. Suzy Zail's first work of fiction for young adults, *The Wrong Boy*, has been included in the 2015 USBBY Outstanding International Books list and was short-listed for Book of the Year in the Older Readers category at the 2013 Children's Book Council of Australia Awards. In 2015, her novel *Alexander Altmann A10567* was recognised as a CBCA Notable Book. Suzy's books have been published in Germany, the UK, US, Sweden, Italy and the Netherlands.

Follow her online at www.suzyzail.com.au or on Instagram @authorsuzyzail.